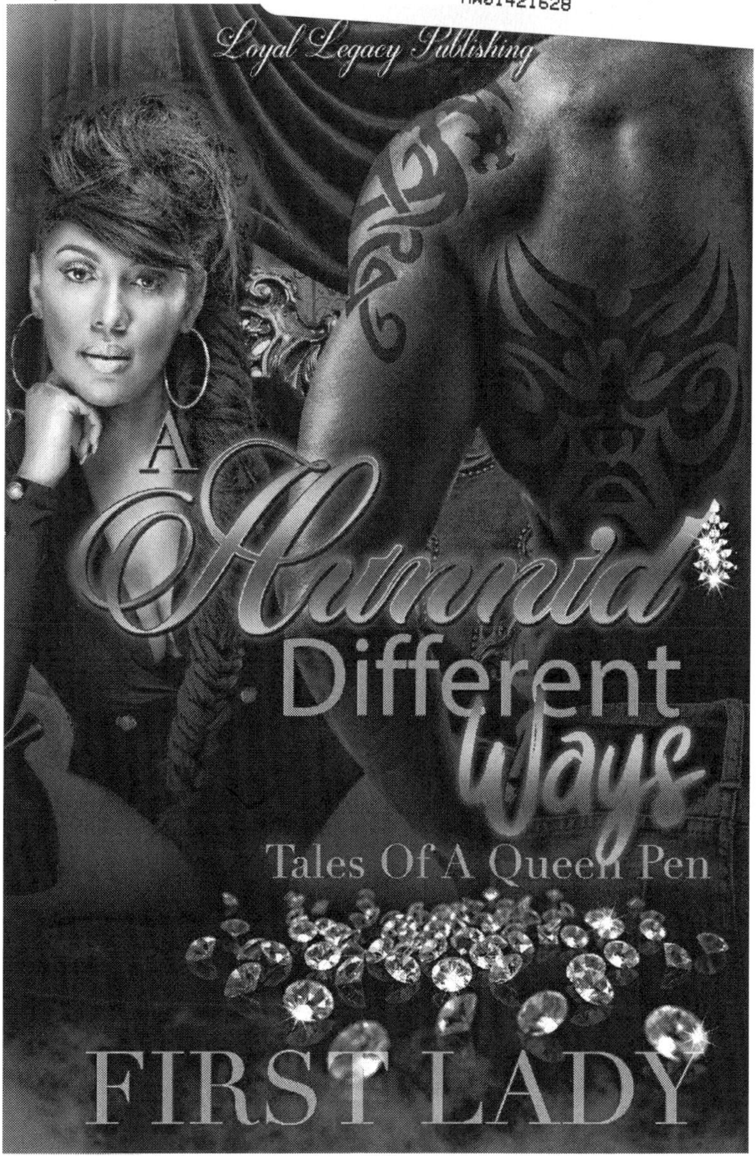
Loyal Legacy Publishing
A Hunnid Different Ways
Tales Of A Queen Pen
FIRST LADY

**A HUNNID DIFFERENT WAYS
TALES OF A QUEEN PEN
-A Series Written By-
AUTHOR FIRST LADY**

Copyright© 2018 by Loyal Legacy Publishing
Published by Loyal Legacy Publishing
Join our Mailing List by texting Loyal to 64600 or click here http://optin.mobiniti.com/Py8J
Facebook: FIRST LADY

This novel is a work of fiction. Any resemblances to actual events, real people, living or dead, organizations, establishments or locales are products of the author's imagination. Other names, characters, places, and incidents are used fictitiously.

Cover Design: Tina Shivers
Editors: Tamiko Covington & Venitia Crawford

All rights reserved. No part of this book may be used or reproduced in any form or by any means electronic or mechanical, including photocopying, recording or by information storage and retrieval system, without the written permission from the publisher and writer. Because of the dynamic nature of the Internet, and Web addresses or links contained in this book may have changed since publication and may no longer be valid. The views expressed in this work are solely those of the author and do not necessarily reflect the views of the publisher and the publisher hereby disclaims any responsibility for them

DEDICATION

I dedicate this book to my brother Wilson Townes Jr, Bro you are my whole heart, there is nothing in this world I would not do for you or your kids. I am so proud of you, you been through so much and you're still standing. You hit rock bottom because of your alcohol addiction but, you turned your life around tremendously.

You are a great father to your children and great grandfather to your grandchildren. You are the best uncle to my children. Even in your addiction you were at every football practice and every football game for my son. When their father could not be there you stepped up. I am forever grateful.

You are the strongest man I know, I remember growing up watching you provide and take care of your family. I thought to myself, I want a man like my brother. A stand-up man, your addiction set you back but, it was a major comeback. I always got your back regardless of what you're going through, that's what a big ill sister is for lol! Your kids are my kids and, my kids are your kids we share responsibility, our bond is definitely unbreakable!

I AM MY BROTHERS KEEPER!!

ACKNOWLEDGEMENTS

First, I want to thank my heavenly father, without you none of this would be possible, **PHILIPPIANS 4:13 I CAN DO ANYTHING THROUGH HIM, HE WHO GIVES ME STRENGTH!** That's my favorite bible verse, this verse touches my soul. I recite this verse daily.

My parents **Wilson** and **Eleanor Townes** you two are my heart, Y'all made me the strongest, creative and beautiful woman I am today, I love you both!

Brian McPherson Jr, Brazil McPherson and, Brooklyn McPherson, my babies you are my motivation , everything I do is for y'all, I take motherhood very seriously, when y'all get older you will understand why I'm so hard on you, Why I be on you about certain things like school, Education is very important, I want y'all to be better than me, Always respect adult and have good manners very important, One thing nobody can take away from you is your education, Always strive for the best *LOVE ALWAYS, YOUR CHOCOLATE MOMMA!*

Big Brian Nigga you get on my nerves lol but, you know

you are my ride or die, ever since I was fifteen years old you were my best friend whether we are together or not, we have a bond that no man or women can break, we have each other's best interest at heart, we been through so much together, even when I don't tell you, I appreciate you, You know I'm stubborn and sometimes just a meanie, I remember telling you about my book and how your daughter broke my laptop, I told you to get me a basic laptop, you came to my house with a brand new Apple MacBook Air Laptop, You made sure I had everything I need to achieve my goal, I will always love you, My headache and blessing !

Lula, Twanda and Antione Snyder we rock this family thing I love y'all!

Tay'ara Burton, Shanice Townes, Kiana Townes, Jiliyah Townes, Wilson Townes lll, Tamesha Towns and, La'Keita Snyder. wherever I go ya'll go with me, all of you put a smile on my face and years ago when going through some tough times, it was all of you that kept me smiling and laughing and forget about my pain, I love y'all with all my heart *FAMILY OVER EVERYTHING* Ohhh...**Serenity** baby I didn't forget about you our new addition to the family, You and your mother

Sylvia Jay are a blessing to this family I love both of you!

To My Bestie, My sister, My friend for thirty plus years **Melissa Williams (My Ride or Die)** Always there for me and my kids, If I want to go to the moon , you'll be like well what time we leaving sis lol down for whatever I'm tryna do, thank you for helping me promote this book, me and you been through alot of trials and tribulations together and we overcame a lot in life, we strong sis, we cut from a different cloth then a lot of these women out here make women want to clone us lol I know Momma Lois is looking down on us smiling, speaking of Momma Lois in 2011 I had a dream Momma Lois she just appeared on night just standing there, we had a stare off, I figured I'll speak first I had a gut feeling her appearance had something to do with me always making sure "I AM MY SISTER'S KEEPER" I got Melissa I said, Momma Lois nodded her head and smiled at me, I will never forget that as long as I live, we are like twins when I hurt you hurt and vice versa, I never had to question your loyalty, you never let nobody say shit about rather I'm right or wrong, you will check anybody about me I love you until the death of me sister !!!

Tiffani Wiggins When I met you five years ago we

became best friends instantly, our sense of humor nobody understands and that's a good thing what's understood between us don't need to be explained to nobody, no matter where we work or live we always keep in touch with each other daily, that's a special connection we have, you are a great Nurse and Creative Pastry Chef, thank you for all your support I love you!

Tawanda Morand *(BOSSLADY)* Thank You for being a great role model and teaching me the importance of work ethic and accountability in the workforce, always keeping it a hunnid with me. Rather I like what you said or not I always respect it. You are a strong black educate woman. Why wouldn't I listen to you.

I never take anything that you lecture me about as criticism. I assimilate everything you say, one thing you said to me five years ago that always stuck out was: Your current job is like an interview for your next job. So always be your best. You also told me that you didn't see Nursing Assistant being my last stop, you see me doing something else. I think you was right Boss Lady. I had a hidden talent for writing...**I LOVE YOU MRS.TAWANDA MORAND**

Darlene Frasher You are so intelligent and Mrs. Darlene you gave me so much info on the author world, you are amazing person, and I thank you for your kind words, you motivated me to go harder every conversation I have with you I learn something!

Sister Black **Deshawn Williams** thank you for everything you did for me thank you for believing in me I appreciate you so much Shawn! My childhood friends **Valerie** and **Tia Bey**, **Jazmine Ross (Bell)** and **Sonya Johnson** Thanks for your support I love y'all! Ohhh...**Kevin Easley** my nigga I wish I could use an emoji lol when you told me you believe in me I believed you, I remember being nervous about my submission to the publishing company and you told me you got this thanks for the support Kevin!

Makeya Johnson Ms. Aspinwall you are always in heart, thanks for supporting me even outside of this book stuff Love you cuz! **Sierra Rucker** we have a connection I liked you when I first met you because we both meanie's lol just kidding thanks for always supporting me and being me critic Love You Cee!

Surmala Stephens you get on my nerves middle cuzzin swear but that's what family do and why you're the middle cuzzin lol thanks for all the support love! **Isaiah Thomas** (Cuz) the life of the party My F$&@! % cuzzin I love you thanks for the support!

Maurie Ford we be rocking these resting b#$@&* face huh lol thanks for your support coolest anti-social person I ever met lol! **Keisha Jones** my chocolate cuzzo thanks for all your support! **Ericka Pinno** I hope I smelled your name right Oh well I call you E.Peezi anyways lol aye I bothered you constantly with my changes in the book and you always kept it a hunnid with me thanks for the support love you E.Peezi!

Marlene Green You my baby thanks for the support Mar you got a special place in my heart I love you Mar! **Karli Mathews (Karli Red)** I probably got on your nerves trying to fix my book in Microsoft word and you helped me thanks for the support! **Lee Marvin Parham** how could I forget you thanks for your support my nigga for life love you Lee ! **Darlene Hopkins** The wild Child, free spirit thank you for always having my back and supporting my vision, Photo shoot gon be outta this world I love you Dar!

Mercedes Ruffin To the best promoter in the world I am

blessed to have you on my team thank you for always supporting me and being my critic I love you Benzo! **Alicia Water** Last but not least; To the best hall partner in the VA Healthcare System. You have my back hunnid percent. When I explained to you I wanted to write a book. You had my best interest at heart. You edit all my work, you gave me your honest opinion when I brought different ideas to you! Gave me sooo much support, I love you Alicia Waters. Thank you for being there! If I forgot about anybody on 1South, Thanks for your support! #TEAM1SOUTH!!!!!!

Table of Contents

Dedication

Acknowledgements

Synopsis

Chapter 1: Chyna

Chapter 2: Chyna

Chapter 3: Chyna

Chapter 4: Chyna

Chapter 5: Chyna

Chapter 6: Chyna

Chapter 7: Chyna

Chapter 8: Chyna

Chapter 9: Chyna

Chapter 10: Rasheeda

Chapter 11: Boss Hog

Chapter 12: Gunna

Chapter 13: Chyna

Chapter 14: Legend

Chapter 15: Chyna

Chapter 16: Bianca

Chapter 17: Chyna

Table of Contents (Cont…)

Chapter 18: Lucci

Chapter 19: Gunna

Chapter 20: Kristen Weiss

Chapter 21: Boss Hog

Chapter 22: Chyna

Chapter 23: Legend

Chapter 24: Chyna

About the Author

To My Family:

Townes and Snyder *Love everyone with all my heart Thanks*

for all the support!

SYNOPSIS

Chyna Jackson is a sexy twenty-two-year-old better known to the streets of Philly as Hunnid. She became Queen of the streets when Chyna's Aunt Deana gets into some unexpected legal trouble. Suddenly Chyna inherits her Aunt Deana's twenty-five-year-old drug empire without warning.

Legend is Chyna's twin brother and he is dealing with his own issues. When he learns the deceitful activities of his girlfriend he is completely devastated. While Legend is dealing with his girlfriend secret his sister is dealing with taking over the drug empire.

Legend never wanted no parts of the drug game, but Chyna and Aunt Deana's enemies emerged, forcing Legend in the throne seat. Things are getting crazy. Enemies are closing in and the snakes are closer than Chyna could ever imagined. Take a ride with this short feisty gangsta chick from Philly. A story filled with lies, deception, intimidation, corruption and murder. You can live a thousand years, but you will never meet another chick like Hunnid!

Chapter 1

HANDING OVER THE BUSINESS

2008

Chyna

My ringing phone woke me up from my sleep. I sat up in my bed in search of my phone. Damn it stop ringing! I searched under my plush comforter for my IPhone 3. I still couldn't find my phone, fuck it. I laid back down. As soon as my head hit the pillow my phone started ringing again. Damn this better be an emergency. I am trying to sleep, I got outta bed to see if my phone was on the floor.

Shit I am still drunk from last night fucking with Gunna drinking Henny ughhh. I notice my phone lighting up under the bed. Now a bitch gotta crawl on the floor. My phone stop ringing once I grabbed it. I put my passcode in to unlock my phone. I looked in my miss calls damn Auntie called me like three times. I tried to call her back but my phone ringed again. Damn it's her again.

"Hello Auntie, you cool?" I looked at the time and realized it was 1 a.m. in the morning.

"Damn I slept the whole day away."

"Naw Chyna come get me ASAP I'm in some shit!"

"Where you at"? I said fully awake.

"Twenty Fourth Street by Starlett Bar." Aunt Deana said.

"Okay Auntie I am on my way."

My Auntie Deana was a queen pen and for the last 20 plus years now. Aunt Deana had the streets on lock, a real boss, and a highly respected BOSS BITCH.

I am trying to figure out who would be stupid enough to cross her. My mom didn't like me hanging around Aunt Deana. She said she was a bad influence, but I hung around her anyway ever since I turned 14. Aunt Deana been showing me the ropes. My mom would be mad as hell if she knew her sister had me around illegal activity.

On the real, I love the thrill of this street shit. I was eager to learn the business. My mother Debbie always did the right things in life a real stand up citizen. My mother went to college straight after high school to become a Registered Nurse. She married my father even though the nigga wasn't shit.

She had twins with the nigga as his wife. Me and my

brother Legend is two minutes apart. We don't look shit alike either. I'm five feet even while Legend is six feet two inches. I look exactly like my mother Debbie and Legend look just like my father the late great "Derrick Jackson". I am the oldest and I take that roll very serious ha…ha...yup two whole minutes older just call me big sis!

Now Auntie Deana was a different story. She had three kids by three different men, never worked a day in her life. Always been a street bitch and hustler. Deana started hustling when she was twenty-five years old. Her boyfriend Leon was better known to the streets as Black. Leon was a King pin who got killed in a car accident. Aunt Deana knew where all his money and work was stashed. Black trusted her that much. The rumor was that she had him killed to take over his business. None of which can be or would be confirmed. Aunt Deana isn't gonna tell nobody shit. She took over Black empire with an iron fist!

Deana didn't take no shit either. She had a full team of old school hustlers and they had a team working under them. These days Deana didn't get her hands dirty. Years ago, she was known for killing niggas at the meetings that didn't have her money or if they were late to a meeting. She makes them work without pay. I laughed about how crazy she is and definitely about that life!

I grabbed my Nike sweat suit and my Nike slides. Grabbed my keys to my 2008 Nissan Altima that aunt Deana brought me last year for my 21st birthday. My mom was so mad Auntie bought me that car.

I tiptoed down the steps, so my mom won't hear me sneak out. Shit Auntie always getting me in trouble with her sister. I reached the bottom step and release a sigh of relief. As soon as I touched the door and opened it, I tripped over something round. I looked down and it was my two- year old Pitbull Ryder's toy. DUMB ASS DOG! I stepped over it and looked up the steps to make sure my mom didn't hear me.

I ran to my car like I was in a lifetime movie, running from a killer. I jumped in car and easily shut the door. As soon as I pulled off it started raining. *"Damn, here I come Auntie!"*

Fifteen minutes later I arrived at the Starlett bar. I had a glimpse look at Auntie. She had on a black hoodie and black leggings. I can see her long lashes. Her damn lashes were long as fuck! Why it looks like she dressed to kill a nigga I shook my head.

Aunt Deana jumped in my car and pulled her hoodie off her head. "Chyna, I fucked up its all bad. I am going have to sit it down. I know that nigga set me up niecey!" I looked over at my aunt with a puzzled look and raised eyebrows. "Why? How?"

"Chyna, Auntie going have to sit it down for like three, four or five years. It ain't about the time you know I'm the toughest bitch that ever lived." I shook my head up and down agreeing with Auntie on how strong she is.

"My empire is what I am worried about. Chyna baby girl you gonna have to hold shit down until I get out." Aunt Deana said. "Aww… shit you know I gotchu," I said to Aunt Deana like this was simple; little did I know in the next couple hours I would be a Queen Pen.

"Naw Chyna I ain't talking about commissary and visits. I'm talking about you running my empire until I get out jail. There ain't shit I can do about this shit I'm into. They got me this time. It's all good though niecey I know you can do this, take me to the Ihop on Route 19 we can grab something to eat. I'll tell you how I got into this bullshit, and how you about to be Queen Pen." Aunt

Deana said.

I made a left turn onto Route 19, for the rest of the ride me and Auntie rode in silence, I looked over at her and it look like she was in deep thought. I started to ask her what's on her mind? Fuck it I'm gon let her daydream in peace. I pulled up to the IHop restaurant on 24th and parked. We got out the car once we were inside the waiter seated us quickly. "Order what you want Chyna I am going to use the bathroom" Aunt Deana said.

I checked my phone while Auntie got up out the booth to use the bathroom I had a message from Gunna:

Bestie Gunna: Wyd I just rode past ur crib. Ya car gone. Wtf u at?

Me: U aint gonna believe this shit but meet me at my crib tmrw around 12 p.m. shit just got real

Bestie Gunna: Oh yea see you tmrw

Me: Ite

As I locked my phone Auntie Deana slid back into the booth. "Chyna baby you are just like me. You a real bitch and hard headed like I am too." She laughed. "I think you shoulda been my daughter. Instead God gave you to your punk ass mom." Aunt

Deana laughed. I laughed right with her. She always called my mom either a punk or a scary ass bitch. Auntie often called her names because my mom didn't want anything to do with her illegal activities.

"I want you to hold shit down." She whispered low like we were being watched. "Your brother…" Aunt Deana said and shook her head. "I love him to the death of me. That's neph but he ain't strong as you. He got your mother's scary ass tendencies."

"Now you remember that bitch ass nigga Ray that I do business with?" Aunt Deana ask. As I was about to say yes, the waiter approaches the table.

"Hello ladies my name is Sarah." The goofy waitress said with a wide smile. "May I start you guys off with a drink?" "Yes, I'll have a sweet tea and Auntie what you want?"

"I'll take a water!" She said with an attitude! I guess because the waitress interrupted her telling me what happened. "Okay you guys ready to place your food orders or, do you guys need more time?" The waitress asked, still smiling at us all goofy and shit.

"Naw we going to order now." I said. "I'll take the steak

and cheese eggs and fried potatoes, I want my steak well done too." I said to the waitress."

"Give me the same thing." My Auntie told the waitress.

After she wrote what we ordered down she put her pad back in her smock pocket and grabbed our menus. "Your order will be right up." She said and walked off smiling.

Aunt Deana looked at me, "Damn that dick got her smiling like a mutha fucka." Auntie said harshly.

"How you know she isn't just happy?" I questioned looking at my phone again wondering why Dontae hasn't called me today!

"Chyna please only dick would have a bitch smiling like that trust me. It ain't this wack ass job!" I bust out and started laughing "Mann… Auntie you're a whole mess leave that white bitch alone."

Auntie threw her hand up like forget that bitch. "She just better makes sure my food is right!" She spats.

"Back to what I was saying Chyna that fuck nigga Ray set me up." He said he had a potential clientele and you know I NEVER get my hands dirty. He asked me for ten extra birds to supply these niggas. I asked him did he trust these niggas. Because if they don't come up with my money it's his debt. Raymond told me they were official. So I fronted him the work. Two months later I wanted my damn money. I gave his ass 60 days to get rid of the shit which he agreed to." Auntie said frustrated as she told the story.

"He kept giving me the run around about my money. Chyna you know how I hate to have to repeat myself. Its blood shed time. I told Ray you don't got my money, so you know what that mean now right? Ray told me I'm gon have your money. I cut him off and hung up on him I don't have time for that niggas coulda, woulda, shoulda! I didn't give a fuck about the police I had them on payroll, but they start disappearing having me wonder what the fuck was going on. Shit's crazy right neicey?"

"Hell, yeah Auntie something is off." I knew them cops been on payroll for years that's why Auntie was always ten steps ahead of the law.

When I looked in Auntie eyes I put my head in my hands because, for the first time in my twenty-two years of being around Auntie looked worried. The waitress came and brought us our food. "Is there anything else I can bring you ladies?" The waitress asked.

"Naw we good." I told her. Auntie wasn't finish telling her story. "So, what happen to the cops you had on payroll?"

"I don't know Chyna, When I looked into it nobody seen them in about a month now. So now the cops that ain't on payroll keep fucking with me." Auntie said with a deep sigh.

"I can't find Ray nowhere he went into hiding, so you know what that mean, Shit I don't give a fuck niecey I already killed his wife." Auntie said. While shrugging her shoulders, "I thought that would bring him outta hiding. I was wrong I still can't find the nigga. Guess he said fuck his wife too! He didn't even attend her damn funeral." Auntie said while chewing her food. I sipped my tea, I was trying to process all this shit she was telling me.

"Anyways Chyna I got pulled over. Never in my 20 plus years of being in the game; have I ridden dirty. Maybe when I was with Black I held shit but, I wasn't the target. He was the King Pen back then, so I would do shit to take the heat off him. I held shit and, transported shit. Once I took over the business I became a target so no more holding or transporting drugs and guns! Just imagine how I felt when the cops pulled me over and they found two keys of dope and a 9mm in my trunk" Aunt Deana said defeated.

"What?" I screamed, and I spit out my tea. Tea went everywhere, all over the table. I grabbed napkins to get the tea up. I thought, *"Damn this shit is getting deep."*

"Auntie I know you send young niggas to do your drops." I was mad as fuck now. I gotta keep the empire running and find out who's out to get Aunt Deana. *"Something ain't right!"* I thought.

"At first I thought it was Mayor Weiss." Aunt Deana said. "I used to fuck him here and there just to keep my empire above the bullshit. I had cops on payroll, and judges. Lil Mikey got booked and he had a lot of work on him. Mayor Weiss made sure all that shit went away and they threw the case out, lack of evidence." Auntie said.

"Mayor Weiss son was upset to learn about his dad extra activities and threatened to get Mayor Weiss fired."

"Foreal he gon give his dad up. What he mad for?" I asked

as I drunk the rest of my drink.

"His son is racist, and he know that his dad helps the minorities in the community and he don't like that shit."

"There gotta be some other reason Auntie." I said, and side eyed her.

"Aite Chyna on some real shit I fucked up. Your cousin Sage is the Mayor's daughter. I fucked him one day. I was drunk. Chyna on the real" Auntie said sounding like she in her twenties.

"That morning after pill they got out today. Shit I sure coulda used it back then." She laughs. I was running the streets so heavy then. I didn't even pay attention to my body. I missed like four periods long story short I passed out one day, at a meeting with Fontell, I went to the hospital and found out I was four months pregnant with the Mayor's baby. Just thinking about that shit now got me mad. I was so stupid, but shit happens. I don't believe in abortions, so I decided to have Sage."

"She doesn't even know that's her dad either. She thinks her dad died and we gonna keep it like that.' Auntie said in one breathe. "I think his son knows Sage is his sister because the Mayor told me awhile back he was receiving unknown calls saying you got a baby by that nigger bitch."

"He's being black mailed by his son?" I questioned.

"Yea Chyna he probably found out about Sage, I got a private investigator looking into the whole Weiss Family, I ain't heard nothing back yet." Aunt Deana said.

To say I was speechless is an understatement. I put my hand up to my mouth in disbelief. "Wow!!! So, what makes you think he ain't snitch on you?"

"Trust me Chyna that man loves me. Shit look at me I can't blame him." Auntie said while rubbing her hands up and down her breasts and thigh area. "He the fucking Mayor and I'm a street bitch. We can't be together. I just fucked him to get shit done but other than that it ain't nothin but business for me." Aunt Deana said.

"So when you gotta turn yourself in?" I asked Aunt Deana. The waiter brought the check and Auntie Deana gave her the money. "It's Friday so I gotta have a meeting to let everyone know you're taking over Chyna. Monday I'm gonna turn myself in."

"Monday?" I asked, shocked at how soon this shit was

gonna happen!

"Yes, is that a problem?" Aunt Deana ask me with an attitude. Bitch act like she was handing over a legitimate business.

"Naw that's cool. I'm gon bring Gunna in on this with me. Is that cool?"

"Hell, yea it's cool. That's your right hand. I trust her plus she will kill for you with no questions asked. That's one gangsta ass bitch. You gon need her on your team."

Chapter 2

SATURDAY THE TAKE-OVER

Chyna

Auntie sat the meeting up with her crew. When I walked in I saw ten of her top lieutenants, old school players and the youngins in attendance. I felt like the old school niggas was gonna try and give me problems and not accept the fact I'm about to be the Queen of this shit. I'm gon sit here and watch how this shit play out. I looked at my Aunt and she was so pretty. She still had a youthful look and she didn't look a day over 35.

She was wearing an all-white fitted blazer, white linen wide leg pants and, nude patent leather Christian Louboutin on her feet. "Can I get everyone attention?" Aunt Deana asked. The room grew quiet when Aunt Deana raised her voice. As I looked around the room the old school drug dealers was casual dressed in dress pants and button-down shirt, Gucci shirts and ties. While the younger drug dealers had on sweatpants, jeans, Jordan's and Gucci sneakers. You can tell things changed in the game I laughed to myself.

Everyone got quiet and focus on what Aunt Deana was

about to say. "So y'all all know I'm about to go to jail Monday."

"What...how what happen?" Several niggas asked, everyone in there was shocked or pretended to be. I watched people faces as my Aunt spoke and one nigga that wasn't really saying anything was Jason he was just looking around looking nervous. I got my eyes on him. Dumb ass nigga didn't even play it off.

He just sat there while everyone was asking questions. "Aite aite shut the fuck up while I'm talking." Aunt Deana said angrily. It was getting so loud in the room everyone was in an uproar.

"Look I'm not going into details, just know that I'm about to lay it down. My niece..." As soon as she said that. I seen a couple niggas drop they head and say, "HELL NAW!"

"Oh hell yea bitch ass nigga. My niece is taking over in my absence. If you don't like the shit, then go cop elsewhere." Jason stood up and said, "Deana how you gonna pass all of us up that's been doing this shit as long as you have. You hand it over to a kid. She is a baby Deana fuck this; I'm out."

Aunt Deana reached behind her back and grabbed her little twenty-two handgun and shot Jason right in his left leg.

"Bitch ass nigga you don't tell me how to run my shit. I'm glad you feel that way. I was firing your snake ass anyways. Get this nigga away from me." Aunt Deana said to her bodyguard Bolo. Jason was on the ground crying like a bitch and holding his leg.

Bolo was 6'9, 300 lbs., solid ass nigga. Bolo picked Jason up and threw him over his shoulder like he was a sack of potatoes.

"Stop fucking crying nigga. It was a leg shot you be aite." Bolo said to Jason while laughing. "Anybody else got a problem with my decision." Aunt Deana ask?

Uncle Rich spoke up he was 6'1, dark skin, and bald head. He kinda put you in the mind of actor Ving Rhimes. I called him Unc since I was little. He been doing business with Auntie for a long time, so I respected him. He never came at her wrong and he always respected her. "Deana you know I'm cool with it. I know Chyna and over the years, you taught her everything she know about the game ever since she was fourteen. So, her taking over is just like you being here." Unc said.

I'm about to retire. I'm handing everything over to my nephew. I'll still be around if Chyna needs me." Yea I know that Unc I said. He gave me a hug and whispered in my ear.

"I also knew if Deana didn't shoot Jason in the leg, he woulda been dead by the end of today." Unc said and smiled. I looked Unc in his eyes, "You fucking right Unc." I said.

"Ya gangsta ass don't let nobody get away with disrespecting Deana." He kissed me on my cheek. "Chyna you got my number. We will have lunch soon to discuss this more. Plus, I want you to meet my nephew Lucky. "Aite Unc."

"I gotta go my wife is sick in the hospital. Deana if you need me for anything.". Aunt Deana cut him off and approach him for a hug.

"I know Rich I'll call you!"

"I love you Deana." Unc said to Auntie. "I know you do Rich. I love you too tell Vicky I said get well soon."

"I sure will."

"Back to what I was saying anybody else got a problem?" Auntie asked and adjusted her blazer and fixed her sleeves. *"Arrogant ass bitch I love it."* I thought to myself and smiled at Auntie.

"Naw!" All the niggas said in unison. Aunt Deana hand all Lieutenants a burner phone. "These are the only phones that y'all will use to contact Chyna. All the info that you will need is already listed in the contacts. I'll see y'all in about four years don't disappoint me. Don't fuck with my niece either. No matter where I'm at I still got power to do whatever I want to y'all." Aunt Deana said and left the room.

They all nodded their heads and took the burner phones. I stood off to the side still observing everyone. Unc was right later on tonight if Auntie didn't do anything to Jason. I was going kill his ass for acting like a bitch and, talking back to my Auntie like he ain't have no respect. Once I leave here I'm going to go holla at Legend, Boss hog and Gunna. I'm little sad Auntie about to lay it down but, she's tough she gon be aite. I'm gon miss her doe. I don't want to disappoint her either.

Chapter 3

SAVAGE LIFE

THREE YEARS LATER 2011

Chyna

I walked out my house to see these dumb ass police sitting in a late model blue Ford Taurus. I started laughing to myself. They been watching me for like three weeks now. Jazlynn and I was having lunch and they rode past the restaurant we were in. Jazlynn told me their names and told me they are detectives. Good thing I really don't get my hands dirty. I decided since; I got some time to spare today. I'm gon go fuck with them, I approached the car. It looked like they were sleep. As I got closer to the beat up blue Ford Taurus and looked inside. Sure, enough they were sleep.

Head leaned back mouth wide open. I laughed how the fuck you on a stakeout and you sleep. Rule number one never sleep on the job. Especially if you gonna fuck with a gangsta ass bitch like me because, I love trouble. My twin brother Legend told me I was a risk taker. Yea he right because he was the cautious twin. I had to toughing that nigga up especially if he's gonna be on my team. The little nigga worries too much just live life!

I knocked on the window hard, they both jumped and looked at each other with a shocked expression on their face. The driver wipes his eyes while the passenger yawned and stretched his body.

"Wake up boy's good morning." I said and smiled. I motioned my hand for them to follow me. It's show time boys let's take a ride! The two detectives look at each other shocked at how bold I was. That was the Aunt Deana coming outta me not giving a fuck.

I walked away laughing because I knew they would follow suit why else would they be here? I walked to my all white Range Rover that I barely drove and after today I am gon sale it. I decided I'm going take them on a little ride to fuck with them. I rode through all the toughest neighborhoods in Philly. Mantua, Strawberry Mansion and Hunting Park. I hopped out my Range in the Hunting Park and small talk with a couple young niggas. I know this made the cops nervous. They try to avoid areas like these. Next, I went to the grocery store yup Walmart, I spent over an hour buying groceries I didn't even need!

I went to the mall drop like ten bands on bullshit. I walked past them outside of the True Religion store I came out with bags smiling. "Damn you see something you like, next stop nail shop fellas." I said, and I put my fingers up in the air. I did a Kenya Moore from House Wives Of Atlanta twirl, showing off all my pearly whites. "Let's ride!"

I took them to a nail shop I never went to before. I ain't stupid. All these places I am taking them today I never go there. Silly rabbits I love playing tricks! I went to a hair salon that one of my customers wife own and carried on a bullshit conversation.

"Hey girl, how are you?" I asked Shelly?

"Oh my god Chyna." She embraced me with a hug so tight. I seen the way the cops were looking through the window. What's so funny; is from outside of the shop it looked like we were bestie's, I love it.

"So what brings you by" Shelly asked?

"The vacant space next door. I was thinking about buying and turning it into a nail shop." I lied. Shit I looked dead in Shelley's hazel eyes like I was serious. Shelly smiled "Oh yes honey that would bring me so much business." Shelly said all excited.

Shelley was what you call a (BBW) Big Beautiful Women. She was so pretty, hips and ass for days. Her husband was a junkie he was bringing her down stealing her hair money, stealing equipment out her shop, trying to sell it in the hood and she knew it too. I guess it's til' death do them part huh? Fuck all that.

I came out the salon the cop was leaning on my Range Rover. "Chyna why you got us on this wild goose chase? Won't you just come down to the station and tell us all we need to know about your Aunt's drug cartel. That you are currently running while she in jail." I made my voice sound like a white girl.

"Soooo you really want me to go downtown to the precinct and offer me coffee, a McDonald's meal and cigarettes. So, I can just answer all your questions about whatever you think I know?" The cop started smiling and got excited like he was winning. I use my pointer finger for the cop to come closer to me. The smell of coffee and cigarettes invading my nostrils *"EWW"* I said in my head.

I whispered in his ear "I AM NOT GOING NOWHERE NEAR A FUCKING POLICE STATION OR ANYWHERE

ELSE TO TALK TO YOU ABOUT SHIT!" If looks could kill I would be dead black ass bitch. The cops face turned beet red. I hopped in my Range and pulled off. When I came to a stop sign at the intersection. I noticed a card laying under my window wipers. Bet money that cop put that bullshit there. I put my truck in park and got out. I snatched that card from under my window wipers. I looked at the business card. Written in bold blue letters. Detective John Snowden 215-682-9999. I ripped the card up and got in my truck and pulled off, "CHYNA WHITE AIN'T NEVER BEEN NO SNITCH!"

Chapter 4

DIDN'T SEE THIS SHIT COMING

6 MONTHS LATER 2012

Chyna

"Babe turn the music down my phone ringing." Dontae told me. We on our way to have dinner with my connect Fontell. Dontae didn't know Fontell was my connect. Technically Fontell just ain't my connect, he is my Godfather. That's what I told Dontae. Fontell is just my Godfather. I don't discuss my drug empire life with Dontae.

Dontae and I have been dating for almost two years. He so fucking sexy, light skin, about 6'4, nice build goatee and low fade. Dontae looked like actor nigga Omari Hardwick, I swear to God he do.

I turned Future's hit song, Turn Off The Lights down in my Dodge Charger rental car. Dontae grabbed his phone and slid his finger across his iPhone 4 screen. "Yo." He said into the phone and then his facial expression changed quick. I was trying to eavesdrop, but I wanted to trust my nigga of two years but, shit nowadays trust is rare to find and I'm having a bad feeling about how Dontae acting. Damn I should of listen to my twin brother Legend I couldn't get me and Legends conversation out my head!

"Chyna watch yourself around that nigga he seems sneaky. Some shit ain't right with ol' boy. I've had my people look into him. I ain't found nothing but he could be good at being a fuck boy and covering his tracks just be careful. I got a bad feeling in my gut every time he around" Legend said and bent down to my small frame and kissed me on the cheek. "Aite bro" I said. I watched Legend walked out my mother's kitchen shaking his head. Legend was worried I'm going take his advice this time. *"Hard head make a soft ass and I gotta observe Dontae a lil bit better."* I thought.

Dontae kept his conversation short by replying one word not a whole sentence and then push the end button. "Damn babe you cool who was that?" I asked Dontae. He ran his hands down his light skin face and turned to look at me with a straight face and lied. I felt the deceit as soon as it came out his mouth.

"Yea everything good." Dontae said and, he turned the music back up. I knew this mutha fucker was lying about something we had like thirty more minutes before we made it to

Fontell house. Like I said before my Godfather Fontell was my connect but, Dontae didn't know that. Well I hope he don't know hmm… that got me wondering. I've been really hiding my life from him mainly because of my Queen Pen status. Dontae and I don't live together. I always take him to my condo in downtown Philly. I don't really trust nobody, but I refuse to get played like I'm a BASIC ASS BITCH. I feel the less you know about me the better.

I looked to my right and the sign said ½ mile left is the gas station. "Why we stopping?" Dontae asked with a raised brow. "Babe I gotta pee so bad." I said. I played it off good and did the I gotta pee so bad dance in my seat. "Get me something to drink while I use the restroom." I hollered as he went into the store.

I round the corner like I was going in the outside bathroom. Once I seen Dontae go in the store. I ran back out the bathroom, to the car and grabbed his phone. I look at the last call. I had a bad feeling about this. I read the number off. Damn a 215-682-9999. I remember this number. I instantly went from worried to mad. I peeked in the store he was still in there grabbing drinks.

I hurried out the car once I put the phone exactly how

he had it. I ran back to the bathroom. I took my iPhone 4 outta my back jean pocket and dialed Gunna's number. What I found out next blew my fucking mind I can't believe this shit! Man…fuck I'm gon have to kill this nigga!

The scene looked kinda funny when I came out the bathroom all the cars looked like unmark cars (police). I dialed Gunna number. "Yo what's up Chyna" Gunna said into the phone.

I whispered, "I think this nigga set me up bestie." I said in one breath! "I can't explain right now but I gotta get the fuck outta here. I'm at the gas station on Vera Road 40 minutes from the city." Gunna sighed real heavy through the phone. "I gotchu Chyna meet me close by Fontell's a block down."

"Okay how you get away?" Gunna asked in a worried tone?

"I don't know. I'm in the bathroom right now. I can't go back out there I got a funny feeling that those are unmarked cars!" My palms were sweating, and I was in need of a fat blunt to calm my nerves. I paced the bathroom floor.

"Fuck I gotta get the fuck outta here Gunna! I'm gon call you when I get close to our meeting spot. Hit Legend and Boss

Hog and let them know what's up." I said quickly into the phone while peeking out the bathroom door.

"Aite be careful" Gunna said and hung up.

I eased the bathroom door open again and peeked my head out the door. There was a black Kia Sorento. This skinny brown skin chick was sitting in the driver side with her one leg out the truck driver's side door. She was texting on her phone not paying attention to her surroundings. I looked to the left then right to make sure nobody was watching. Shit knowing a gas station in this suburban area of Philly, there were cameras watching. I got to be discreet as possible. When I looked to my right I seen the same detective that was following me months ago. John Snowden was drinking his coffee and approaching my rental car. He was talking to Dontae and they seem to be previously acquainted with each other.

I saw Donate point to the bathroom. FUCK I gotta go in a hurry. It seemed like everything was moving in slow motion. I started shaking my head and my blood was boiling. This lame ass nigga Dontae is a fucking snitch. How else would he know that detective? I stepped closer to the brown skin chicks truck. I bent down to her ear. "Don't fucking scream." I whispered. "Don't look at me either." I said through clench teeth. I made that bitch jump in her seat.

I slid my 9mm from the back of my Express jeans to my side. I got real close to her so that on camera it looks like we just on some lesbian shit. I took my right hand and grabbed her face like I was about to kiss her. I looked into her eyes because she looked real familiar. Shit I come across people all the time but, I don't forget a face or a number. She knew exactly who I was by the shocked expression written on shawty face.

"Please Hunnid don't kill me." Shawty said and start crying. "Bitch I ain't gon kill you. I just need your car."

She shook her head up and down and whispered, "Okay just don't hurt me." She keeps saying don't kill, don't hurt me. It was annoying the hell outta me. I gotta get outta here before I shoot this crying ass bitch. "Goofy ass bitch I just said I'm not gon hurt you." I said trying calm down.

"What's your name?" I asked her.

"Kenisha Henry." She said nervously and slid out the driver side and I slid in. I looked in the rear view mirror and notice John

Snowden walking towards the bathroom. I started the ignition, I looked at Kenisha.

"Aye keep your fucking mouth shut." I told her. She nodded her head up and down in agreement. "I'll buy you a new car thanks boo!"

I pulled around the back of the gas station. I knew there was an exit. As soon as I got down the hill I started doing seventy mph. I used my burner phone and dialed up Gunna. She answered on the first ring.

"You cool?" Gunna asked with her raspy deep voice sounding like a nigga. I still can't figure out why and how Gunna sound just like a dude. "Yeah, I'm in a black Kia Sorento. I should be there in about twenty minutes." I said, and I looked in the rearview mirror. I notice a black Chevy Impala following me. "Fuck Gunna this black Impala is following me." I said still looking in the rearview.

"This shit is all bad Hunnid drive that fucking car don't let that car get close to you." Gunna said hollering at me! "I'm trying Gunna I'm doing ninety mph now and I can still see their headlights." I said angrily.

"If I don't be at the meeting place in twenty minutes you know I'm locked up." I said and made a sharp turn. This Sorento was damn near on two wheels instead of four. I was driving the hell out of the Sorento.

"I'm coming to get you." Gunna said.

"No Gunna ain't no need of both of us going to jail." I screamed into the phone at Gunna!

"Hunnid what I am I gon do without you by my side?" Gunna asked in a worried tone.

"Hold shit the fuck down Gunna, you got this!" I said. I push the end button and kept driving.

Gunna was in her feelings. I understand we were like Bonnie and Clyde. You wouldn't see one without the other I trust her with my life, I love Gunna! The day she saved my life. That situation made our bond stronger.

A few years back these niggas tried to rob me. My cousin's boyfriend was the culprit. There was three of them and Gunna killed all three of them niggas before they even made it pass my garage.

I was driving so fast through this small hick town. I'm

hitting pot holes, but It didn't slow me down. It started raining I put the windshield wipers on. I looked around and notice I was closer to my destination. I looked in the rearview again. It was the same car tailing me. I hit some back street, I don't know if this bitch reported this truck stolen. Think Chyna, *"Jesus take the wheel."* I thought to myself. I look down in the cup holder. Ohhhh...I smiled this bitch had a freshly rolled blunt. I know her getting carjacked and then your weed gone too. Yea shawty having a fucked up night! Not as fucked up as I am though. I'm gon make sure I throw something extra to her ass, when I get a chance. Show her my appreciation for the ride and the blunt!

I contemplated on rather or not to blaze this weed. I needed to smoke but, I don't know if this bitch laced this weed or not. People be doing the most in 2011. I need to smoke I thought this might be my last blunt for a while. I found a lighter in the console and lit the blunt. This weed was good as fuck. It tasted like Gunna weed though! I was high as fuck, blunt hanging out the side of my mouth.

Now the rain was coming down hard. I really couldn't see. I put the car in reverse to make a left down the street. A car came outta nowhere. When I got closer to the end of this street. I seen them blue and red lights flashing. *"Fuck they trying to corner me."* I said to myself. I continued to back up and crashed right into the side of this car. I put the car in drive and tried to proceed down the narrow street. There were two cars coming up this street. I kept driving if these cops wanna play (chicken) let's get it then!

I still was smoking my blunt, the weed had me feeling numb. I felt like Cleo on set it off. I was doing like fifty mph down this street with four cop cars coming towards me. All of a sudden, the tires were being shot out POW... POW... POW! DAMN that shit definitely slowed my ass right down. I was still trying drive too! It was no use my black ass was caught, and Dontae was the reason. I don't care if I found out he a cop. I'm still killing him.

The cops pulled their guns out and pointed it towards the truck. "Please exit the vehicle with your hands up!" The cop screamed! I laughed to myself and continued to smoke my blunt I was thinking in my head, *"They gon fucking wait."* Moments later I opened the door with my hands up. The little bit of blunt I had left was still in my mouth. The cop had his gun pointed at me while searching me but, I threw the gun I had on me out the window good luck finding it. Once the white cop realized I didn't have any weapons on me. He flashed the flashlight on my face and I showed him all my pearly whites.

My eyes were bloodshot red. He took the blunt out my mouth and threw it on the ground and I laughed. "Aye cop you shoulda hit that shit. That was some fire ass weed."

He looked at me and smirked. "I hope you enjoyed it because it will be your last smoke for a long time young lady." He said and laughed so hard in my face like he told the most funniest joke in the world. My smart ass laughed right with him.

"Cracker boy don't nobody put fear in my heart but God. So do what you gotta do. I don't give two fucks." I said sounding more confident than Whitney Houston when she stated that crack is whack, crack is cheap. She makes too much money to ever smoke crack.

"I bet you gon care about this." He smarted off.

He looked over at the black impala. The passenger door opened up. Bitch ass nigga Dontae emerged from the car smiling and approached me.

"Baby don't be mad at me. I'm not really Dontae. I am

detective Carl Rays an undercover cop. "It was my job to act like your man." He said with his chest poked out like he did something, and I laughed right in his face! I shrugged my shoulders. "You think you just won?" I asked Dontae?

He walked behind me. "Chyna Jackson also known to the streets as Chyna White & Hunnid. You are under arrest for drug trafficking and attempt to deliver." He grabbed my hands and put the handcuffs on me. Dontae read me my rights.

"You have any last words." Dontae asked me? "Yea FUCK YOU!" I said, and I spit in his face.

He smacked me so hard that my cheeks were swelling. I laughed and played that shit off like it didn't faze. My cheeks were stinging but I never showed any pain. He was pissed that I wasn't mad. Whatever happened... happened I can't re-do it. I shoulda been more careful but; it's life lessons and I'm gon fight until the end. I wonder how much evidence they got on me because I didn't do illegal shit in front of Dontae and I never talked business on the phone. If I did I always used untraceable phones. *"They talking about drug trafficking and attempt to deliver. Nigga deliver what? I got young niggas for that shit."* I thought to myself.

I am eager to know how this shit play out, I know somebody planted some shit on me. "Don't you ever spit on me again you lucky these cops are out here. I woulda beat your ass to death and say it was self-defense." Dontae whispered in my ear. "Nigga shut up and take me to jail. What's the fucking hold up?" I screamed.

He aggressively placed me in the back of the black Chevy Impala. Dontae shut the door and went over to the vehicle I was driving. Donate and two other cops was searching it. I hope they don't find nothing in there. I stole that car I prayed the bitch ain't have shit. If they find some shit, it's on me huh FUCK!!

"You ain't no cop Dontae." I screamed as Dontae was getting back in the Impala. All the cops looked over at the Chevy Impala wondering what was going on. This time he was in the driver seat. I was sounding like LL Cool J when he played God in the movie, 'In Too Deep' and he told Omar Epps you ain't no cop J-Reid!

Another cop got in the passenger side. He was a young white cop. He just laughed at me. "Shut up Chyna you did enough tonight. You need to focus on the time you about to do." Dontae said sounding frustrated with me. Nigga said that shit like I was going be scared *"Nigga I ain't getting life."* I thought to myself! "Nigga you was eating my pussy and ass every night you played your part good very well I ain't mad at you." I said with a slight giggle!

Dontae turned his head around as he made a left turn almost swerving into the guardrail turning onto the highway. My little statement made him lose focus on the road.

"If I gotta tell you one more time to shut up. You gonna be in the emergency room before you go to jail." He said with so much anger it made the white cop look at him. "Ohhhh somebody mad huh?" Dontae slowed the car down and for the first time the young white cop spoke.

"Let's just get her to the precinct. You already in enough trouble for withholding information on this case. I don't think assaulting the suspect is a good idea." The cop said and shook his head. "You can't afford no more mishaps, or you can be taking off this case." Dontae nodded his head to the cop and wiped his hands down his face.

I wonder what evidence he withheld hmm...he probably

was falling for me hard and was mixing business with pleasure. After a while he couldn't separate the two. That's what good pussy will do to you. I looked out the window and was thinking hard trying to unravel this mess is going be hard. *"Why are they gunning for me and who is Dontae?"*

The ride to the precinct was hilarious. I am about to do some time and my dumb ass had jokes typical Chyna. Once my high come down things gonna get real. I can hear Legends voice now. *"I told you Chyna. You hard headed."* Once my high come down and I'm gon be mad as fuck!

Hour later at the Precinct...

I was sleepy by the time I reached the precinct. My high was coming down too. Reality started to set in. Dontae should get an Oscar for his performance. Dontae pulled up to the 17th precinct. Dontae open the door and helped me get out the car. The white cop that was with him just stared at me as I was getting out the car. Donate eyes roamed my body. "No..No cop boy you fucked all your chances up." I said to Dontae while sticking out my tongue. The white cop turned around and looked from me to Dontae. He had me hemmed up on the car.

"Bitch if I tell you one more time." Dontae started to say but, I mean mugged him and looked up at the precinct building reminding him where the fuck he was at. *"Do it."* I was thinking this will help my case.

"Tell me Dontae how hard your dick is right now?" I asked. Dontae still had me hemmed up on the car. He was losing his grip.

"Nothing Chyna." Dontae said, and he let me go.

"What Dontae? Tell me… how hard I got your dick right now? Yea I see your dick pointing at me." I said laughing at his weak ass. Dontae ignored me.

The white cop grabbed my arm gently and started walking me towards the precinct. Leaving Dontae just standing there in a daze, his erected dick was still poking out his pants. I kept a side smile on my face just to make him mad. "You sure love pissing him off." The white cop said as he opened up the door to the precinct.

Jeremy put her in the interrogation room number two. The

fat white detective said to the white cop. Who I just learned his name is Jeremy. He grabbed the keys and unlocked the door. He flicked the light on and uncuffed me. My wrist was hurting a little. I had to rub them to soothe the pain. The door open and in walks Dontae avoiding eye contact. "Chyna you want a blanket or something to drink?" I ignored him I didn't want anything from Dontae. Joke time is over.

"Chyna we gotta talk." Dontae said and scooted his chair up to the table and folded his hands. What's crazy the nigga is sexy as fuck for three whole seconds just now! Fourth second that attraction quickly went out the window. I know y'all thinking why I would still find him attracted after all he did to me but; trust I'm just stating facts.

Dontae shoulda let me be. I know that's crazy thinking. Like he had options. Oh well he shoulda came and hollered at me maybe we coulda work something out. I woulda made him rich if he woulda kept his mouth shut and, kept me ten steps ahead of the law. Naw he had to do the right thing. I'm gon destroy everything that mean something to him. I just stared at him. "Oh so you don't got nothing to say?" Dontae asked getting agitated.

Again, I stayed silent he slid his chair out and stood up. He came around to my side of the table bent down and whispered in my ear. "I know you mad but guess what Chyna this was the hardest thing I had to do in my career. For what it's worth I'm sorry! I really believe that if we were in a different life your gangsta ass woulda been my wife." Dontae said emotionally.

I still sat there playing with my fingers. Dontae walked out the door. I turned around and looked at the door. Damn nigga caught feelings. Well they wasn't strong enough. If so I wouldn't be in this shit in the first place. About twenty minutes later a short skinny black Detective came in the room. Why don't they just send me to jail? I ain't telling them shit. They wasting their time.

"I'm Detective Steve Neal I just want to ask you a couple questions." He said and sat down. I noticed he had a yellow folder, he opened the folder. He laid out over ten photos of me doing hand-in-hand transactions. I looked at the pictures, that is definitely me. I would never do no hand-in-hand transactions. I had other people on my team for that. I was only present for big shipments. The way I organized the shipments is through the grocery store, my Godfather Fontell own. Fontell is Mob connected but he play the background. Only people know about them meetings or even present is Gunna, Boss Hog and sometimes Legend.

These pictures gotta be photoshop. The day I had that outfit on I wasn't even on no drug activity shit that day. The second picture that was the day Bianca open up her hair salon so no drug activity that day. The third photo was Gunna's birthday. I remember she brought me them badass Nelly Bernal heels that I had on in this picture. I only wore them once which was on her birthday. I was on no drug activity that day somebody set me up but, how could I prove it?

"What are you smiling for Ms. Jackson? You are going away for a long time." Detective Neal said.

"LAWYER!" I said still smiling.

"You won't…" Detective Neal started to say. I cut him right off again. **"LAWYER."** I loudly repeated. The cop looked annoyed by my outburst. He closed the folder and got up out his seat. "You are making a big mistake." He said and stormed out the interrogation room. I sighed heavily. What the fuck is going on here?

I put my head down because I knew it would be a long time before they come get me to take me to jail. It was cold as fuck and truth be told my black ass was hungry. I ain't taking nothing from them they might spit on it. I took them on a wild chase. Then I spit in Dontae face. Fuck a meal. I'll just suck it up.

It felt like hours later, but it was just under an hour. When I walked passed the clock earlier it said 9:45 p.m. When the detective came back in the interrogation room to get me. I walked past the clock and it said 11:10 p.m. These cops tried to be on some First 48 type shit coming in with a photoshopped folder of fake evidence. Silence is what they got. When you say nothing, they can't use shit against you in court.

I just came to the conclusion that Dontae photoshop those pictures to cover his ass. I walked passed Dontae's desk I seen a picture of his girlfriend or wife and a baby. I want eyes on that bitch. If I can't catch him wifey gotta go. I'll spare the kids life. I got a little bit of a conscious left for kids. Dontae looked at me with sadness in his eyes as I walked past. I just kept my poker face on held my head up high like I was going home.

Aunt Deana always told me in this street shit you have to

keep your weakness in a jar. Don't show it in this game or your weakness will make it easy for people to get to you. As the officer escorted me to the waiting car. The ride to the jail was short. All I kept thinking about was Legend. I said a silent prayer that my twin is okay, out here in these wild Philly streets without me. I trusted Gunna and Boss Hog but ain't nothing like me out here.

"Aite Chyna" I said to myself. *"It's survival of the fittest in here."* I went through intake and was told I wouldn't see the Judge until Monday. The female C.O. told me to take all my clothes off. She searched me thoroughly and made me squat and cough. The female C.O. gave me orange jumpsuit, shoes t-shirt and a sports bra.

She took me to the level of the jail where all women were jailed. The C.O. was tall about 5'10, short haircut. We got on the elevator. She looked at me and smiled. I mean mugged the shit outta her. Bitch didn't look familiar fuck she smiling for. I'm going to jail ain't shit to smile about.

"Hunnid." the C.O. said. I turned my head slowly. I didn't answer her. Nor was I shocked, she knows who I am. I looked over at her with my brow raised. "I don't care what nobody says about you. Your good in my book." I turned my head back around and watch the elevator floors move. I don't care what she's talking about. Take me to my cell.

The elevator stopped, and the C.O. leaned over. "You don't remember me, but I remember you. Couple years back my grandma electricity was about to get cut off. You seen the man on the pole about to turn them off and you gave him $1000 to leave them on. That was some real shit Hunnid. I will never forget that because, we were struggling financially back then. I definitely couldn't help her." The C.O whispered to me.

I proceeded to walk out the elevator and she stopped me. "Hunnid whatever you need in here legal or Illegal I gotchu." She said. I gave her a small smile. We walked a short distant to my cell. To my surprise I didn't have a cellmate. I walked in the cell and looked over at the C.O. She gave me a side smile. "Thanks yo." I said. "Taylor." The C.O. said. I looked at her. "What you say?" I asked her with attitude. "My name is Taylor." She repeated. "Aite good looking out Taylor."

I didn't sleep all night. I needed to talk to my brother. I tossed and turned all night on the flat ass mattress. Morning came, and it was time to go eat breakfast. Even though I didn't want to eat this bullshit a bitch ain't eat shit since yesterday. On my way down there, I saw Taylor.

"Hey Hunnid." She said all bubbly. "What's up Taylor. I need you to do me a solid" She smiled before speaking. "Yes of course anything." Taylor said. "I need to talk to my brother like yesterday, I need money down here."

"Okay what's his number?" She asked me. Taylor took a pen and piece of paper out her shirt pocket? "It's 215-328-4949 tell him I need money but, shit I don't know what they gon do at court never mind the money. I might be shipped off soon anyways but, to be on the lookout for my call.

"Oh call Gunna too." I quickly said. I gave her Gunna's number "Tell her the same thing."

Taylor moved her hand in a motion to tell me keep walking while we talk. "Hunnid I'm gon call your brother and Gunna. I'll let you call them later off of my phone." Taylor said. "Aite cool I'll see you later then." I said to Taylor. As I finished walking down the steps to go eat people was screaming my name. I just threw my hand up, I hit the last step and Sasha approached me. She was a booster from my hood.

She was a badass booster we basically grew up together. "Hunnid what the fuck you doing in here?" She asked me. "Bitch what it look like? What you want Sasha? I ain't in the mood." I told her. Sasha put her hands up in a surrender stance. "Hunnid I ain't mean it like that. I'm just surprise to see you down here." Sasha said. "It's just some bullshit." I said and observed my surrounding. Me and Sasha walked to get in line to get a breakfast tray.

"Hunnid I got caught stealing again and they tryna give me two years." Sasha said. "Damn you know after so many times getting caught they get tired of seeing you." I said to Sasha while looking at this nasty ass jail food. A bitch wanted an old western omelet wishful thinking doe that ain't happening. "I know… fuck it is what it is" Sasha said and shrugged her shoulders. "Yeah that's how I feel too Sasha."

We got our food and sat down just talking about bullshit. "Hunnid what's up." Some bitch walking pass my table said and waved. I just ignored her. These fucking groupie ass bitches I don't know y'all. Sasha laughed at me "Hunnid you crazy as fuck you know that." Sasha said. "Shit who don't know that." I said and laughed. "I'm glad I grew up with your crazy ass and we always been aite." Sasha said. "Fuck these bitches Sasha."

We continued to eat these bullshit ass breakfast. Sasha was always cool I didn't really fuck with too many bitches but, Sasha was cut from the same cloth I was. She got hers by any means necessary. She fought bitches, she been to jail numerous times. I know because I looked out for her a time or two on a lawyer. What I like about her was she never looked for a handout. So she did pay me back when she got her money up.

"What level you on?" Sasha asked me. "I'm on 4B." I said and took a sip of my bitter ass orange juice. "Oh I'm on 4C." Sasha said. "Aye Sasha you got phone time? Let me use your shit to call Legend." I eagerly said to Sasha. "You know I gotchu Hunnid." You looked out for me when nobody would." Sasha said.

"You ready now?" I asked Sasha? "Yea let's go." We got up from the table and went straight to the phone. Sasha put her Pin number in and doc number to use the phone. I got on the phone dialed Legend's number it rings twice and the recording about three-way calling is prohibited blah… blah.

"Hello." Legend said in a deep raspy voice. "Nigga what's good?" I said, excited to hear my twins voice.

"Damn Chyna you good? He asked me. "Yea bro I'm good you should know me by now. Legend I go to court on Monday at 9 a.m. I don't wanna talk to mom yet doe." I said.

"I was over there this morning. She's worrying herself to death. Please call her so you can hear your voice" Legend said.

"Yea you right. I'll call her later. I gotta go bro make sure you at that hearing. I'm gon try call Gunna and see what's up with her. She might not answer because its early."

"Hell, yeah Gunna probably just got in the house.'" Legend said, with a slight chuckle. "Bro just tell her Blue gets Green." I said. That is our code to let her know she gotta do the shipment and meet with Fontell her and Legend. "I gotchu sis. I love you and keep your head up" Legend said.

I hung the phone up. I had Sasha to put her info in again. I dialed Gunna number it went straight to voicemail. *"Damn Gunna be on point."* I said to myself in my head. I slammed the phone down.

"Gunna M.I.A ain't she? Gunna probably laid up with

some bitch". Sasha said and rolled her eyes.

Gunna use to mess with Sasha and Gunna is always with a different chick. Sasha was always fighting bitches over Gunna. Sasha just got tired and eventually moved on.

"Yea Gunna be wildin sometimes. I'll just hit her up later on. Fuck it." I said. "Aite Sasha I'm gon go lay down and take a nap. I ain't get no sleep last night because of that bed." I said and turned to walk away. "Thanks for the phone calls." I said over my shoulder and went up the stairs. "I'll see you later then Hunnid." Sasha screamed up the steps.

I knew she was about to get in her feelings about Gunna and I ain't in the mood. I'll call Gunna later from Taylor's phone. I got to my cell and laid down. Monday morning came so fast. My bond was revoked judge said I'm a flight risk.

Three months later

Three months later my case went straight to trial. The C.O. came and took me to the holding cell for inmates waiting for court. My court hearing started at 9 a.m. I looked at the wall clock its 11a.m. Fuck I'm still sitting here. What the fuck? "Ughhh." I sighed. I don't understand why they schedule a hundred niggas for the same time at court. They have us all just sitting here. My patience were running thin.

My lawyer came over to talk to me about an hour ago. He told me to basically take the plea. There is no way to tell the pictures were photoshop. Plus, Dontae is testifying. The judge is not going to listen to me when you got a cop on the stand. I was fucking livid. Mad is an understatement.

The plea was five years. If I fight it I would be facing ten to twenty years. They got me this time. The judge going believe his own before listening to me. I know when all this is over I am definitely gon have another lawyer look into this case again. It ain't adding up.

The State of Pennsylvania is going pay for me being wrongfully accused. I said that shit like I was a stand up citizen, like I have a 9-5 and pay taxes. I laughed. I play way too much. My name being called snap me outta my thoughts. I was dressed in black Gucci high waisted pants, Gucci white button down and, all black suede Gucci pumps. I looked back and saw my mom,

Legend, Boss hog and Gunna in the court room.

My mom looked disappointed in me, but I never lied to her. I ain't gon say that, I'll say I never lied to my mom as an adult. Around the time I turned twenty two, I just kept it a hunnid with her. Sorry mom I'm a street bitch. I didn't want nobody to tell her nothing wrong about me especially if it was lies. My mother blamed Aunt Deana for my street shit but truth be told I believe it was always in me. Aunt Deana just figured if I'm going be in this shit she gon teach me.

Granted though I'm in jail now I don't regret this at all. In this street shit, mannn... shit happenings. I take risks, and this is some of the consequences to this shit. Will I ever grow outta of it? Maybe one day but, it won't be no time soon. Even after this bid I ain't gon want outta this drug game. My mind is too corrupted, and I live for this type of this shit. This Is what Money Mitch meant when he said he loves the hustle, shit me too. I can't see myself working 9-5. I'm just in too deep.

The judge called my name "Chyna Jackson vs The State of Pennsylvania please rise." Once everyone was sworn in. "How do you plead?" The judge asked me. They crossed examine

Dontae nigga straight lied. Telling the court, he seen me making drug transactions. I didn't even say nothing. That pussy ass nigga sat across from me and couldn't look me in my eyes.

I turned around and looked at my family especially my mother. The look in her eyes was telling me she was over my bullshit. The mother in her wouldn't let her turn her back on me. I looked at Legend. He was shaking his head telling me to fight it but, the fight I was going against was tough. I rather do the five then be looking at ten to twenty years. I was already a target because of Aunt Deana, I would never get a fair trial. How can I try to fight some shit going in blind? It's time to go lay it down. I turned around and cleared my throat. "I plead Guilty your honor." I said, and I adjust my blouse like it didn't faze me.

"No..no it's not right." My mother Debbie screamed. I saw tears coming down her face and she turned and ran out the courtroom. I nodded my head at Legend to go check on our mother. Gunna facial expression was blank when I looked at her. She knew what was up. I'm cool. I looked at Boss hog and he mouthed to me. "Keep your head up sis." I gave him a head nod.

"Ms. Jackson do you have anything to say." The judge

asked me? "Naw I don't got nothing to say. Y'all already had yall mind made up before today. I don't even know why there was a hearing. Matter fact y'all minds was made up before I was born. I don't have no say so in this case. There is a vendetta y'all got against my family. That's why I'm here. So just take me to jail. I'll deal with this later, trust me this ain't the last time y'all gon see me and, when y'all do see me again it won't be on the sentencing side." I said with a calm voice like I didn't care!

"Are you threatening the court Ms. Jackson?" The judge asked me. I looked up at the old white judge "See what I'm saying all that I just said, and you took it as a threat. You still didn't receive the message just take me to jail yo" I said and shrugged my shoulders!

"A sentencing hearing will be held in thirty days from today you may be dismissed." The judge said. The cop came over and handcuffed me. I looked over at Legend consoling my crying mother. I heard Legend say, "Be safe sis. Keep dat head up. I AM MY SISTER'S KEEPER." I looked at him over my shoulder as the officer was escorting me out the courtroom and said, **"You fucking right!"**

Chapter 5

FIVE YEARS LATER

February 2017

Chyna (It's almost release time)

I got almost six months until I'm released. Gat damn that will feel so good being home! I've been in Muncy Women's Prison for five years. Dontae got on the stand and lied. I'm still killing his ass. Nobody been able to catch up to him yet but; trust me I will. Whoever fuck me over it can be a family member, friend or cop whoever it is I'm killing them. My twin bro was on the streets holding shit down. Nigga ain't came see me in three months but was sending money up here for my commissary. It was my money any fucking ways. Legend better get his ass up here. I need to know what's going on out there with my trap houses and my money. My Best Friend Gunna was holding shit down back home and keeping my commissary full.

I got in so many fights up here when I first touchdown. I had to fucka couple bitches up from D.C and New York. They ain't know who I was but shortly found out. I ran shit back home. Never been a punk bitch, always hold my own weight with or without a gun. "What's up Chyna you got a visit." C.O Brown came to my cell and told me. I jumped down grab my mirror to check my hair.

I wore my hair in two French braids. My hair was what you call a decent grade of hair. It wasn't that good but, it wasn't nappy either. It was very manageable without a perm. My hair came to the middle of my back. My chocolate skin was glowing my ass got fatter and my titties were on point. Damn jail did ya girl right. I was five feet even 170lbs no stomach because, I work out in here every day. Too much time on my hands what else was I gonna do. Besides smuggle drugs in here and get this money.

Before I got here bitch had a kangaroo pouch. My titties was 34B when I first came. Now I'm a 36C. *"Damn bitch."* I smiled to myself about how much my body filled out in this jail. I am a short feisty bitch. I don't have a filter. I never did you either love me or hate me. People often said I look like Cameron's girlfriend JuJu naw she looked like me. I smirked and jumped up from my bunk.

"Come on Chyna before I cancel your visit girl." C.O Brown said and smiled at me knowing damn well he was playing.

I kept his pockets laced, So I can smuggle this shit in here. He knew better than to try me. "Okay Brown don't get cute before I cut your half breed ass off and lace somebody else's pockets." I said with an attitude.

"Chyna you know I'm just kidding pretty lady just come on your brother is waiting for you. Hey Chyna that shipment is still coming tomorrow right? C.O Brown asked. I gave him a funny look and tilted my head to the side. "Oh I'm only asking because I thought something was wrong that's why your brother is up here." C.O Brown said.

"Naw I'll let you know when shit ain't on schedule, you know that."

"Why you really come to my cell for earlier? Huh…" I asked him with my mouth twisted and my head cocked to the side. I never fucked C.O. Brown, but I let him give me head occasionally. I respect all sexualities but, I wasn't being gay for the stay. He said, "You know what I really wanted." He smiled showing all his not so perfect teeth. "I'll think about it later." I said. "Now take me to see my brother Brown before I change my mind."

He walked me to the visitation room. Brown unlocked the doors to the hallway that separated the area. I smiled when I saw my twin brother. He was looking so handsome. Legend was tall, dark and handsome. He put you in the mind of actor Lance Gross with a beard. Legend was a younger version of my dad. God rest his soul! Legend got hazel eyes, fresh cut lined up, fresh cut bread. He had that Philly look.

"What's up twin?" I said to Legend. He looked sad as fuck as he hugged me. "Chyna I'm aite. How you doing? You look good." Legend said. I'm like…"Thanks but you don't look aite. Talk to me lil brother."

He rub his hands down his face and picked his head up. "Little what I tell you about that little brother shit. Chyna you only two minutes older than me." He said with a smiled. "I think Bianca getting high." Legend said sounding defeated. My eyes got big. "Bro why you think that?" I asked stunned.

My sister-in-law Bianca been with Legend for like five, six years and always held him down. Bianca was a bad bitch looking like Waka Flocka wife Tammy. She is an accountant. She used to be our accountant up until six months ago. Legend really didn't tell me what happened. He just replaced her. All she did was smoke weed and drink.

"What the fuck? Did somebody lace her weed with bad shit bro? How do you know this?" I asked Legend. He licked his lips and shook his head before answering. "Look Chyna one of my young niggas you remember little Ghost?" I nodded my head up and down. "Kache' little brother, right?"

"Yea he seen her and Velvet over there buying drugs not weed either Chyna." Legend said.

"Bianca tried to be slick and send Velvet in there to cop for her. So it wouldn't get back to me but I ain't dumb. The little nigga told me he always see them over there buying coke. Sis she's getting high off coke and bad. I tried to reason with her. She tried to say she ain't getting high. Talking bout niggas are lying on her and she's a bad bitch. You know what I told her? You was a bad bitch you starting to look sick." Legend said with fiery dripping off his tounge.

I cut my bro off. "Nigga you need to be there for her she is ya rider."

"I knew you was gonna be on her side" Legend said.

"Naw it's not even that doe. You know I rock with Bianca on any bad day because, she a real ass bitch. She was never with you for money. Always was about you and our family. You need to get her to rehab before it gets worse. Do you ever wonder what made her start using? Maybe she's trying to numb pain from her past. Shit it might started because Bianca was dealt a bad deck. Her mom was on drugs and a bonafide whore and her father never came around after he left when she was younger." I said displeased about this whole situation.

"Chyna, I love her. I'm trying to help her. I tried everything. You can't help nobody that don't want to be help. When you talk to Bianca weeks ago did she tell you she went to rehab but didn't finish the program? When Bianca came home, she found out I mess with some bitch. She beat the chick's ass; the chick called the police and Bianca went to jail. I posted her bond. When she got out she stole my drop top and crashed into a fire hydrant. When I caught up to her she was in a crack house high outta her mind." Legend said while rubbing his hands together.

I was 38 hot I can't believe he was just giving up on her. "Legend you got another bitch. You letting this shit go too easy.

She was with you before this money. That's rare to find. She's the type of bitch you keep. What you embarrassed huh? I understand she wildin but, you don't know what other demons she fighting? You care about what these niggas gon say when they find out huh?" I beat on the table as I talked to Legend. C.O Brown came over "Chyna just keep it down some." I waved him off fuck them!

"Chyna" Legend called my name. I held my hand up to cut him off because I wasn't done talking. "Nigga you know I'm gon keep it all the way one hunnid with you. I'm disappointed in you nigga. How the fuck you gon just let her deal with this shit by herself? You gotta do everything you can to help her. I'm gon call her later see what's up with her. If I find out this is about a bitch and that's why you acting funny towards her because; a bitch is involved I'm cutting you off. It's gon be strictly business. I'm not telling you to be with her but be there for her." I whispered to Legend with intense eye contact. I had to calm myself down. Ain't shit I can do for Bianca while I'm in here.

"Cut me off?" Legend questioned with his voiced raise. "Lower your fucking voice nigga." Need I have to remind you who the fuck you talking too. I said seriously." Chyna on some real shit you feeling yourself and I never wanted to be in this drug shit anyways." He stop talking.

"What bro?"

"Never mind Chyna. I'm just frustrated because she keep lying about shit. My money coming up missing. I'm starting to think I can't trust her. I put her out my house last week. I had twenty stacks missing out my safe." Legend said.

I looked at Legend like he just made some shit up. "Sis she ain't the same person she was when you was home. I'm gon try to do everything I can for her because, she definitely rode with a nigga." Legend said and drop his head in his hands. I sighed, *"I can't wait to touchdown."* I thought. "Other than Bianca what's up out there?

"You remember Boss hog cousin Lucci that's from the Eastside?" Yea I vaguely remember. What about him Legend?" "He got a lot territory on lock over there on the East Side. He gon partner up with us." Legend said like he ain't gotta run shit by me first. "How the fuck you gon leave me out and just make decisions without me huh Legend?" I asked Legend and took a swig of the bottled water. "Chyna I'm not." Legend rubbed his hands down his face to keep himself from getting mad at me for jumping to conclusions.

"I just wanted to expand and cover all sides." Legend said. "I thought you wanted out Legend but yet you making boss moves. Make your mind up." I told him.

"I just want you to make enough money to leave the game Chyna. By expanding to different areas, we can make more money. After I make what I need I'm out Chyna. It's getting old. I'm only doing this for you and lil side money." I side-eyed Legend.

"Nigga you doing this for the money too. Bro you love this shit. You talking about side money. Shit nigga side money is a couple thousand. We past that; Once we expand we gon be past millions." I said excited. "You right sis money too but, let me get outta here." Legend said and stood up. Put that nigga Lucci on your visitors list. We will all come up here to visit you. Everyone can get acquainted together." Legend hugged me and kissed my cheek. It was bitter-sweet watching my twin brother leave. *"Back to survival of the fittest!"*

Chapter 6

SHE GOT MY BACK & I GOT HERS

Chyna

I got to my cell and went to sleep for three hours. My jailhouse bestie Rasheeda came back from her visit with her lawyer. As soon as I heard the clicking off the door I sat up and rubbed my eyes, stretching my body. Rasheeda greeted me.

"Hey bestie." Rasheeda said sniffling and wiping her eyes." Hey boo what the lawyer say? Was you crying for what?" I asked her. Rasheeda looked at me with a concerned look on her face which got my attention.

"Sheeda what's wrong?" I yelled at her. She picked her head up and looked at me. I saw tears coming down her face. I quickly got off my bunk and hugged her. "Chyna!" She cried out. "They trying take my baby saying my mom too sick to care for her. You know my sister Passion don't give a fuck about me or Skylar" Rasheeda angrily said.

"They can't get in touch with my aunt who live in D.C. Skyler is going to foster care." Rasheeda cried out and punch the wall. I grabbed her and wiped her tears.

"We going figure this out. What happen with your mom though?"

"She sick Chyna she got stage four cancer. You wanna hear something crazy as fuck. My mom never told me that she was sick. I ain't seen her in like four months. When I talk to her weekly she said she be working different hours at the hospital and busy with Skylar. I didn't think nothing of it. Why would she lie to me about her health?" Rasheeda asked, sounding devastated by her mother's actions.

"Well I think she just didn't want you to worry too much." I said genuinely.

"I'm gonna be so lost if my mother dies and my daughter is taken away from me." Rasheeda said.

"Let me make some calls real quick. I'll send Legend over there to check on your moms. Then I'll talk to my mom about keeping Skylar until you get out of here." I proudly said. Rasheeda looked at me shocked but actually I owed her.

When I first got to this jail I was always fighting, fighting to live, fighting for my respect and fighting to get money in here. One fight I almost lost my life. I was fighting four bitches and I was fucking two of them up. I got hands like Mayweather real shit. Aunt Deana taught me how to fight. She didn't play that punk shit. Ever since I was twelve all up to seventeen. I had boxing lessons twice a week, Aunt Deana took me to the gun range weekly. She taught me everything about ounces, pound, zips and kilo's. I learned so much at a young age. I honestly think she seen her jail shit coming. She been preparing me to take over her empire at a young age. *"That's crazy!"*

These New York bitches was trying to kill me, I only knew Rasheeda by passing she kinda resembles the actress Tika Sumpter. Rasheeda was in here on a drug charge. She got caught transporting work for some nigga she worked for. Rasheeda was using the phone at the time but had a clear view of what was going down.

I always noticed her, and we were cordial but; like I said a lot of shit was going on when I first got here. All I know is I was fighting by myself and getting the best of these two bitches. Left, right upper cut laid that bitch out flat. The other bitch was feeling bolt She came for some action. I dropped kicked her so hard made her spit up her lunch.

Rasheeda punch that bitch so hard in the face they both fell. The fourth girl tried to stab me. Rasheeda slice that bitch up. I'm sitting here smiling now while thinking damn my bestie is lethal. We fuck them bitches up. We both was in the hole for like ninety days and six months was added to our sentence. That's why I'm not home yet. Bitches be hating in jail and out on the streets. Rasheeda was loyal to me and I wanted to return my loyalty.

"I don't know what to say Chyna. Damn how could I ever repay you?"

I grinned at her and said, "LOYALTY!"

Chapter 7

TROUBLE IN PARADISE

Legend

I was sitting in my 2016 Red Range Rover outside of my two-story home. I was contemplating if I wanted to even get out and deal with Bianca ass. I just left the jail visiting Aunt Deana. I seen Bianca's 2016 Infiniti Q50 parked in the driveway. Damn I gotta get my girl together. This shit bothering me. The ringing of my phone took my out my thoughts. I looked at my iPhone 7 and seen Lucci's name flashing. I sled my finger across.

"Yo what's sup nigga?" I yelled while smiling. I fucked with the nigga Lucci. He met him through my right-hand Boss hog. Lucci is Boss hog first cousin. Lucci was a real street nigga wild as fuck. They really don't make niggas like him anymore.

"Nothing just called to check on you. I ain't talk to you in a couple days." Lucci said. "Yea I'm good Lucci I told sis to add you to her visiting list so yall can meet."

"Oh, yea what baby girl say. I heard she feisty as fuck and really don't like fucking with new niggas." Lucci said with a slight chuckle. "Well that's true she doesn't but she trusts me and

Boss hog decision so it's all good." I expressed!

"Aye on some real shit I can't believe that's your twin. Y'all don't even look alike. You tall as hell. I remember Chyna is short as fuck. What the fuck happen nigga? You ate your food and hers in the womb?" Lucci said laughing hysterically. "Fuck you! Fat ass nigga." I said. I laughed at his joke myself because it was weird. Who I am to question God's makings?

"When you trying to go?" Lucci asked me while he was inhaling the weed he was smoking.

"Nigga if I'm on the list by the end of the week. Is next Tuesday good?" Lucci asked me.

"I'll let you know tomorrow what's good." I told Lucci. "Other then that you good doe?" Lucci asked me. "Mannnn...I'll holla at you tomorrow. Meet down Club Lex. We gon discuss the bullshit I been going through over some drinks and rotation." I said.

"Okay cool." Lucci said.

"Aight bro be safe out here." I said seriously to Lucci.

"Always nigga." Lucci said and I ended the call.

I slid my phone in my pocket and got out the car. As soon

as I was about to pull my keys out the door swung open. There stood Bianca. I slowly lifted my head and our eyes met. Bianca looked high off of something other than weed. I was so mad, I could feel my temperature rising every second that I looked at her junkie ass.

"Are you just gonna stare at me like I'm a fucking statue? Are you going speak to your woman of six years?" Bianca asked, standing there in the door way, with her hands on her once thick hips. Bianca has lost at least forty pounds. Bianca held up six fingers like a nigga was retarded. I was gonna laugh but, this shit wasn't funny at all. I looked at her attire. She had on some skinny jeans and a Nike white tee that used to fit like a glove. Now it looks like somebody was playing tug-a-war with her t-shirt. Her eyes and nose were red and puffy.

"Are you high Bianca?" I asked her. I tried to slid past her to get in the house. She ignored my question. I moved her to the side to get in the house. "I just smoked a blunt with Velvet. Gat damn you always riding me Legend. You ain't my dad." Bianca screamed.

I dropped my keys on the kitchen counter and went to the

fridge to get a bottled water. As I was drinking my water. I watched Bianca out the corner of my eye. Bianca every move was snappish. Bianca was jittery couldn't stay still. I remember when things wasn't like this and we were happy, a power couple. Now shit is weird. We barely spend time together. We ain't have sexing months. When we are in each other's presence all we do is argue. Bianca was still shaking like she nervous about something. I put the water down and walk over to her and looked right in her pretty green eyes.

"Bae why you shaking?" I asked Bianca. "I'm just a little cold; I think I'm getting sick." Bianca nervously said."

"It's hot as hell in this house; how the fuck are you cold?" I ask Bianca with a raised eyebrow. "Bianca you know I love you." I said while getting in her personal space. I grabbed her hands. "Whatever you going through, you know I gotchu and you can be honest with me." I softly whispered in her ear.

"Legend I'm just not feeling good and I'm going to the bathroom." Bianca said. She let my hands go and walked around me. I grabbed her hands.

"Bianca are you getting high off of something other than

weed again?"

"What?" Bianca screamed. Now she had tears in her eyes like I just told her I was gon leave her.

"Nigga I'm bad bitch. What I look like getting high? NIGGA PLEASE!" Bianca yelled loudly and getting in my face.

"Why you act and look like an addict. Your movements are different. Your body is changing. I got money missing and our relationship is falling apart." I told Bianca. As soon as I said that now we were having a screaming match.

"You don't know what you're talking about. I'm just stress the fuck out that's why I'm losing weight. Fuck you Legend." Bianca said. She was whimpering so bad. Tears were just pouring down her pretty face.

"You care more about the streets than me." Bianca screamed at me. She took off running towards the bathroom, slammed, then locked the door.

I stood there froze in the kitchen like man what the fuck just happened. Why she get so mad? I'm gon just go upstairs to my office and calm down before I fucking kill this bitch. Every time I think about her stealing off me, I get mad all over again.

After making a few phone calls and reading some emails, from my Auto body shop customers placing orders. I decided Bianca been in the bathroom long enough and we need to get to the bottom of this shit. Either she going to rehab or I gotta let her go.

How can I be that nigga in the hood selling all the weight and my wife getting hella high in these streets? You can't help somebody that don't wanna be helped. I know I sound lika confused nigga but, this shit is stressing me out! She is denying everything like the first time she shoulda stayed in rehab. I believed her the first time when she claimed it was just a faze. Naw that was a lie. Now I really know it's an addiction.

I closed my laptop and went to go find Bianca. The bathroom door was still shut. I turn the knob and it was locked. I knocked on the door bang…bang no answer. What the fuck? I started knocking harder on the door and hollering.

"Baby open the door, so we can talk." I heard nothing I started knocking again Bang...Bang...Bang "Bianca baby." I put my ear to the door I didn't hear no movement. Damn did she fall asleep I kicked the door boom, boom the door gave in.

I tried to open the door wide enough, so I could get in.

Something was blocking it. I looked down and it was Bianca's feet. I squeezed through the door and looked down. Bianca was on the floor. I shook her she didn't move. I felt her pulse. It was faint. I grabbed my phone out my pocket and dialed 911. While I cradled Bianca small frame body in my arms.

"911 what's your emergency?"

"Yes can I have a paramedic to 1132 Babcock Road my girlfriend passed out in the bathroom. She is breathing but she's unconscious." I said to the 911 caller.

"Okay sir how old she is?"

"27" I answered quickly. "Can you tell me what happen?" 911 dispatcher asked. "Can you just send somebody here? What the fuck is all these questions! I found her in the bathroom like this. I screamed into the phone, mad that the 911 dispatcher was tryna play 21 questions.

"Bianca baby please wake up" I said getting worried she wasn't moving. My heart was beating so fast. "Sir can you tell me if she hit her head." 911 dispatcher asked? Yo by the time y'all fucking get here my girl gon be dead." I angrily spat to the dispatcher. "Calm down sir. I'm just trying to get some information on the patient to help Emergency response team." Dispatcher said. "Well stop asking me stupid questions. Where is the fucking paramedics?" I screamed! I kissed Bianca on the forehead. Damn how did shit get this fucked up?" I questioned myself. I heard a knock on the door. I stood up while still holding Bianca. Gat damn they finally here. I quickly went to the door.

I passed my big ass portrait of me and Bianca four years ago. That's when things were good. *"What happen to us?"* I asked to no one in particular. I reach the door and open it. I put her down and let the paramedics do their job while I answer series of questions. One medic asked me "Is there any drug abuse history?" I paused yea man I think she using cocaine and drop my head while speaking to the paramedics. After checking her vitals, the Paramedic gave her some medicine through a IV. "What was that you giving her through the IV?" I asked the paramedic.

"Benzodiazepines this is to decrease the chances of her having a seizure after an overdose of cocaine." The paramedic replied. I tried to remain calm, but a nigga was on edge. I was so fucking scared of losing Bianca Moments later, Bianca's eyes flutter and a nigga was so happy. At that moment I knew I was still in love with Bianca no matter what the situation was.

"I gotta get her together" I thought to myself. I watch as they put her on the stretcher and got ready to transport her to the hospital. I grabbed keys and my phone and followed them to the hospital.

Chapter 8

I'M THAT NIGGA

Lucci

"What's up y'all? I'm dat nigga Luciano Wilkins known to the streets as Lucci. I'm dark skin standing about 5'11, tatted up and, a chubby nigga. I got that Philly beard swag neatly trimmed. I got too much sauce. I'm the nigga to see on the East Side of Philly. I run shit. My uncle Rich retired and, handed me over his portion of the Eastside. A nigga pockets been getting fatter ever since. I'm about to partner up with my cousin and his right hand. What surprised me is Legend sister Hunnid was the one really running shit. I used to hear niggas say Hunnid did this, Hunnid did that, but I never knew Hunnid was a female. I must of not being paying no attention either. *"I never heard the word SHE"* I thought.

I'm thirty years old, I been hustling since I was Fifteen. Right now, I'm not ready to stop until I see millions and not just one million. I got out the bed to take a leak and my phone start ringing. I walked back to my bedroom and grabbed my iPhone 7 plus. I looked at my phone thinking, *"This goofy bitch Essence."* I swear for the life of me I don't know why I still be fucking with this bitch. *"Naw I know why."* I laughed. Essence has that bomb ass head. Available pussy anytime bitch is a slide but, swear up and down I'm gon wife her.

"Yoooo." I yelled through the phone. "Hey baby when can I see you? What you doing? Why didn't you call me back last night?" Essence said annoying the fuck outta me. "I looked at my phone while I lite my blunt and sighed. "Damn Essence you work for the federales. You know I don't answer no question. You ain't my woman." I said and blew the weed smoke out. "Yea not yet Lucci. You know I'm almost there." She said with confidence.

"Essence you will never be my woman. I'm not gon keep having this discussion with you! Now if I feel like it later, I'll come through but if not, I'll see you when I see you." I said and ended the call. I didn't even give her a chance to reply. I'm tired of these bitches. I need a real women all these bitches good for is a nut and a smack on the ass.

My ex shit I thought her smut ass was the one. She prove me wrong by fucking my nigga from my crew. How the fuck you mess with the help doe? When you got a boss nigga but, I was running the streets heavy. I wasn't running that much that I didn't notice a change in her sneaky ass. Then she tried to blame her baby on me. I ain't never fuck the bitch raw but anything possible. I asked for a blood test. Shit came back 99.99999 percent not mines. Every time I think about that shit I get mad.

Let me get in the shower get dress gotta meet up with Boss hog and Legend to go see his sister Chyna. At first, I wasn't going go. I hate jails but, this is Chyna's empire. I gotta meet her and see what's up with her. Boss hog said she real thorough bread. I seen Chyna once about five years ago before she got locked up. She was riding this bad ass Kawasaki Ninja HR2 motorcycle that Legend painted flat black for her. That bike is nice. I wonder if Legend still got Chyna's bike? She stopped passed Legend auto body shop, when I was there getting a paint job on my old school Chevy Caprice. she probably don't remember me.

I met Gunna already and I swear that's a nigga. Gunna harder than a lot of niggas. I handled my hygiene. I decided to put on my Polo light blue jeans and Polo white tee White Jordan's Retro. Sprayed on my Guilty Gucci cologne and grabbed my phone keys off my dresser. I got in my all white Audi 8.

I called Legend Ring...Ring. Legend answered on the

second ring. "You ready?" Legend answered his phone and said. "Damn nigga yea."

"I'll meet you at your crib in fifteen minutes." I told Legend. "Aite cool." Legend said and hung up. We didn't do too much talking over the phone. I pulled up to Legend crib twenty minutes later. I beep my horn moments later Boss hog and Legend were walking out.

They got in the car and slap hands with me. We always did this handshake that was for nobody but us. "What's good y'all? What's the address?" I asked Legend.

Legend ran the address off to me while I put it in the GPS. "Yo Legend how Bianca doing?" Legend shook his head from left to right. "I put her in one of the best rehab places Green Leaf Rehab Center. She going be there for like ninety days again. That shit broke my heart Lucci." Legend sadly said.

"I know that shit hurt bro but, you gotta be there for her. Even if you don't wanna be with her no more support her." I seriously said to Legend.

"I'm trying Lucci but this bitch doing the most. I'm not going turn my back on her. Even doe she did me dirty these past couple weeks." Legend said.

"Nigga sis gon be aite, I got faith in Bianca but, I also feel you. Who wants a junkie as a wife and we supply that shit in the hood daily, that's a lil contradicting if you ask me." Boss hog said and scratch his chin.

Two hours and forty-seven minutes later passed and we were pulling up to the jail. We went to check in and grabbed some shit out the vending machine. Since it was like 70 degrees outside we sat at the picnic tables outside. It's March and this weather don't know if it wanna bring spring out or keep winter. Two days ago it was 30 degrees that's crazy! Seven minutes later I seen the most beautiful women ever walk over to the table. No makeup, no lashes, her hair was in two braids to the back. Her skin was flawless. Her eyes was hazel. OH MY GOD! She is fine. Come to think about it. She kinda look like Cameron's girl JuJu, I love a dark skin female.

"Damn nigga close your mouth. It's just my sister. You can't have my sister Lucci. I fucks with you my nigga and all dat, but I don't play bout my sister." Legend said sounding like he was Chyna's dad. "Nigga she grown. You always cock blocking.

Sitting over there looking like Dr. Phil. Mind ya business and let them be great." Boss hog said and pointed at Legend.

"Fuck you!" Legend said and laughed at Boss hog.

She was staring at me like I was looking at her and I swear I felt a connection.

"Damn chill." I told myself. You don't know her like that. Shit ain't no such thing is love at first sight.

Well second sight I don't know if Chyna remember me. We didn't get formally introduce. Now is my chance! "What's up bro?" Chyna said then hugged Legend and then Boss hog.

"Damn Hunnid you got thick ass fuck in here." Boss hog said. She waved Boss hog off. "Shut up nigga all I do is eat and workout, but I look good don't I doe?" Chyna said. As she said that her eyes were on me. I was thinking in my head. *"Yes you do."* Legend interrupted my thoughts.

"This is Lucci, Lucci this is my twin sister. Chyna better known to the streets as Chyna White and or Hunnid!" Legend said formally introducing us. "Damn Legend just throw all my alias out there." Chyna said and laughed. Chyna reach out to shake my hand and I gently grabbed her hand but, I held on to that mutha fucka too long. She cleared her throat. "Can I have my hand back?" Chyna said sounding a lil irritated.

I was mesmerized by her beauty. Legend smack my hand down breaking the grip I had on Chyna hand.

"Hating ass nigga." I laughed. "Business nigga" Legend said. "This ain't love connections. We here on business. You over there trying boo love with my sister. Y'all are not a good match." Legend shook his head. "Lucci on some real shit Chyna is a female version of you." Legend preached. I start playing with my beard looking into Chyna's hazel eyes. DAMN I think I met my match!

After going over business and meeting Chyna's cell mate I notice how my cousin Boss hog was looking at Rasheeda. After leaving the jail. I dropped Legend and Boss hog off. I couldn't get Chyna off my mind, her chocolate skin tone, high cheekbones, pretty smile oh and how can I forget about that body. It was banging. She's street. She get money by any means. Just the type of female I need in my life. All these bitches I'm entertaining now is just to past time. They too fucking needy or just want to be in a niggas presence just because a nigga getting money. Bitches ain't good for shit. I fuck with J'Onna she was aite for the moment nothing serious.

I been fucking with her about six months now and she cool. J'Onna want us to be more. I just can't do it. She just keep asking me when we gonna make shit official. I told her don't try to force me into a relationship. Aww when I told her that, then she tried that... I'm pregnant shit. I shut that shit straight down. I took her to a walk-in clinic around the way. The bitch that run it I fuck from time to time. Pregnancy test came back negative. From that point on I looked at J'Onna different. She sneaky. Why would she lie about being pregnant? Who raised these hoes?

I'm talking all this shit on her but I'm still fucking her. I laughed to myself why wouldn't I. J'Onna gave head like she was runner up to be my wife. She need to start giving head classes that shit would be a success. Thinking about her head game had my dick hard, I was on my way home but shit that daydream had me bust a U-turn in the middle of the street.

I pulled my phone out and scrolled to J'Onna name and tap phone icon to call her. The phone ring once and she answered. "Hey baby." J'Onna said sounding sexy as fuck my dick was on brick now. "Chill with that baby shit. Open up the door. I'm coming through." I said through the phone. "Ughhh…whatever Lucci" J'Onna said. I was at J'onna crib in less than ten minutes.

I was at that bitch's door, condoms in hand, and ready to fuck. J'Onna answered the door with nothing on but some gold heels. She had a video vixen body, titties sitting up high, and a small waist. Her baby making hips damn near had my mouth watering to get between her legs. "Hi daddy." She said and grabbed my hand and led me to her bedroom. While we were taking the steps. I was enjoying the view in front of me.

Her hips sashayed left to right to a perfect rhythm. Her dark skin was glowing from the glitter she had all over her body. We got to her room. She pushed me against the wall and unbuckled my jeans. She got down on her knees. Took my already hard dick in her mouth and, started going in circles on the head of my dick. She was massaging my balls at the same time. "Damn J'Onna suck that shit." I said with a lustful expression. She started moaning and inserted my whole ten inches in her mouth without gagging.

J'Onna mouth was so warm and wet. Her tongue was so long and thick. She then started deep throating real fast with no hands. No gag reflex "Fuck Ma." I said while grabbing on to the back of J'Onna head very aggressive. I had a hand full of her jet black curly hair.

This shit here reminds me of that song Moneybag Yo Have You Eva. *"Fuck on her, then get her hair done, fake love I don't care none."* I started laughing. I busted right in J'Onna mouth "Ohhh...shit damn Ma turn over." I said outta breath. She looked at me and licked up the rest of the cum on my dick. Nasty ass bitch I love it. I aggressively flipped J'Onna over. I pushed her face down. "Get that ass up in the air." I said. "Okay daddy." J'Onna said. I slid the magnum on and enter J'Onna from the back. J'Onna was taking this dick so good. That's why I fucked with her, she doesn't run from the dick she take all of it like a G.

I gripped her hips and was slamming my dick into her roughly. "Oh Lucci... I love this dick fuck me harder." She hissed. I looked down J'Onna was super wet. She was throwing that ass in a circle. At that moment for some reason, I started thinking about Chyna sexy ass pounding into her sweetness. I was in a world of my own giving J'Onna death strokes. "Damn Lucci slow down she said. "Take this dick Chyna Doll" I said ...damn that accidently slipped out my mouth FUCK. "CHYNA who the fuck is Chyna?" J'Onna said and jumped off my dick. Snapping me back to reality.

I wiped the sweat off my head. "What you talking about J'Onna?" I asked tryna play dumb. "Lucci you just called me another bitch." J'Onna screamed. "Bitch are you crazy?" I said while taking the condom off.

I was turned off now and this is all my fault. I know this bitch ain't Chyna. This whole situation made my dick go soft as hell. I'm tripping I went in her bathroom and did a quick wash up. J'Onna came banging on the bathroom door but, I locked it. So I wouldn't have to talk about the it. I opened the door and she was still there.

"How the fuck you going disrespect me Lucci" J'Onna said and started crying.

I ignored her because I think J'Onna really think I'm her nigga. "Move the fuck out my way I don't hit women, but I'll hit a bitch." I said. Her eyes grew big "I'm a bitch now Lucci? You are so wrong in so many ways. How could you be getting the best pussy in the world and calling me another woman's name?"

J'Onna asked me still crying, screaming at me. I just looked at her delusional ass. "Aye ma you just answered your own question." I said with no emotion. "What?" she asked angrily.

She was now leaning against the wall. I started getting dressed. "Well if your pussy was the best. I wouldn't be calling another bitches name." I said with a bright ass smile to make her mad. I grabbed my keys and started to leave. "Fuck you Lucci." I hate you she said and following me down the steps.

I stopped at the front door and opened it. I looked back at her standing on the last step with her hands on her head. Tears showcasing her face. "Now I'm I right or I'm I right I said over my shoulder?" Then I left out the door. J'Onna screamed "Ugghhhh don't call me no more Lucci." I just got in my car and started it up. When I looked up I noticed the bitch was outside butt naked. Crazy bitch was still crying and ranting on "I hate you Lucci. You gon be mad when another nigga want me. Fuck you!" She said. J'Onna kept going on and on before I pulled off.

I rolled down the window just to fuck with her, I took my phone out "J'Onna" I called out my window. She looked up at me I snapped a picture. I'm uploading this on Facebook Ma! You look stupid." I said to her cracking up.

"Noooo... don't Lucci." She said and ran in the house. "Stupid ass bitch." I thought and pulled off from J'Onna house.

I looked at my phone and I had ten missed calls. Three of them were from Queenie that's what I nickname my mother some years back. I pushed play to listen to the message:

"Lil nigga I know you seen me call you. I ain't seen or talk to your black ass in four days. You probably with one of them thottie ass bitches. Lil boy you ain't too old to get your ass fucked up. I cooked for your black ass too ham, collard greens, mac n cheese, fried chicken and peach cobbler. I know them bitches ain't cooking for you. These lil hoes now-a-days don't know how cook. Son what they there for huh. She laughs holla at me son I love baby boy... Queen !"

I laughed while listening to that message. The rest of my missed calls was from Bad Ass and Legend, I'll call them back later. My mom Queen was a special kinda crazy. I been running the streets these past couple days. Just open up new territory, thanks to Chyna with the connect. Damn I meant to call my mom back a couple days ago. Better yet go pass her house. I took the exit to get to Queen's. I saw Queen's money green Infiniti XJ35 truck sitting in the driveway. I parked right behind it. When I first started really getting money, I bought this house for Queen. The house was in foreclosure I brought it for $3,070 a brick Victorian I put like $80,000 into that house and now the house is worth $250,000.

I got out the car, use my key to enter the house. As soon as I got in the door the smell of soul food invaded my nostrils. "Hmmm... it smell so good in here Queen...Queen." I scream and put my keys on the hook in the foyer. "Ohhh...could it be the son I've been trying to get in touch with for four days." My mother said all dramatic. She was standing in the kitchen and putting her hand up to her mouth tryna be funny. "You play too much Queen." I said and grabbed her face and kissed her cheek. I hugged my mother tight like I ain't seen her in years.

My mom smiled. "Where you been son?" She asked with her hands on her hip. Queen was very short women only standing 4'10, dark skin, short haircut. She kinda put in the mind of a dark skin Jada Pinkett in the face but she had a workout body. It's funny because my mother never worked out a day in her life. I went to kitchen table. "What's up mom." I said smiling. "What you been up to beside trapping?" Queen asked me. Yea my mom wasn't stupid she knew what I did. She didn't really like it but what could she do. I'm grown ass man, I made sure she was good and never brought harm her way.

"Not much." I said.

"Oh you cheesing too hard tell me what's new?" Queen said. "I met somebody, and I think she gonna have me locked down. I don't know if I'm ready for that yet. I was just with J'Onna and we were fu- I was about to say but stopped talking." I forgot who I was talking too. I never cuss around my mom. I had the upmost respect for her that's why I call her Queen. She is my Queen and that's the way I treat her. I never lied to her I kept it real. Our talks were always deep. "I meant sex with her." I said trying clean it up because I almost cussed.

"I called J'Onna Chyna while we were having sex." I said. Queen gave me a stern look as she made my plate. "Who the fuck is Chyna" Queen asked? She sat my plate in front of me. I looked at the plate my mouth watered in anticipation, I couldn't wait to taste Queen's food.

"You want some fried chicken Luciano?" She asked me calling me by my government name. "Yea let me get a couple wings." Queen gave me six fried wings and an ice cold Mountain Dew out the fridge. Queen treated me like a King. Queen sat the bar high. So For me to wife a chick she gotta top this. Fuck that! "Chyna is Legend twin sister." I said to my mom.

My mom looked at me shocked. "Legend got a twin sister?" Queen ask. Why I ain't never meet her?" Queen asked with raised brow."

"She been locked up for five years." I said and bit into my chicken. "Jail what the fuck did she do?" Queen asked. "Getting that money I'll let her tell you her side of the story.

"When y'all meet." I said to Queen. Smiling and stuffing mac n cheese in my mouth. This food is fire, "HOLD UP!" Queen said. She pointed her finger at me with a serious face "Ain't you and Legend working together?"

"Yea and?" I said. "Why would you wanna run with somebody never mind I'm gon mind my business!" Queen said. I took a sip of my drink. Queen gave me a disturbing look.

"Queen we will revisit this convo again. When Chyna get

out." I told Queen. "You must really like this girl to wait for her to get out." Queen said.

"You know mom I don't care nothing about these women out here. I seen Chyna for the first time like five years ago. I was getting my car painted at Legend's Auto body shop. It was brief but, when we looked in each other eyes it was like time stopped. She is so beautiful. She get money at any cost. She something like me and when I'm around her I can't stop staring at her."

"The connection I feel when I'm around her Queen I can't explain it. Like today I went to the jail to visit her with Legend. We just kept staring at each other. Crazy part is mom in jail ain't no weave, no lashes or makeup. When I looked at her it was just natural beauty." I said feeling excited. The look Queen gave me spoke volumes and I know she was shocked about the shit I just told her. I never talk about a woman the way I just talked about Chyna.

"You really serious about this girl?" Queen asked while cleaning up the kitchen?

"Yes, Queen I am. You believe in love at first sight?" I asked Queen. "Son let me tell you something about love. You will know when it's real because your heart will tell you. You will start doing shit you never thought you would do, to keep the one you love. That include cutting these other hoes off. To answer your question… yes son I think love at first sight is possible." Queen said and kiss me on the cheek.

I hugged her tight. "Aye Queen you better get ready to be a grandma because, if I get a chance with Chyna I'm definitely getting her pregnant." Queen smacked me on the back of neck and said, "Shit the bitch gotta get out first Luciano!"

I looked at my mom and said, "She is mom in a couple months. I'm counting down like a kid waiting on Christmas!"

Chapter 9

LUCCI ON MY MIND

Chyna

Damn this nigga swaggy as fuck I love a confident ass nigga. I ain't mixing business with pleasure. I remember him before I got locked up. He was at Legend's Auto body shop. I was on a mission but, we did have a stare off. I played that shit off like I didn't know who he was; but I'll kept it strictly business. I don't do relationships anymore. I'm done with niggas. The nigga I was fucking with for two years turned out to be a cop. I am a boss bitch so y'all probably wondering how the hell that happen right? The shit happened and now I'm like fuck niggas.

When turned my attention back to the little meeting as I turned around I seen Rasheeda on a visit with her lawyer. I signaled C.O Brown over to the table. I got up to meet him halfway! "What's up Chyna?" He asked, and his eyes roamed my body. "Nigga this ain't what you think it is. Calm down can you do me a favor?" I asked the C.O Brown. "Hmmmm!" He rub his chin and said, "I might what you need?"

"When Rasheeda get done with her visit can you bring her over here to meet my bros?" I asked the C.O. "Aite Chyna I gotchu." He winked and walk away. "Brown I'm gon give you something extra on top for doing me a solid." I said. "Naw Chyna you know what I want." He said and licked his lips and I smiled. I walked back to the table. "What was that about?" Legend ask with his eyebrows raised?"

"It ain't what you thinking bro chill. I just want y'all to meet somebody." I said to Legend not tryna reveal the truth.

"Is she cute?" Boss hog asked through a side smile. "Nigga all you worried about is fucking!" I said to Boss hog. "Hell yea why else would we wanna meet the bitch." I wasn't even shocked by Boss hog comment he has no filter and even me being gone for over four years he still ain't change. I laughed, "Never mind your silly ass wouldn't understand." I said to Boss hog.

"Shit I'll understand if she ain't cute you wasted our time." Boss hog said sounding so serious. "Nigga you sound dumb." Legend said to Boss Hog. "Chyna why you want us to meet her?" Legend asked.

"Look I fucks with Rasheeda she helped me, when I got into a fight with these hating ass hoes up here. Her mom dying of breast cancer and the courts is trying send her daughter to foster care. I wanted to help her."

"Ohh Aite Chyna I'll make some calls to a lawyer and see how we can go about it." Legend said. "Thanks Legend I was thinking mom could care for her daughter until she gets released. She gets out two weeks after me." I told them.

"Anyways back to business what is this meeting really about?" I asked, and I looked up. Lucci and I eyes met again. This chocolate ass nigga had dimples with a Philly beard and he is a lil chubby but, his fucking swag and confidence OH MY LAWD! There go that feeling again. *"What is this nigga doing to me? He never even touched me. Damn Hunnid get it together!"*

"We gon split up the East, West, North and South. I know you wanna still keep your side cause Gunna got shit on lock. I'm gon handle the North side. Lucci the East and Boss hog will handle the Souths side. We got new product coming in getting those things for 16.5." Legend said rubbing his hands together. I smiled and look at my brother. "How the fuck you getting that white that low?" I asked Legend while opening up Lucci's bag of chips that was sitting on the picnic table.

He eyed me "Damn shawty you just gon open my shit

without asking?" Lucci asked me. I twisted my mouth. "What's yours is mines." I flirtatiously said. Lucci winked his eye at me. "You mutha fucking right shawty and this is only the beginning." Lucci replied sounding so fucking cocky. I love it. I looked at him and laughed. "You a confident ass nigga ain't you?"

"About some chips doe you feeling yourself boo." I said to Lucci. We both laughed.

"Shut the fuck up. I don't wanna hear shit about y'all linking up, hooking up, creeping or spending money. This is about business. Nigga you can't have my sister. I done told ya ass. I'm not going keep telling you Lucci." Legend said. I rolled my eyes at him.

"Lil nigga I'm grown fall back." I said to my brother. "Back to what I was saying" Legend said.

"God dad is back in business. He had to lay low for a while." Legend said. Oh yea how is he doing? He sent me some money and a letter. I don't be trying call him. I keep my distance just in case they watching my call list.

"He said come by the house when you get out" Legend said.

I started rubbing my hands together and thinking about my released date. "Boss hog how is business for you over there?" Ohhhh.... shiiit everything good sis. Shit coming together real nice. I got about six shooters and about thirty workers and ten blocks. Two niggas to each block I got two lieutenants. I really sit back and watch. I'm done getting my hands dirty only if it's necessary we going get these millions and buy legal shit." Boss hog proudly told me.

I shook my head up and down agreeing to Boss hog. Thinking it is smart to get out eventually. Lucci shit is almost the same. "Yea I got two lieutenants. I had five blocks but with your help and my unc retiring from the game. I extended it to ten blocks. "Who ya unc"? I asked Lucci. Rich that use to work with y'all Aunt Deana" Lucci replied. "Oh yea small world" I said with a shocked expression. "Shit with them thangs coming 16.5 I had to open up more territory." Lucci announced sounding business savvy. I like that shit too.

"You know what Gunna be on straight boss shit. Her two trap houses close to $150,000 monthly." Legend said. "$150,000?" I asked while smiling proud of my bestie. *"Hustling ass bitch."* I thought. "Yo that's 150 each trap house or that's the subtotal?" I asked Legend?

"Naw sis that's subtotal for both. Low house does better than the high house" Legend said and took a drink of his water.

"Why is that?"

"Sis the low trap is in a good area and the high trap the location ain't good. We looking into moving it doe. I know that was your next question Chyna. I'm on it already. Plus, Gunna still got that weed shit poppin. Yea she doing her thing. Fierce and Flower houses we had to work together. 1st week I run them, 2nd week Gunna run them, 3rd week Boss Hog run them, 4th week is your wannabe baby daddy over there." Legend said and pointed to Lucci.

They were add on trap houses. Shit was suppose to be a trial run, but they made so much money I kept them open. Until… we find two stand up niggas to run them." Legend said.

"Okay Legend I see you got shit handled. I trust you with the decisions." I told Legend. My twin act like he really doesn't like this hustling shit but he making boss moves and opened up new territory.

We sat there and discuss business for another twenty minutes this whole meeting had me in my feelings. Damn I wish was home. I got mad all over again. I can't wait to hit these streets.

"I heard Mankind got this lil nigga name Dallas working for him he like his lil minion!" I told them. "Yea I heard that shit too Chyna." Boss hog said. "Anybody can die, Mankind better teach the lil to stay outta grown folk's business." Boss hog said. My brother and Boss hog are like hot and cold they look at shit different Boss hog is a hot head nigga but, Legend is more business and less street he ain't really a punk. He just evaluates situations before he reacts and me, Boss hog, and Gunna just don't give a fuck.

Legend shook his head and was about to get up when Rasheeda approach the table. "Rasheeda this is my twin brother Legend and his right-hand man Boss hog" Rasheeda shook their hands.

"This here is…" I said, and I paused.

"Her future husband" Legend intervened. Lucci waved Legend off.

"Rasheeda where you from?" Boss hog asked.

"I'm from New York but, I got caught up in Philly. So that's why I'm up here." Rasheeda said. "Oh yea? How long you been here?" Boss hog asked. "I been here for five years now on a drugs charge." Rasheeda replied and shifting her weight from left to right.

Boss hog eyes got big as hell. He tapped his hand on the table. Sit down shawty we don't bite. Rasheeda laughed and sat down. "Rasheeda was you hustling or holding work for somebody? What's your story?" Boss hog questioned."

"Actually…" Rasheeda said and paused. She took a seat at the table. "I was desperate to make some money because my daughter dad wasn't good for shit. He put me and my daughter out his house and I had to moved back with my mother. I was struggling and a little impatient. I was tired of depending on my mother or the state to care of us. After filling out several job applications and none of the jobs I applied for called me back for an interview. I met some nigga through my sister and, started transporting drugs for him. I got caught up one day on a traffic stop going back to New York." Rasheeda said.

"Yo the nigga that you were transporting for did he look

out for you or your daughter while you been in here?" Boss hog asked Rasheeda.

"Rasheeda I have to take you back in." C.O. Brown said as he was approaching the table. Rasheeda looked at Boss hog and smiled showing her deep dimples.

"No he didn't... not even my daughters dad. If it wasn't for Chyna and Legend I would be fucked up in here. I refused for my mother to send me money up here. I told her I rather her just use that to take care of my daughter."

Rasheeda stood up from the table "Aite bestie. I'll see you later. Nice meeting everybody!" Rasheeda said. "Trust me bestie we won't have to do this too much longer." I told Rasheeda.

When Rasheeda left the crew was ice grilling me hard as fuck. "What damn don't just stare?" I seriously said. "First I wanna just say sis I like shawty. She ain't even tell on the nigga that got her in this shit." Legend said impressed.

"I'm digging the fuck outta shawty. Damn sis put me on!" Boss hog said and rubbed his hands together like he was plotting. "Yea she solid as fuck bro" I told Legend.

The visit was ending so I stood up from the table. "I luv

y'all." I said. I hugged Legend and Boss hog. " Luv you too sis." Boss hog and Legend said in unison.

Lucci just looked at me and walked away. Bipolar ass nigga he going be the death of me. "Dat nigga is crazy sis don't worry about him. He's on his period" Legend said and laughed! Lucci grilled him.

"Fuck you nigga… well brother in law!" Lucci said fucking with Legend. Legend facial expression changed quickly, and he stop laughing.

"Aye nigga I will beat the fuck outta you about my sister." Legend said to Lucci and mean mugged him. I watched them walked through the doors still arguing and I shook my head them niggas crazy. He is fine as hell but, *"I'm not mixing business with pleasure."* I said trying to convince myself.

Chapter 10

WAITING ON BESTIE

Rasheeda

I got back to my cell waiting for Chyna and thinking about that fine ass nigga that she introduced me to Boss hog. Then I suddenly felt sad because who would want me. *"Yeah, I'm pretty but I'm in this shit hole waiting to be released and I don't have custody of my daughter."* Chyna walked in taking me outta my thoughts. She was laughing her ass off!

"What's so funny bitch?" I asked her.

"Sheeda!" Chyna said and hopped on her bunk. "First that nigga Lucci is fine as fuck got my pussy wetter than a fountain. Then Boss hog kept asking me questions about you. We in here doing this time. Niggas really ain't in my forecast right now and probably never will be again. I got trust issues. Plus, I'm too much in love with my money and this street shit. Boss hog my bro. I love that nigga like I love Legend, but Boss hog is a whore." Chyna said as her eyes rolled up in her head.

"You got a point bestie you been through some shit. To trust a nigga again even if he friends and business partners with you and your twin." I replied.

I look down at the pictures on the wall of my baby girl

and started crying. "Damn Chyna I failed her as a parent." I said through tears.

"Naw Sheeda you didn't. All you did was put your trust in a pussy ass nigga. He failed you and your daughter. You tried to make money the honest way and it didn't work. You just went into survival mode. You tried to get money another way to provide for you and Skylar. You didn't fail Skylar. I know you feel that way because you're in here but, look at the chain of events. Fuck it in a couple weeks, you gon have a chance to make it right. When Skylar get old enough tell her your story. Tell her not to ever put her life into a nigga's hands." Chyna said and clapped her hands together getting her point across at this moment she turned into Hunnid on me.

"That niggas day will come." Chyna gangsta ass said. I looked up at Chyna. A sinister grin spread acrossed her face. No words were spoken. As I matched her grin and nodded my head. I gather my things together to take a shower. After I showered I was in deep thoughts. I gotta prepare myself to sign my Parental rights over to Chyna's mom, so my daughter won't be in the system.

I trust Chyna and her family because they been there for

me from the moment me and Chyna met. I just gotta accept the fact that someone else other than my mother is going have guardianship over my child. I finally made it upstairs to the third pod level. I entered my cell and Chyna wasn't in there. I figure she must went to the shower.

Flashback

I remember when I first met my baby's dad Malik in 2008 S550 at the gas station. *I was pumping gas into my all black 2004 Acura Legend. I was sitting there watching the pump. Only five dollars of gas went in my tank. The gas pump stopped.* "I know fucking well I gave the clerk a twenty shit." *I thought. I went back in the gas station to ask the attendant what happen.*

I bumped right into the finest man I ever laid eyes on. Six feet four inches and brown skin. Damn come to think of it. This nigga looked just like the internet comedian King Keraun. "Damn lil mama watch where you going sweetheart." *He said defensively. He was handsome. I was speechless, so my words were caught in my throat.* "Cat got your tongue what's good? I know I'm a fine ass nigga but…" *He said and licked his lips.* "I usually never have women speechless until I put this dick in their *life." He said real cocky.*

Now that brought me outta my trance. "I'm sorry I wasn't paying attention." I nervously said. "That's obvious." He said while smiling and undressing me with his eyes. I'm dark skin, round face, chubby cheeks and pretty wide smile. 5'8 super thick and I weigh 210lbs. I had baby making thighs. On this particular day I had on a yellow fitted Maxi dress. This dress fit me like a glove. The yellow looked so good on my skin and the tie-up brown sandals from Aldo's.

My hair was short, wild, wet and wavy weave part down the middle. That made me look like I had Cuban in me. I tried to walk around him, but he grabbed my waist. "Can I get your name since you scuffed up my Jordan's. I just cop these today." He said with a straight face. I started laughing and looked down. There was no scuff on them damn sneakers he running game. I thought. "Since you made up that weak ass lie to get my attention It's Rasheeda." I laughed and replied.

"Rasheeda and Malik I like that." He said while checking his ringing phone. "Aye look lil mama I gotta go. Give me your number. I want to take you out and get to know you

better." Malik said in a rush. I was all smiles and gave him my number.

He didn't call me for like two weeks. Malik and I finally went on our first date. He was nice and attentive. Six months into dating him, I moved to Philly with him. He wined and dined me. Shopping trips, vacations and a 2008 Mercedes Benz but, the honeymoon came to an end quickly. Malik changed. He started putting his hands on me for any and every little thing, I tried to leave but, good dick and being in love will blind your ass from the truth.

He was controlling. See Malik had two sides to him. Malik was the good side of him sweet and caring but, when he was Mankind he was the devil. After several attempts of trying leave him. I ain't gon front a bitch was scared and just figured this is gon be my life. I thought I would get the courage to leave eventually. Well that didn't happen because I found out I was pregnant. That shit was like a blessing and a curse.

"He trapped me," is all I kept thinking. Mankind would beat me while I was pregnant with Skylar. He didn't give a fuck. One night he got mad because one of his workers was stealing *money and he came home and took it out on me. "Rasheeda get your dumb ass down here." Malik screamed. I jumped at the sound of his voice that's how scared this nigga had me.*

I rolled my eyes and ran downstairs. "Yes Malik?" I said sounding innocent. "Did you cook today? I don't see or smell no food in this bitch." He roared, and the bass of his voice echoed. "Malik... Skylar have an ear infection and she's been cranky all day." I told him and nervously, playing with my loose strings of my hair. "Answer the question bitch?" He screamed. Malik screamed so loud I'm pretty sure the neighbors heard him.

"No!" I said while shaking nervously because, I knew what was next. I seen it in his eyes. Malik got up off the leather sofa and grabbed my neck. He started choking me so hard. I swear to God I saw stars. What gave me the strength to really want to leave this time was Skylar's cries. "I gotta do better by my daughter this can't be my life." I thought. I tried to get outta the strong grip he had on my neck. "Stop, Malik please the baby is crying." I said sobbing. "Bitch let that baby cry, her lungs need to get strong anyway. I'm fucking talking right now. Don't nothing or nobody come before me, not even that damn whining

ass baby. You got that bitch?" Malik said with malice dripping from his tongue. I slowly nodded my head up and down. This nigga is crazy. Nothing Malik says or does surprises me anymore.

"I be out in these streets hustling, robbing, stealing and killing so you can have this good ass life you're living. All this name brand shit and that fucking brand new Benz you driving. A nigga can't get a home cook meal?" He asked me. Malik continuously slapped me in the face. Every time he named something he did for me he would hit me. After about the tenth slap to the face and yes I said tenth. The tenth slap brought me outta my daydream. Most times when Malik would beat me I would zone out and start daydreaming. It's like I was numb to the shit this abuse been going on for so long.

This day I got tired and for the first time, I swung at Malik with all my might and my fist connected to his jaw. Blood flew out the side of his mouth. Malik was so astonished by my actions. He paused, and it was like time stood still. I don't know who was more surprised me or him. "Bitch you hit back? Huh bitch you hear me?" Mankind said through clenched teeth. He wiped the blood from his mouth with his shirt. Sweat was pouring down his face.

I was trying my best to escape the next slap and get away from him but, this wasn't Malik I was dealing with this evening this was Mankind. Yes, we lived good but; I didn't want none of this. All I wanted was his love and respect. Fuck this material shit. He thought since he brought shit, and this was his crib he could treat me any kind of way. That's exactly what he thought. I allowed it for three years now.

Malik looked at me with hatred in his eyes and sat on the couch and put his face in his hands. "See bitch look what you made me do huh?" Malik said all emotional like he was the victim. "Oh here come game" I thought! I just knew for sure he was gon hit me back. Now he tryna make it seem like, I made him put his hands on me. "What the fuck they are your hands but whatever.

I ran upstairs to get Skylar. She was in her crib crying so hard, she was shaking. Ughhh I hate his ass. As soon as I said that. He came rushing in Skylar's room.

"Bitch y'all gotta go." I looked at him in disbelief.

"What? Malik what are you talking about?"

"Bitch get out my crib. You hit me back. That's a no in this house. You disobeyed me. You and that baby gotta go." When I say my whole world shatter like how could you put your mother and child out. Yes, I wanted to leave but; I needed a plan and today I don't have one. My mom is all the way in Jersey. "No money, no car, how the fuck I'm gon get there?" I thought to myself, packing up me and Skylar shit.

"I'm so confuse bitch. Get it together you wanted to leave here is your way out." I said coaching myself.

"Bitch you ain't good for shit but, a nut. I can't believe I couldn't get a meal outta your lazy ass." This crazy ass nigga said. "A meal? Malik, I cook everyday are you delusional?"

"Where are we gon go this time of night. My mother lives all way in Jersey?" I said with tears coming down my face.

"Bitch I don't care how you get there but you or that baby ain't staying here. Plus I'm tired of my other bitch who I really wanna be with sleeping by herself at night. She cooks meals for me daily and she obeys orders. Malik said like this shit was okay.

To say I was livid is an understatement. I said a quick prayer and finished packing Skylar bag. Then I went to my room and packed up my bag. From the corner of my eye I saw Malik standing in our bedroom door way, "Hoe don't take none of that shit I bought. Skylar can have all her shit but, you." He pointed to me. "You can only take two outfits and one pair of shoes." I didn't wanna get beat anymore so I just did as I was told.

My face hurt so bad it felt like I was jumped by four bitches. Fuck that shit. That can't be the case because I knocked bitches out back home in New York. I was considered a problem but, to Malik I was soft. Tears just pouring down my face.

I called my mom and she told me she would drive here right now and get me. I told her I'll be at a hotel until she gets here. My mother gave me her credit card numbers over the phone, so I can get a room for the night. I called a cab to pick me and my baby up.

I looked back at Malik and he didn't even kiss Skylar goodbye. "Cold-hearted nigga." When I got back to Jersey I was broke as fuck and needed money quick. I wasn't trying to be a burden on my mother. I met some nigga through my sister

Passion and I transported drugs for him every weekend. I made $3000 for every drop. I had to do what I had to do for me and Skylar. Thinking back on my life had me a little stress. *"Suck it up Sheeda you made it this far. You strong."* I kept telling myself. I jumped on my bunk and laid down sleep took over me.

Chapter 11

LET ME INTRODUCE MYSELF

Boss Hog

Damn I didn't get a chance to introduce myself before the muthafuckas in the story started talking. I am 28 years old my government is Raheim but, I'm known to the streets of Philly as Boss hog. I'm 6'7 Brown skin, thin frame. Ya'll ain't gon believe but I favored the rapper Fabulous me and that nigga had similar swag. I got the name Boss hog when I was a 17. I was just a runner for Aunt Deana. She said I was always in Boss mode. Telling all the other runners how and what to do. Auntie Deana gave me that name ***Boss hog***!

When Chyna took over I really started making money I had my own team. I'm a fucking boss and I demand respect no matter where I am. I'm a wild, loud, play too much, hot headed at the same time type of nigga. When Chyna took over we expanded Aunt Deana's areas. We now served the whole Northside. Instead of the two areas that Aunt Deana had and that took work. There was a nigga name Howard old school player still running a hoe strip. Pimps still do exist damn. We bullied our way into that area. Old school Howard ain't been seen. Since we made him leave his strip. "I wonder what happen to him hmmm…dead man can't tell no tales." I laughed.

Niggas already know how I feel about Chyna and Legend. They're my fucking heart and I'll paint any city red about my family. My phone ringing took me outta retention. "Yea doe." I dryly answered the phone. "Raheim why you just now answer your phone. I've been calling you all day." Kenya annoying ass voice came through the phone. I instantly got mad "Yooo don't call my phone questioning me about shit." I could hear Kenya sucked her teeth and exhale loudly.

"Ughh Reheim you make me so mad treating me like a regular bitch. You weren't saying that when I sucked your dick last night." Kenya continued to scream. I smirked, "Exactly no words exchange because you know what it is. I'll call you anytime to top me off with the sloppy." I calmly said. "I swear to god Boss hog I'm not fucking with you…" Kenya tried to say.

I cut Kenya right off and hung up. I went to my contacts on my Galaxy 7 plus and found Kenya's name and blocked that bitch. I don't tolerate that bullshit with these nothing ass bitches out here. FUCK HER!!! Back to my story.

I've been knowing Chyna, Legend and Gunna since grade

school. We always been close. We lived right next door to each other and our mothers were good friends too. When Chyna first started hustling me and Legend didn't think it was a good idea because she a female. My sister proved us wrong. She put in work and do shit I never seen a nigga do. Chyna's ass was barely five feet tall, but she had the heart of Giant.

I rolled over on my California King mattress and Gucci sheets. Yea a nigga was eating good in these streets. Never thought I would see a day a nigga I could sleep on Gucci sheets. I looked at the time it was 9:08 a.m. Damn Kenya called me early as fuck.

I was drunk and tired from last night. I came home and stretched out on my bed. Pussy was far from my mind. I smelled food cooking like bacon or some shit Tayla must be here. I was so drunk last night I didn't even know she was here. I jumped out of bed and went to handle my hygiene and took a shower.

I took a peek into my walk in closet fuck it. I bought some shit yesterday from the mall. I just cop dem Gatorade Jordan Retro 6, Secret Stuff t-shirt and Levi jeans. AP watch and pinky ring no chain. I got dressed headed downstairs. When I got to the kitchen Tayla was dressed in a pink maxi dress, barefoot twerking while cooking. I laughed to myself This girl always dancing.

"Baby sis what you cooking?" I hungrily asked. Tayla jumped and grabbed her chest. "Oh shit you scared me. What the fuck Raheim?" She reached out to hug me and gave me a peck on my cheek. "I'm just cooking eggs, bacon, fruit and toast." Tayla replied. "Ohhh...shit a nigga hungry too." I said all excited. She swung around and looked at me. "Nigga I ain't cook you shit this is for me." Tayla smart ass told me. "I know you better go back outside and find your mind because you definitely lost it. If you think you going come in my house uninvited cooking food and not feed a nigga." I said and grabbed me some orange juice out the fridge.

She rolled her eyes and made me a plate and smiled. "Bro you know I wouldn't do you like that." Tayla playfully said. "Yea I thought so." I laughed, Tayla play way too much. "Your bitches should be over here cooking for you bro. What these bitches for?" Tayla asked with her face twisted into an ugly scowl. "Pussy and head." I replied as I stuffed a piece of bacon in my mouth. "Hmmm...better get you a real women bro." She said while sipping her pineapple smoothie.

"Yo you need to worry about why that nigga Geno is at my door. Worry about that." I seriously said. The lil nigga do work for me. Matter fact that's my nigga but for some reason I feel like some funny shit going on right up under my nose. I look at my security monitor on the wall. I seen this nigga Apple Red Benz parking in my driveway.

"Oh, he just came over here to say hi."

I smirked at her like yea right. I put my plate in the dishwasher. "Tayla I'm a street nigga. You can't run game on me. Try again why is here?"

"He wanted to take me out to lunch. Since I'm on break from school. I figure I'll spend some time with him bro. Is that okay?" Tayla asked patiently waiting for my response.

"No, it's not. Let me go holla at the nigga real quick." I said and walked off. Geno rang the doorbell as soon as I made it to the foyer. I opened the door he smiling from ear to ear. "What's up Boss man?" Geno said, and he gave me a brotherly hug. Geno tried to go into my house. I pushed him back." "WHOA!!!" He said wondering what the fuck is going on. "Let me holla at you real quick" I told him.

He looked confused. Geno was not a soft ass nigga. He was a wild lil nigga been loyal to me. Geno is five years older than my sisters and he got as many bitches as I do. I gotta see what's up wit it.

"What's up with you and Tayla?" I questioned.

"Yo Boss man it ain't what you think." Geno said with a serious expression on his face. "I like your sister a lot. That's why I tried to come over here before you left to ask you if it was okay. I rather it come from me. Then you hear rumors." Geno expressed. I shook my head. "How long y'all been talking? Did you fuck my sister nigga?" I asked while folding my arms across my chest and leaning against the porch waiting for his answer.

"Naw nigga I ain't fuck. I'm tryna get to know Tayla. She a different breed then these bitches out here." Geno seriously said. Boss hog Tayla tryna get her education. She work full time and Tayla is creative and her conversation is something that is very interesting to me. Tayla don't talk about the shit these heaux out here be talking about. Fucking, sucking niggas with money and these heaux be in everybody business talking about muthafuckas but don't got shit their selves."

I looked at this nigga like I was talking to somebody else. I seen this nigga in action with bitches. "Aite my nigga my fault. I'm gon fall back I see you serious." I told him. I proceed to walk in the house after I slap hands with Geno. He pushed me back and look me in my eyes. "We cool Boss?" Geno asked. "Yup just don't hurt my sister or it's gonna be wild wild west out this bitch." I told Geno.

"I'm not but this is coming from a dude that treat bitches like shit." Geno replied. "Yeah that's true but they ain't my sister nigga." I replied in a calm tone. "Yeah you right." He shook his head." Then Geno followed me inside the house.

I went in my crib, grab my keys, and my phone. I peeked my head in the kitchen and seen the way Geno and Tayla conversation was just flowing. Both of them looking in each other eyes. "I'm out. No fucking in my crib" I boomed in my dad voice. Tayla rolled her eyes and Geno dropped his head and then looked up. "Bosssss!" Geno emphasized. "You know I got more respect for you then dat chill nigga. We bout to roll out anyways." Geno replied.

I didn't even respond I just left out. I hopped in my cocaine white Range Rover. I'm going to check out the traps houses first. I always come through at random times no schedule. I want niggas to be on their P & Q's at all times. Geno run this first trap house. I made him lieutenant a year ago and he always impress me. I pulled up and got out my Range.

He got a nigga at the door with walkie talkie's on. One nigga at the back door. When I stepped inside and looked around every nigga was in this bitch working. I love it. He had his cousin and three other bitches cooking. They didn't have to be naked. Just no pockets but they were his family. He trusted them.

I seen the lil nigga Bad Ass coming down the steps. He was a 17-year old lil nigga on the rise but, Geno still made him attend school. "What's up Boss hog?" He said. I laughed because he sounded like Lil Boosie and favor him too. No lie that's why Geno named him Bad Ass. He was a short lil nigga standing five foot eight inches and a box haircut. Only difference Bad Ass was light skin.

"What's up Bad Ass? What you up too?" I greeted him. "Nothing about to go to my girl's crib." He said while counting his money. "You saving your money or you blowing it on dumb shit?" I asked him. "Naw Boss hog y'all taught me well. I'm stacking my money up. I don't trick on these hoes or buy dumb shit he told me. "I'm tryna get in the studio." Bad Ass said. "Good come

see me tomorrow." I told him. Bad Ass was smiling hard. "You gon holla at Ol 'boy about some studio time?" Bad Ass asked excited. "Just come see me tomorrow." I told Bad Ass.

Bad Ass been bothering me about some studio time for months now and I wasn't taking him seriously. Now days everybody wanna be a rapper I thought it was a phase he was going through. Until I heard him rap for the first time at an open mic night down Club Lex. I don't know why Gunna snuck his seventeen-year old ass in the club. I slap hands with him and left out I checked the scene before I got in my ride and pulled off. Next stop see what's up with Legend crazy ass.

Before I took the half hour drive to Legend's crib. I went to get me some blunts from the corner store. I parked and got out check my surroundings. I seen Gunna leaving the store with some thick, bad ass, shawty with red hair, Gat damn that bitch fine. "What's up nigga?" I said and Gunna slapped hands with me and smiled showing her two rows of gold fronts.

Gunna had on some Jordan's that just hit the store today. All white Nike joggers and a sports bra and a Pittsburgh Pirate baseball jersey and a matching Pittsburgh Pirate fitted. Gunna be fly as fuck. "I ain't up to shit about to go holler at this nigga about Hunnid's bread. He tryna spin me but Boss hog you know what it is." Gunna said. I just shook my head. *"Somebody about to die."* I thought.

I looked over at the shawty Gunna had with her. She was eye fucking me and Gunna caught her ass eye fucking me too. "You wanna go with my nigga or something you eye fucking the nigga. Check it I got shit to do Boss hog." Gunna said and lifted her fitted hat and put it back on her head. "I'm out." Gunna said and got in her Porsche truck.

Shawty started to get in the passenger side of Gunna Porsche truck but, the door was locked. "Baby can you unlock the door?" Gunna looked over at shawty smiled and pulled off. Shawty looked at me. "You must have just met Gunna. She don't play about disrespecting her. You just lost your chance baby girl." I laughed and went in the store. "Hmm… what you about to do?"

She asked me with her hand on her hip. "Whatever I'm about to do, don't consist of shit with you thirsty ass. Move on shawty."

I walked away from shawty and went in the store grab peach wraps and a juice. While I walking to get in my truck. I seen one of my workers Loso in the car getting head from the bitch that was just with Gunna. Loso head was laid back on the head rest enjoying himself. I laughed, and he open his eyes and through his hands up. *"These heaux is for everybody."* I said to no one in particular as I drove off.

I got to Legend house in twenty minutes still laughing at Gunna, her ass is wild as fuck for that shit. I parked next to Legend money green Mercedes Benz. I walked around back because I knew this nigga was probably out back smoking that good. As I approached Legend he got up.

"What's up nigga?" I slapped hands with him doing our twenty-year old signature handshake. We've been doing since the third grade! "Nothing much Boss just sitting out here smoking on this good!" Legend said and took a seat in his lawn chair. "Let me hit that shit." I grab the blunt and puffed on that shit so hard. "Damn nigga you hitting that shit hard as hell. All aggressive and shit." Legend laughed.

"I needed this shit." I said while blowing smoke outta my mouth. "What's up with baby sis? She good you cop that house for her? I'm going grab that cocaine white Mercedes Benz truck she wanted just as a welcome home present." I said as I passed the blunt back to Legend. He threw his hands up. "Nigga you can have that shit. You smoked damn there the whole blunt greedy ass nigga." Legend playfully said.

I got that house for Chyna, but I don't think it's gon be finished by the time she come home. The plumber ran into some issues with the line, they gotta re-do the whole thing over." Legend expressed. "Damn bro so where she gon stay here until they get done. Don't be acting like Chyna's dad either." I said. "Boss Chyna needs to stay outta trouble before she get herself killed."

I laughed and continuing smoking the rest of the blunt. "On some real shit you know Chyna is not gon sit still or fall back from this street shit. Especially since she still didn't figure out who framed her and Aunt Deana. Chyna love trouble when she get out I feel sorry for the hood because, she gon paint the city red. She gon murks something. Keep fucking with her It might be you. That's just in her my G." I told Legend.

"Yo what's up with Bianca? She admitted into Greenleaf Rehab center after that night she overdosed and almost died on me." Legend said emotionally. Legend looked worried. I never seen Legend look like this before. I know this is killing him to find out she was getting high. "So how you feel?" I asked Legend.

"I'm mad as fuck because, I sell the shit I know the signs. Bianca doe bro…" He said and paused for some reason. "I didn't know she was addicted to cocaine. Thinking about that shit got me mad all over again." Legend angrily voiced.

He started pacing the floor. "I hope she make it through rehab this time. I think you was just in denial. You ignored the signs trying give your girl the benefit of the doubt. That's what happen when you love someone." I told Legend. "I got her at the best rehab." Legend said ran his hands down his face. Legend went to his bar and pour himself some Grey Goose. "I never thought Bianca would be getting high." Legend kept repeating over and over.

"Legend just don't turn your back on her. Legend took

another shot of Grey goose and said, "I won't. Chyna already on my ass about this shit. Talking about if she find out I turned my back on Bianca she gon cut me off and just do business with me." Legend said. I laughed because Chyna ass was crazy for sure.

"Boss hog you know when I first got in this drug shit. I just wanted to make enough money just to open up several auto body shops. My first love is cars. When Chyna went to jail I had to step it up." Legend sadly expressed. "Yea I know Legend but we getting real money now. You still feel that way?" I asked him. Legend looked at me with a serious facial expression and said, "Yes I do."

"Oh and Boss hog Chyna told me if she find out I'm acting funny towards Bianca about a bitch. She gon shoot me!" Legend said and started laughing but I didn't.

He stop laughing and said "Nigga ain't that shit funny?" "Naw Legend it ain't. You know why because Chyna lil ass crazy. She will really shoot your ass with no remorse. You know how close Chyna and Bianca is and if Chyna said that she meant it." I explained to him.

Legend stared off into space and said "Boss I think Chyna

think her ass in the MOB or something. That's how she be running her shit. She don't play. Let me get outta here. I'll come through later, go over them numbers with you, and Gunna. Then we gon to Club Lex Moneybag Yo is coming through. Pete called me yesterday to see if we coming through." I said to Legend and I gave Legend a brotherly hug. I hopped in my ride. I'm trying to turn up later. I need some pussy let me see who gon be the next victim. The chick Rasheeda crossed my mind I wonder what baby girl like outside of them bars. I smiled and started my ride up.

"Naw Boss leave that girl alone she got enough shit going on in her life."

Chapter 12

DON'T PLAY WITH YOUR LIFE LIKE THAT

Gunna

"Ohhhhh... shit! Lick that shit. Damn I'm cumming!" Light skin screamed in ecstasy. "Let that shit go baby girl." I replied. I had this thick ass light skin bitch legs in the air eating the shit outta her pussy. Light skin was so wet damn. I flipped her ass over after. I put the strap-on around my waist. I slid in behind her. "Hike that ass up" I demanded.

"Okay baby." She said in her sexy ass voice! I was giving her long deep strokes. I was spreading her ass, so my stroke would go deeper. "Hmm... baby this feel so good damn." She said and squirted all over the strap-on. I slid out of her and laid down to lite my half a blunt. Light skin unhook the strap -on and started eating my pussy. I inhaled the smoke and enjoyed this pleasure damn. I love smoking and getting head at the same time. Light skin gon fuck around and make me wife her. I laughed to myself. Naw I ain't wifing nobody let me introduce myself.

I'm Ashanti Jones better known to these Philly streets as Gunna. I am a swagged out ass lesbian. Yea I know y'all wondering why they call me Gunna. Well just know my aim is on point and I shoot to kill. Niggas fear me. I am Hunnid's right hand. She upstate doing a five-year bid. I can't wait for Hunnid to get out I miss her so much.

"Gunna...Gunna!" Light skin snapped me out of my daydream. "Damn ma you the best." I said complimenting her head game. I slowly got up to go handle my hygiene and brush my teeth. I took good care of my gold teeth and I don't play about a clean mouth! As much pussy I be eating I should huh! I got in the shower and hurried and washed. I need to check my trap spots. Ain't no half stepping when it comes to getting this money and keeping my soldiers in line.

I stepped out the shower and went to get dressed Light skin was still here. She was sleeping so I woke her ass up. "Bitch ain't no napping in my spot! Aye ma you gotta roll." I said while putting some army green cargo shorts, army fatigue button down white wife beater and, Timberland boots on my feet. She stirred in her sleep then wiped her eyes. "Gunna you ignorant as hell. All that good head I just gave yo." She tried to say but I cut Light skin straight off because she was doing too much talking!

"Bitch you got five minutes to get the fuck out my crib. You don't make the rules!" I said starting to get mad. She hurried got her shit on and left out the room without looking at me. She said "Fuck you, wanna be a man so bad you are a…" I grabbed my gun from my dresser. Before she could finish her sentence. I ran up on that bitch. Grabbing her by her neck.

I put the gun to her head! "Bitch I killed for lesser shit than you spitting at me right now. I am trying to be nice by just telling you to leave. Now if you don't want to die take your ass on and I kissed her on her forehead and smiled. Light skin looked nervous as hell. She turned around and tried to walk away. I smacked her on her ass real hard. *"Damn she gotta fat ass!"* I thought. *"Damn I forgot to get her number."* I hopped in my Maserati coupe!

First stop was lower house. All our traps got names to separate them. My lil nigga Atlanta was top lieutenant of this trap. He was twenty-five years old. I pulled up to the spot and parked around back like I always did. There was one nigga watching the door and the other niggas was outside shooting craps. I know these niggas ain't shooting craps while money is to be made somebody about to die. Where the fuck is Atlanta at any fucking ways? I grabbed my monster drink out the cup holder and slid my phone in my pocket.

I entered the house and slap hands with the nigga that was guarding the back door. "What's good Gunna?" Jamal asked me. I heard a thump, "What the fuck was that?" I asked Jamal. Niggas was in there shooting craps and you know how Atlanta is. He don't like slackers. Jamal was a fat black nigga standing about 5'10, bumpy ass face and big lips. "Yea I was about to cause hell when I seen that shit. Niggas on the clock." Jamal nodded his. "I already know Gunna how you get down." He said laughing! I got further in the house and heard sniffling and crying.

I rounded the corner and Atlanta was beating the shit outta, one of my runners. "Sit him up in the chair." ATL I said calling Atlanta by his nickname. "Get up pussy." ATL groaned. ATL was a tall lanky nigga. I swear he had to be 6'9, 180lbs if that, high yellow, real long dreadlocks to the middle of his back. ATL kept his locs neat.

Past four years he been working for me. I never seen none of the workers fuck up… always on point. I think the nigga were mixed with something. I don't care what he said. He always beg the differ that he wasn't mixed with something.

He was a good worker, I like how he handled business. ATL picked the worker up by his shirt and swung him in the chair, we had in the dining room. ATL swung him so hard I didn't think the lil nigga would make it in the chair. I laughed then rubbed my hands together smiling.

"What's going on?" I questioned ATL. "This lil dumb ass nigga keep breaking the rules in here. He shooting craps in front like we ain't already doing Illegal shit. Drawing unwanted attention. ATL expressed frustrated. ATL got mad all over again and punch the Ol' boy in the face. "I'm sorry ATL damn. It won't happen again." He screamed out in pain. He was holding his face that was quickly swelling up.

I know it won't, ya last day is today without pay. ATL said and looked at his ringing phone. "I gotta take this call Gunna."

"Oh, it's cool I gotta holla at youngin anyways." As I approached the youngin he guarded his face. "Put ya fucking hands down. I angrily said to young boy. "Don't shoot me." He screamed. A menacing laugh escaped my mouth.

"Now why was you outside of my trap house shooting craps?" Before he can speak I pulled out my 9-millimeter. POW! "Why you shoot me?" He yelled out in pain.

POW......I shot him in the other leg for question my decisions. "Gunna." He continued hollered out in pain. "Shut the fuck up before I end ya life, stop crying." I said through a laugh. Youngin was mumbling something under his breath. I turn around and ATL was just standing there. "Gunna I had it." ATL said all calm. That's why I fucks with this nigga. He don't let shit scare him or get to him; my type of nigga. "I know you can handle it but, you had to take a phone call. I took care of it. Lil nigga be aite."

"Just clean this shit up. I didn't wanna kill the youngin just teach him a lesson. This is a grown folks business. I'll holla at youngin in a couple days see where his head at. He was just our errand boy anyways." I voiced to ATL. Youngin was this lil nigga name Jalen, that would always wanna be around us. I didn't let him hustle but I'll give him lil odd jobs to do keep money in his pocket. His home life was fucked up but, he can't be doing dumb shit in my spot.

If I wasn't gay I will give ATL some pussy. He the first nigga I ever found attractive. I put my gun back in my waist line. I looked over at ATL. He still had a blank expression. I slapped hands with him. "I'll holla at you later. You coming through the club, tonight right?" I asked ATL making my exit out the trap house.

"Yea I'm gon be there. Hold up Gunna." ATL said in a low tone. I answered my ringing phone and left of the back door. I checked my surroundings before getting my car you never know when a nigga waiting in the trenches to do the unthinkable. It was now one in the afternoon and I still had to my hair braided. I felt my phone vibrating it was the chick that braid my hair. "YO speak to me." I said through the phone. "Gunna you still coming to get your hair braided. You was supposed to be here an hour ago." Kache said with a frustrating voice. "Yea I got caught up in some shit my fault yo. Yea I'm still coming through is that okay? I'll throw you something extra for your time."

"Naw it's cool." Kache said with her sexy ass voice.

She sound like one those bitches that be on the sex hotline.

"You know what I want." She said seductively. "Oh yea shit I'm on my way then." I said eagerly. Kache and I mess around from time to time nothing major.

Two hours later my hair was braided. I got my nut off too, smoked a blunt, went home showered. Dress in Moschino white jeans, white and gold Moschino belt and a t-shirt that say Hustle or Die in gold letters. On my feet is some white and gold customize Nike Foamposite. I checked myself in the mirror and nodded my head up and down. "Yes sir I'm pulling bitches tonight." I said while smiling while rubbing my hands together. My Gold teeth shining bright I grabbed my Rolex watch and around my neck was lightweight gold rope chain. Now it's was time to go. I put my keys and phone in my pocket.

Ten Minutes Later….

I was sitting at the red light in traffic. The street nigga in me looked at all cars around me. I turn to my left green Chevy Tahoe. I did a double take because I know my eyes was deceiving me. The undercover cop Dontae in the flesh. Legend or I have not been able to get any information on his crooked cop ass. I looked over he looked unbothered and focus on the road. I should just give him a dome shot but, that idea quickly left, when I thought about it come on Gunna that's a cop. It's broad daylight. Furthermore, Chyna wanted to handle herself. Chyna will be home in couple weeks any fucking ways. The light turned green I pulled my phone outta my pocket; to take a picture of his license plate. "Pussy ass nigga I been looking for his ass for over four years." I said to myself and zoomed in on his plate. I can't wait to tell Chyna about this shit. It took all of me to not but a bullet in his head. I can't wait to tell Hunnid. This nigga just riding around Philly like shits all good.

Never mix business with pleasure and that's what Dontae did. I truly believe he caught feelings for Chyna. Shit why wouldn't he my bestie is bad. Dontae couldn't bring himself to do his job. Dontae had to make the ultimate choice and Chyna wasn't it.

I pulled up to Legends house and got out the car. I tried the door it was open. *"Damn nigga ain't locking his doors."* I walked in his crib. *"Why the fuck the nigga got the door unlock its real out here."*

"Legend!" I yelled out. "Gunna" Legend answered. I can tell my bro was smiling from the way he said my name. "I'm in the kitchen." Legend yelled. "Nigga why the fuck you got the door open?" I asked Legend. He was running the money through the money machine but, stop and gave me a serious grin. "Gunna I seen you on the camera pulling up. What you thought, I just let niggas have full access to me like that naw. You and Chyna did way too much shit out here on these streets I know better." He seriously said.

I laughed at him and took a seat. "Where Boss hog at?" I asked looking around. "He in the bathroom. Boss hog always shitting. He better go get checked out." I replied. Legend start laughing loud. "What you laughing for nigga?" Boss hog said entering the kitchen. "You... nigga you always shitting." I said. "Better out than in." Boss hog said snickering and took a seat at the table.

We sat and discussed business counted up the money. We went over monthly gross for each trap house. "Let me tell y'all about this shawty I met." Boss hog said and took the rubber band off the stack of money. "Lil light skin bitch, she was fine, big perky titties and a pretty face. I took the bitch to the hotel. She was talking all this big shit too."

"Naw you just ass nasty nigga." I told Boss hog he fuck anything. Gunna you more of a whore then me and Legend.

"Let me finish my story Gunna you keep interrupting me damn." I waved him off. "Anyways I took the bitch back to the room. She start giving me a lap dance and she started shaking her ass in my face. I got a whiff of something foul. I pushed that bitch right on the floor." I laughed so hard if I was light skin my face would of been red. Boss hog was mad. "Nigga this ain't funny. That bitch foul she looked clean."

"Well looks are deceiving!" Legend expressed while shaking his head. Legend got up from the table taking the money machine with him. "Yo." Boss hog yelled "I wasn't finished counting this last stack of money or finish telling my story." Legend cocked his head to the side and "Boss you take home anything bro. I knew you since I was ten. I know how this story going end. Her pussy was stink but you still got your dick suck." Legend said and bust out laughing as he left out the room.

Boss Hog looked at me "Gunna what fuck you laughing for?" I pointed to him and said, "Your nasty ass. So answer this for me Boss hog." I sat back in the chair crossed my arms across my chest. "Did you?"

"Did I do what?" He asked me and separating all the bills into a pile. "You get head from shawty; after you smelled that foul ass pussy?" "Boss Hog started smiling. "Hell yea, bitch wasted my time. I wasn't gonna fuck her doe."

"Nigga you wild." I told Boss hog. "What can I say they can take the dog out the hood but not the…" Boss hog stop talking mid-sentence and, waved his hand and said, "Fuck it I'm a dog ass nigga!" I got up from my seat I'll see y'all niggas down at the Club Lex.

I left out and got in my Porsche truck. I was fucking with my radio. When Boss hog and Legend approached the truck. Legend grabbed the handles. "Unlock the door Gunna." Legend said with his raspy ass voice. He always sound like he need to clear his throat. I unlocked the door. Boss hog got in the passenger while Legend got in the back. *"I don't know where these niggas going but, I'm getting some pussy tonight. I'm riding solo."*

"Hold the fuck up y'all niggas ain't riding with me. Fuck I look like an Uber. I'm tryna climb in some pussy tonight. I ain't chauffeuring y'all niggas around." I said with anger.

"Shut up Gunna and drive," Boss hog said. "Naw Boss hog you always on joke time." Boss hog said and reclined his seat back. "Gunna how you climbing in pussy. When you got a pussy. You taking this lesbian thing too far." Boss hog voiced. I took my fitted off and turned it around. Something I did when I was irritated. "Y'all niggas always joking until I take y'all bitches." We all laughed. Boss hog pointed at me. "You gotta point but fuck all that. Are we to the club or naw?" Boss hog asked?

I turned around and looked at Legend who was texting on his phone. I kept my truck in park. I shook my head. "Y'all niggas is high." "Yea that batch of weed you got Gunna is FIIIIRRREEEE!!!!" Legend said while smiling! "I don't know why y'all getting comfortable. I ain't pulling off. Take your own whip."

"Aite she mad Boss hog. Let's just ride in my whip." Legend said. Boss hog opened the door and got out my truck. He leaned down and looked at Legend. "Bro you driving." Legend got out the car and I watched them get in Legend's Cocaine white Benz. I pulled off.

I got to the club in less than fifteen minutes. I let the valet take my whip and I walked right pass the line. All eyes was on me bitches calling my name. Shit I'm something like a celebrity to these heauxs. I gave a celebrity wave to all my fans. I laughed these heauxs is so thirsty.

The bouncer Carlos was working the door. Carlos also worked part-time for us as security at my lower trap house. "What's up Gunna?" Carlos said, and we slap hands. "I was just about to text you see if y'all was coming through tonight. You know MoneyBaggs Yo is performing." Carlos said. "Yea the whole gang coming through dey on their way." I said to Carlos. I walked in and Future's Draco was blasting through the speakers!

"Draco season with the bookbag, rat tat tat got a little kick back hundreds on hundreds got a good batch you ain't gon never get your bitch back"

I bounced my head up and down to the music. My favorite bartender was approaching me. She had on black leather corset with leather boy shorts and, black leather thigh high boots. Her name is Phoenix. "Hey Gunna. What you drinking Henny?" Phoenix asked with her head tilted to the side, showcasing the most prettiest smile I ever seen. That smile was so flirtatious it was warming my heart. "You know what I like baby." I said and matched her flirtatious smile.

Phoenix was five-feet nine-inches, light skin, with a nice body. Phoenix was not thick but just enough ass and titties to fulfill a niggas dreams. She was tatted up all on her thigh, stomach and back area damn that shit was sexy. Phoenix was a good girl. She only worked at Club Lex to pay her way through school. She was studying law at Temple University Of Law. I don't want to ruin shawtys life with my fucked-up lifestyle. I only flirted with Phoenix nothing more. "Baby." I said to Phoenix. She turned around smiled wide because she loves when I call her that shit too.

Phoenix turned around with lust in her eyes. "Yes baby?" She replied. "Grab me a bottle of Belaire too meet me in V.I.P." I told Phoenix. I walked through the crowd observing my surroundings. I looked to my left and seen the jackboys are here. You know them type, always tryna rob hardworking niggas or just bully niggas outta they trap house.

Mankind was in the building. He was a low-level hustler. He wasn't broke but, he wasn't getting no money like my team! Mankind mean mug me. *"Ya days is numbered."* I thought in my head. I slapped hands with a couple niggas I knew in the club. I made my way to the V.I.P section. Bad Ass, Geno and ATL was already in V.I.P. I slapped hands with all of them then took a seat on the plush sofa. Club Lex was lit and, the decor was all white and silver.

The dude that own this club Hunnid helped him get this club. Pete use to run with Aunt Deana back in the day and fell off. Pete went damn near broke. He contacted Hunnid with a business proposition and she helped him. Now Hunnid was part owner. Legend talked Hunnid into the shit. At first Hunnid said she was gon let Pete borrow the money. She didn't want any parts in the business. Legend is very business savvy so Hunnid agreed. It's been over five years and the club is still doing good. Moments later Phoenix came back with my drinks. I slipped $200 in her boy shorts and kissed her on her cheek. *"Damn shawty smelled so good."* I thought to myself.

"Chill Gunna." I said in my head. *"She a good girl. Leave*

her alone."

"Thank you, baby." I seductively said to Phoenix. She looked me in my eyes. "Gunna why you be playing me? I see the kinda bitches you be entertaining. They ain't half of what I am." Phoenix said! She had this look in her eyes like I disappointed her. It shocked the shit outta me that she really be paying me that much attention.

I kept it a buck with her. "Baby girl." I said while holding on to her waist. "I'm a wild ass nigga. I don't wanna fuck up your life, hurt your feelings and, you deserve to be somebody's wife. I know I'm not ready for all of that." I honestly said and pointed to my chest. "I respect you enough to tell you that. All these bitches is just for fun. I don't care about none of them." Phoenix dropped her head low.

I grabbed her chin and raised her head so that we were looking in each other's eyes. "Baby don't ever put your head down. You are too pretty for that. Hold your head up high. This ain't a rejection. It's a compliment, go back to work you losing money over there. I know you make big tips in here." I kissed Phoenix on her cheek. Then smacked her on her ass. She slightly turned around and smiled.

"One day Gunna you are gonna be mines and that's not up for debate." Phoenix whispered to me. While softly rubbing finger down the side of my face. "You gon love me." She said and, walked away smiling. Phoenix crazy. She said that shit like, I just told her yes, we gon be together. Truth be told I was just scared of love.

This street shit dangerous. *"Just let her be Gunna."* I had to convince myself to not like Phoenix. I ran my hands down my face and shook that feeling I had for Phoenix off. I went back to my seat on the plush sofa. "Damn Gunna what you do to Ol 'girl." Geno asked me? I smirked at Geno "Nothing lil nigga." I said.

"It didn't look like nothing to me. She is fine as fuck. You passed that up? Are you dumb or are you dumb?" Geno asked while laughing hysterically.

"Fuck you Geno. She's a good girl. I don't want to turn her life upside down with my bullshit." Geno laughed harder "WHAAAAT…Gunna got a conscious." Geno said with his hand over his mouth. Then took a swig of his Henny. "I ain't never seen you spare a bitch's feelings." Geno said. I waved Geno off. "He get on my nerves sometimes." I laughed to myself.

I looked over at the door and seen Legend, Boss Hog and Lucci entering the club. I looked over a Mankind and his squad had jealousy in their eyes. I laughed at them niggas. They mad we get this money. "Take notes niggas." Geno whispered in my ear. "Gunna I'm already on point you know that." Geno was with the bullshit. I slapped hands with Lucci, Legend and Boss Hog.

Boss Hog start milli rocking to Yung MA's 'Ouuuu'…...Legend start laughing and whispered to me "I see that fuck nigga in here. I don't want no bullshit tonight. I'm tryna have a good time tonight." Legend said. "I know fuck them doe." I expressed to Legend. "Who is that light skin nigga with Mankind. Don't he look familiar?" Legend asked me? I squinted my eyes to focus on the young bull. He does look familiar. "He definitely does. Naw I don't know him." I said to Legend.

As I took a last glance at the bull he looks like somebody I know. I said to myself I'm definitely storing his face in my memory. "That's Mankind lil minion. I was telling y'all about when we visited Hunnid Boss hog said his name is Dallas. He in his 20's." Boss said and shrugged his shoulders. "Dallas huh I need more details on this little fucker." Legend said.

"I might have to knock that chip of his shoulder. He feeling himself and getting in grown folks business." Geno said. I just nodded in agreement. Geno have Jazlyn to stop pass the trap. I know you will see her before I do. I gotta holla at her. See what these niggas up too." Legend said. "Aite I gotchu" Geno said.

Thirty minutes had passed, and shit was still calm. We had hella blunts in rotation. Geno was getting a lap dance from one of the strippers. ATL was talking to some nigga that was just as tall as him. *"They gotta be related."* I thought. I looked over at Lucci and he was arguing with some chick. "Yo take your bald head ass somewhere. I got a woman." Lucci said to the chick. "Since when Lucci?" She asked with her hand on her hip. Lucci chuckled "Since...since." But stop mid-sentence. "I don't gotta explain myself to you get the fuck on somewhere."

"You pretty but my women look way better. It ain't worth it." Lucci seriously said. The chick started rubbing on Lucci joystick. He looks like he was enjoying it until reality set in. The chick had a banging ass body too. She was about 5'5 brown skin, very short haircut. She kinda put you in the mind of Meagan Good with deep dimples. Lucci got super mad smoke was coming out the top of this niggas head. He grabbed the chick by her throat. "Didn't I tell your heaux ass that I gotta a woman." Lucci said through clenched teeth.

"I don't want nobody going back telling her I was doing anything with y'all heaux." Lucci screamed in her face, still choking her. She was tryna get his hands off her. Lucci was tryna kill this chick in the middle of the club. *"What's wrong with this nigga?"* I said in my head and I took my fitted hat off and turned it backwards. I jumped up off the sofa and grabbed Lucci off the chick. "Chill nigga what the fuck you doing?" I asked Lucci. "She just keeps following me Gunna. I warned her to leave me the fuck alone. I don't want Hunnid to find out I'm entertaining these bitches. Especially while she in jail." Lucci said sounding serious.

This nigga is a fool him and Hunnid ain't even together. I laughed and turned my attention back to the chick. I was about to address her weird ass and tell her to chill but, I was cut off by the bitch screaming. "HUNNID...HUNNID is your woman?" She asked wearing shocked and scary expression on her face; "Hunnid is crazy!"

"Don't tell her I was trying to mess with you. Don't even tell her we ever met!" She pointed towards herself then pointed at Lucci. "I swear I didn't know Lucci. You better start dropping Hunnid's name. You gon get somebody killed and, I ain't tryna die about no dick." The chick started looking around. Hunnid ain't out, yet right?" The chick asked.

Lucci waved her off and said, "Stay your weird ass the fuck away from me Dawn!" Crazy ass chick stomp her feet like a lil kid. "Lucci don't say my name." Dawn nervously said. Boss hog came over and laughed right in Dawn's face. He grabbed her by her arm and pushed her right out V.I.P. "Dingy ass bitch" He yelled and grabbed his bottle of Douse.

"Y'all niggas need to be on point, instead of playing with these hoes." Boss hog voiced. "Mannn… fuck that bitch Lucci said. "You better learn how to control your hoes Lucci or the crime rate in Philly gon go up." Boss hog said and took a shot of his D'usse. Lucci side eye Boss hog "What the fuck you talking about?"

"You over there running ya mouth. How the fuck you know what happen over here? I pay attention to everything. If you serious about fucking with Hunnid. She don't play dat. That's what I'm talking about." Boss hog said and got up to go on the dance floor.

I got up to go to the bathroom and somebody bumped me hard as hell. I turned around and it was the lil nigga Dallas. "What you looking at nigga?" He said smiling. "Lil nigga watch where the fuck you going or-"

"What… Gunna what you gon do?" He asked with his chest all poked out. Now that I'm up close and personal in Dallas face. He favored Legends girl Bianca. This had me thinking. *"Naw I'm trippin. Maybe it's just a coincidence."* I said to myself, People was walking past, so I couldn't hear what Dallas was saying.

I pushed through three people grabbed his lil ass up by his shirt. I pulled my nine from the back of my shirt and put it to his head. "Lil nigga don't play with your life like that."

"Fuck you. Won't you go put on a dress or som…" Dallas started to say but, I interrupted his comment by hitting his ass over the head with the gun.

"Ughh." He cried out in pain. I repeatedly hit him in his

face with the gun. Blood was everywhere a crowd start forming. Dallas was trying his best to block and guard his face. By the amount of blood gushing out his face, you woulda thought I killed Dallas. Yea lil nigga thought since I'm a female that he could fuck with me. *Naw I'm Gunna you can't fuck with me Dallas.*

Security came, and they yoked him up by his shirt. They knew not to touch me. Legend came over. "What happened Gunna?" Legend asked with raise brow. Legend looked down at my white fit that was now soaked with Dallas blood. "Lil nigga need to learn how to act in public." I said to Legend. "Get his ass outta here." I told security. Security had him by his shirt and Dallas was still holding the side of his face in disbelief.

I looked up and the whole gang came over to bathroom. The music stopped, and all the attention was now on us. Mankind rushed through the crowd "What the fuck happened to my youngin?" He asked looking at all of us.

We all looked at Mankind pretty ass. "Nigga fuck you. We ain't gotta explain shit. "Play with pussy you get fucked huh Mankind!" Geno said with malice. "That bitch hit me with the gun for no reason Mankind." Dallas said spitting blood out his mouth."

"Oh yea so we gotta problem huh?" Mankind asked pointing to Legend.

Geno reached for his gun and Lucci stop him. "Not here G." Legend said in a low tone."

"Oh noooo… dont stop him let's get it crackin. Y'all niggas don't scare me." He laughs. "Y'all work up under a bitch. Don't get me wrong she harder than most niggas I dealt wit. This shit ain't over wit." Mankind said while security was escorting him and Dallas out the club.

"I don't do no talking. Fuck these niggas." Lucci said and walked away. As security was escorting them out Mankind turned around and, had the most devilish smile I ever seen. "I promise you, this shit ain't over and tell Hunnid I'm closer to her than she thinks. So move cautiously. Karma Issa biiittcchh." He said maliciously.

"Bitch nigga we ain't losing no sleep over you." I yelled to Mankind before he exited the door. "What the fuck everybody looking at? Aye DJ turn the fucking music back up." I hollered to the DJ. The crowd was silent, and the DJ started the music.

I walked by the bar I seen Phoenix sitting at the bar with

her head down. I approached her and tapped her on her shoulder. She lifted her head up "Gunna are you okay?" Phoenix asked with concern in voice. "Yea baby I'm always good, I notice her words was slurring. "Phoenix you drunk shawty?" I asked shocked as hell; she never really drink.

My rejection must have caused more shots than she can handle. Phoenix threw her arms around my neck and looked in my eyes. I held on to her waist, Phoenix was sloppy drunk she could barely stand.

"Phoenix you need to go home. You shouldn't be in her like this. Niggas will try to take advantage of you." I said and scooped her up bridal style. I walked past Legend. "I'm about to roll" I said struggling a lil bit to carry Phoenix. I slap hands with him. "You cool Gunna you want me to walk you out?" Them niggas could be lurking. You can't carry shawty out and watch your back. I'll walk y'all out." Legend inform me and turned away from the crowd to take the safety off his gun.

I had valet to bring my ride around back I didn't want Phoenix to get caught up in my bullshit. Legend led the way. I carried her through the kitchen and out the back door. After

Legend checking the surroundings. "Gunna call me when you get to the crib." Legend said holding his gun in his hand looking up and down the alley to make sure the nobody was out there. "Aite I will." I informed Legend.

I put Phoenix safely in my ride. She was knocked out not even five minutes of me driving. I didn't know even know where Phoenix live. *"Fuck it I'll just take her to my crib."* Today events were heavily on my mind. *"Damn What the fuck was Mankind talking about he closer to us then what we think hmmm… there is somebody on our team playing both sides!"*

Chapter 13

FIRST DAY OUT

Chyna

Ahh... shit it's go time. I patiently waited in my cell for my name to be called. Swear I had my shit packed days ago. Rasheeda was in her feelings. "Bitch you good? Rasheeda you only got two weeks left in here, that's nothing. We just did over five years. Don't let these bitches in here see you weak; always remember that." I informed Rasheeda and hugged her.

I pulled back from the hugged and looked in her eyes. She looked sad and lost. "Fix your fucking crown Sheeda." I said aggressively. "It's just we made each other days here better." Sheeda emotionally expressed. "You fucking right." I said. Rasheeda looked over at the pictures of her daughter Skylar. "Have I ever lied to you? Skylar is good. I promise you that." I said with a wide beam spreaded across my face.

My mother got custody of Rasheeda daughter about eight weeks ago. One thing about my mom she has always been; caring and compassionate. "Chyna Jackson." The C.O. called my name. I picked up my bags. "Keep your head up Sheeda, call Legends phone tomorrow." I said peering over my shoulder. "Okay." Rasheeda said in a low tone. I know she was sad but, she better suck it up.

C.O. Stevenson unlocked the door to my cell. I walked the block, bitches was yelling out their cell. "Oh shit Hunnid getting out. It's about to get cold on dem streets." I gave a couple bitches hugs that was cool. One inmate in particular was Ms. Karen D. She was in here violating probation and check fraud. She was smart and was good with washing dirty money. I need somebody like that on my team. I slid a piece of paper with Legend's number in her hand as we hugged. "Call me Ms. Karen." She gave me a head nod. Not wanting to discuss the details about shit.

"Enough Chyna." C.O Stevenson said. "Do you wanna leave or you wanna go back to your cell and stay longer I got shit to do." C.O. Stevenson sarcastically said. He was an old white man late in his late fifty's, short standing 5'9 with gray hair. He was a C.O that went strictly by the book. He was not into breaking rules. He will tell on your ass quick. "Naw I'm ready. Let's go." I dryly responded. "I thought so." He said and gave me a slight grin.

Moments later we reached the door. My adrenaline was

pumping I was ready to smoke, fuck and most definitely ready to do some gangsta shit. I signed for my belongings. The check the C.O. handed over was $4,367. All the rest of them clothes and a pair of shoes I threw away. I told Legend don't send no clothes up here. I'm gonna wait until I get home; to get out these state clothes fuck all that.

I don't want to spend another minute in this bitch. I walked out the doors as a free woman. I turned around and looked up at the jail and stuck my middle finger up. As I walked out I seen my bestie Gunna leaning on an all-white drop top Mercedes Benz. The sun was shining so bright it was mid-September. Gunna was on the phone smiling showing all 32 gold fronts. She had on a red snapback on backwards her braids was freely hanging out the snapback. Patent leather Red Jordan 11 Retro's. Distressed light denim jeans and a throwback Chicago Bulls jersey.

"OMG!" If I was gay I would fuck with her. Gunna had so much swag. She turn straight bitches gay! Gunna put you in the mind of the New York rapper Young MA. Gunna did not have an ounce of feminine in her. "Damn bitch you swagged the fuck out. I see you." I said, and I start milly rocking. Gunna laughed with excitement. Gunna stepped towards me smiling. Gunna still tryna hold up her jeans with a Newport cigarette hanging out the side of her mouth. She embraced me. She pick me up and, swung me around.

"I missed you so much Chyna. We back bestie!" You fucking right." I said and kissed Gunna on her lips, still hugging Gunna. People often thought it was weird or assumed I was into women because I be kissing Gunna in the mouth. Naw not at all fuck people's opinion. That's my bestfriend and I love her.

"Come on let's get outta here, I hate jails." Gunna said after looking up at the jail. We heard females screaming "Gunna...Gunna and Gunna!" Gunna hood celebrity ass blew them a kiss. "Come on superstar stud." I sarcastically said chuckling. I was thinking about when Gunna first told me she was gay. She was scared to come out. Being gay isn't as strong and powerful as it is today. I always accepted her for her. Sexuality shouldn't tarnish a friendship. Fifteen years later here we are, and our bond is forever.

I was about to open the passenger side door. Gunna stop me. "Chyna what you doing this you?" Gunna gestured her head at the car. She flick her cigarette on the ground and, toss me the keys. "Oh yea?" I asked with a surprised look. "This is a gift from me and Boss Hog." Gunna said and came around to the passenger side. I ran to the driver side and got in the car. This car was nice as hell. All white everything, wood grain, back up camera, push start. "A bitch was cheesing."

I put my foot on the brake and pushed the start button. The engine roared. The startup was nice and smooth. *"Damn I'm in luv with this car already."* Thanks to Legend's main hobby as a mechanic. I was in love with fast and foreign rides. Two hours later I had the top down blasting Yo Gotti's Rack it up.

"Gunna I'm getting pampered before I meet up with the team. "Naw Hunnid today we just gon focus on you coming home. Tomorrow is back to business; I scheduled the meeting for 9am tomorrow. Mutha fuckas thought you was gon be gone for ten years. "They about to learn today" Gunna admitted rubbing her hands together like Birdman.

"I just wanna get back to the money and find Dontae. I'm putting a bullet right between his eyes." I said to Gunna. I pulled up to Legend's house. It was a four-bedroom mini mansion. Big ass backyard, built in pool. I entered the house with the passcode that Gunna gave me.

"Chyna call me when you ready. I'm going to collect this money from ATL real quick." Gunna said

"Aite I'll call when I'm done." I simply replied. I opened the door, I heard Gunna calling my name I turned around. Gunna was jogging towards me with a pink box. "Here I forgot to give this to you." She said outta breath. I reached out to grab the pink box. It looked like a jewelry box.

"What's this Gunna you tryna propose to me? You think because I did them five years I like pussy now huh?" I playfully said with my tongue out. We both bust out laughing. "Hunnid open the box. I got shit to do. We got somewhere to be. "Gunna said now sounding serious. I opened the box. I was so fucking excited. My customized black and hot pink Glock 19, 9mm, semi-automatic gun. This shit had a silencer to it too. *"Sweet"*

My Godfather Fontell got it for my 21st birthday. My pussy was getting wet looking at my favorite gun. I was caressing it like it was an erected pole. *"Damn my ass is horny."* I chuckled to myself.

I'll never leave home without it. She was my guardian angel in these streets. "Damn Gunna good look boo. I missed her we gotta get better acquainted with each other. It's been a minute Gunna smiled. Shiiiitt…the way you rubbing all on dat 9 I think you need some dick Hunnid." Gunna laughed loudly, holding her stomach. "I knew that would make your day, I'm out Hunnid." Gunna said and walked back to a silver Jeep Cherokee. *"That must be her everyday ride."* I thought.

"I went in my brother's house. His house was nice. Black and white theme. Huge black and white area rug, biggest white sectional I ever seen, mirrors everywhere a huge portrait of Legend and Bianca in the foyer of the house. I gotta go see Bianca tomorrow at the rehab center. I drop my head. *"Damn sis what happen to you?"* I continued to look around the house, I know my mom decorated this for Legend. There ain't no way he decorate this himself but, it's nice.

Moments later I heard heels clicking against the floor. My antennas went up. I know Legend don't got a bitch in here that is not my sis. and it's my first day home. This bitch about to die today. I seen a pretty fair skin chick with a green flowy maxi dress on. She came round the corner her Juicy Couture perfumed invaded my nostrils. She reached her hand out. "Hello, my name is Shay. Your brother hired me and my glam squad to do your hair, makeup and dress you." She said super bubbly.

She still had her hand out waiting for me to shake it. I was sitting there looking at her hand like it was the dirtiest hand. I mean mugged the shit outta her. Shay had an embarrassed slight nervous look plastered on her face. Once I realize she was here on some business shit and not fucking my brother; I shook her hand. "What's up? My name is Chyna." I calmed down some and greeted her.

Shay took my hand and lead me to the dining area. Her team turned the dining room into a salon. They had everything set up like I was about to star in a movie. I still gotta ask my brother about this bitch but, I'll play it cool. I don't want this bitch fucking up my hair and makeup. I'll have to shoot her pretty ass.

Shay introduced me to her whole glam squad. She sat me in the chair and put a pink cape on me. "Hold up I really don't wear makeup." I voiced and turned around and looked at Shay. "What I need makeup for a bitch skin is flawless." I said and turned back around in my seat.

"Don't have me looking like I should be in a casket instead of a runway. I got an image to uphold." I said with an attitude. Shay smiled nervously at me. "Please trust me. I don't play about my brand or my money. Also, me fucking up your makeup and hair will do both. I'm about my money Chyna. Furthermore, I know how you get down and I love my life." Shay said with her hands up!

Two hours later my nails, hair and makeup was done. They didn't let me see myself until they was finished. Shay assistant Erykah brought the full-length mirror and turn it around. I looked at myself and couldn't believe my eyes. My makeup was flawless Pink lipstick and gold eyeshadow "OMG y'all bitches did thaaaattt!" I yelled. I had on a hot pink Bandage jumpsuit with my whole back on display. The jumpsuit hugged every curve on my body. Gold Privilege sandals. My hair was in big beautiful wand curls, my lashes was popping I never wore lashes before, but I likes.

"Damn bitch we gon do alot of business together I happily said to Shay. I'm happy that your happy." Shayla said while grabbing a little gold clutch purse out this Louis Vuitton suitcase. "Chyna I think this will go real nice with your shoes" Shay suggested. I gave Shay a questionable look with my brow raised. I looked down at the clutch purse like I was too good to wear it. I grabbed the clutch out her hand and was just examining it.

"What's wrong you don't like it?" Shay asked me all disappointed like she fail me as a stylist. It's cute Shay don't get me wrong but, my gun can't fit in there. Hunnid don't go nowhere without her gun! I said while holding my index finger up like I was disciplining a child.

Shay's eyes grew big; Shay was shocked by my statement. "I'm sorry Chyna come again" Shay said like as if she heard me wrong. "My Glock 9 can't fit in that lil ass change purse. I been gone five years y'all got me fucked up" I ranted on. "Ohhhh" Shay laughed nervously. I do have some bigger purses. I don't know if they will match those shoes though Shay said and left the room.

I sat there talking to myself, *I'm not a prissy bitch, any mutha fucking way. I coulda wore some jeans, a bustier and some fucking timberlands. Shit I coulda rocked my fucking gun holster.*

Shay entered the room holding three other purses. They wasn't as nice as the change purse. I hope my gun fit. I went to the living room to grabbed my gun off the TV stand.

When I went back to the dining room. Shay was still standing in the same spot holding them purses. Shay stood there froze in her spot. When she seen my black and pink Glock 9 gun. Shayla dropped the purses and was hiding behind the dining room chair with her hands up. "Chyna what are you doing?" Shayla nervously asked.

"Bitch what do it look like? I'm seeing what purse fit my gun in it. What you think?" I said with my head tilted to the side and laughing.

"I ain't gon shoot you Shay get from behind that chair." You just slayed me. Why would I kill the talent?" I said to Shay, so she can get her life. I grabbed the house phone to call Gunna, but she didn't answer. Gunna never answer, you gotta call her back to back. "DAMN!!!"

I wanna see my mom. I wanna see Legend as soon as that statement left my mouth. Legend ass ran through the door and scooped me up in his big arms. "Legend." I screamed and wrapped my arms around his waist I'm so short my arms don't go pass his waist that shit funny as hell. "I'm so happy you home Chyna." Legend said.

"Legend put me down." I just looked at my brother and started fixing my hair. My hair got a little outta place from Legend picking me up. "Damn Legend your emotional ass messed up my hair." I said playfully. "I'm so happy to see your annoying ass." I said and hit him in the back of his arm.

"Good look bro. Shay and her team are the best. They made a gangsta ass bitch look so beautiful, I love it. You fucking her?" I asked Legend; hands on the hip with my lips poked out waiting for a response. Bianca was my fucking sister and if he on some fuck shit. I don't wanna be involved.

I'm not one of those sister that they play all sides. Hang with all the girlfriends and the side chick being messy as fuck. "Naw Chyna damn why can it be all business?" Legend asked like he was annoyed with my question. "Bro being that my sister-in-law is outta the loop at the moment. You might be out here on some whore shit."

"Chyna I ain't never fuck Shay. I just paid her for her

services. Shay do be tryna get on me though. I don't wanna entertain that shit. I got enough problems with your junkie ass sis-in-law." Legend said with frustration in his voice.

This time I was able to smacked him in back of his head because he tall ass was sitting down. "Don't be calling my fucking sister a junkie. Bianca just going through some shit right now but Hunnid home now. Don't make Hunnid shoot your ass. Chyna love you but, Hunnid don't give a fuck." I said referring to myself in third person.

Legend laughed. "Keep your hands to yourself. Tough ass Hunnid sister or not I'll shoot back." Legend said still laughing at me.

"Nigga I taught you how to shoot." I seriously said with a smirk on my face. Yea true sis I'll give you that." Legend said in his raspy voice.

Boss hog came in the house laughing. He heard me and Legend arguing. "I see ain't nothing change. She still punk you like she did when we were kids." Boss hog laughed holding his stomach like the shit was really funny.

"Fuck you Boss hog go the fuck home why are you here?"

Legend said to Boss hog. I'm definitely ain't here to see your ugly black ass." Now it was Legends turn to laugh. "Fare skin niggas ain't in no more. Y'all might get a chance again in 2030." Legend clapped back.

These niggas always rippin on each other. I love their friendship. They been bestfriends since we was kids. Boss hog was our neighbor. From the first day Boss hog and Legend met they been inseparable. Even when they was in school, if one played football the other one would play. Legend and Boss hog are the total opposite.

Boss hog is wild and a natural born hustler. Legend is laid back and calm but; if you get bro mad enough he will go hard. That's why I always fuck with him. I love to see his gangsta side. "I wish you both shut the fuck up; where we going tonight? I been locked up over five long years. I'm not staying here listen to two grown niggas rip on each other." I said as I went on the porch with the house phone to call Gunna.

When I reached the end of the porch a black on black Maserati Ghibli was pulling up in Legend's driveway. I took my gun out my purse and let it dangle to my side. When I got a clear view of the driver. Aww… shit. It was Gunna pulling up. She hopped out the car smoking on a blunt with a T-Mobile shopping bag. "Here Chyna this is an iPhone and this one is the business phone. Me, you, Boss hog, Lucci and Legend in a group message codes only. You know the routine, we switch up the codes every ninety days." Gunna said blowing smoke out her mouth.

I sat down in the chair to set up my phone. "When you get that car Gunna?"

"Damn bestie you look nice as fuck in that jumpsuit shit. I never seen your ass wear makeup." Gunna said ignoring my question about her car. Gunna said looking me up and down.

"This shit was Legend's idea." I said and tryna do my fingerprint on this new iPhone shit. When I was home the iPhone 4's was out. This shit look like a tablet, big ass phone.

"What you listened to Legend huh? I thought I would never see the day you listen to Legend." Gunna said then pulled out a bag off weed and, started breaking the weed up in the blunt she unwrapped.

"You tryna catch tonight huh Hunnid?"

"Naw Gunna. What the fuck? Catch who?" I asked her

playing dumb. "Hunnid one person you cannot lie too is me. We twins." Gunna said and licked the blunt and sealed it and pulled out a lighter and lit the weed.

"Gunna I ain't thinking bout no niggas. I'm tryna get back to this money." Gunna looked at me like I was lying. I was feeling the shit outta Lucci but, I think it's just lust. I don't know too much about him. Maybe one day I'll find out. *"Don't rush it Chyna."* I said to myself. Gunna inhaled and exhale the smoke out her mouth.

"Yea whatever Chyna, I got my eyes on you tonight." Gunna pointed at me. Legend and Boss hog came outside. "I'll see you in a minute sis me and this lame ass nigga." Legend pointed at Boss hog. We gotta handle some shit real quick.

I stood up out my seat 38 hot. "Nigga I been gone all these years. We only get twenty minutes together and you leaving?" I questioned Legend. "Chill Chyna!" Boss hog said. We got an emergency at one of the traps." Boss hog said.

"Fuck that. I'm coming too let me go grab a bigger gun. "Legend where my AR at?" I asked.

"Naw Chyna chill you ain't been home 24 hours. You

already on some trouble shit. Sit your ass down." Boss hog said. Legend waved me off and got in his Benz. Boss hog followed.

"Come on bestie let's ride." Gunna said over her shoulder. I looked at Gunna funny as she went down the porch steps. Pulling up her jeans blunt dangling out the side of her mouth. Either Gunna smoke a blunt or she got a cup of liquor. I never seen her without drink or smoke. Bitch carry drink and smoke with her at all times like it's a security blanket.

"Bitch if we just riding I can just go put on some sweatpants and a wife beater." I seriously told Gunna. "CHYNAAAA… chill I gotta make a run. I'll bring you back later to change." Gunna said in an irritating tone. Gunna walked towards her Maserati and got in. I got in the passenger. We rode out while listening to *Future's Mask Off* **Percocets, Molly, Percocets rep the set, gotta rep the set, chase a check, never chase a bitch, Mask off fuck it Mask off!**

I was dancing to Future in my seat. Wishing Gunna would pass the blunt. "Gunna passed me the blunt." I sighed.

"I want my own weed." Gunna laughed at my outburst. "I gotchu bestie. I'm in my zone." Gunna admitted. She hand me a bag of the most potent and loudest weed I ever encountered.

"Gat damn Gunna you the shit." I said all excited. I found a wrap in the console. She always prepared to smoke. I rolled that shit up in like 30 seconds. "Chyna you need to be in the Guinness book of world records." Gunna said wit a light chuckle. "For what?" I questioned.

"Shit the fastest weed roller." I cracked up laughing. I miss times like this with my right hand. We pulled up this big ass building, and I continued to smoke my blunt. Gunna got out the car. There was so many cars in the parking lot. I remember this building, before I went to jail. This building was a private K-5 school. *"Why we be going in here?"* I asked myself.

Being nosey I opened Gunna glove department and found mini bottles of Henny. This bitch is a drunk. I opened the mini bottle of Henny. I drunk it straight down. "Urrggh..." I grunted this shit strong burning my damn chest. I was finishing my blunt. Gunna turned around. She just realized I wasn't with her. Gunna walked back to the car and came around to the passenger side. I looked up at her. "I ain't going in there. What the fuck is this? Let's go to the club. I'm ready see some strippers." I said sticking my tongue out. I love strippers I wanna see a bitch slide down the pole.

"Chyna get the fuck out the car yo." I sense Gunna's attitude because she took her fitted hat off and turned it backwards. By now I started feeling the Henny and weed in my system. I got out and followed her inside the building. Gunna opened the big glass doors to this building. The place was decorated all white and diamonds huge balloon arch red carpet. I heard music. It was dark in the room. We were about to enter. All I heard was **"SURPRISE WELCOME HOME CHYNA!"** I was shocked and amazed how they got me I never expected this.

I looked around I seen my mom, aunts, uncles some cousins. My Godfather Fontell and his wife Bella, Legend, Boss hog, Lucci and all the niggas that work for us. My cousin Nia was holding up the wall off to the side. I made a mental note to see what's up with her. I hugged my mom first, she was in tears. "I'm so happy your home safe baby girl." My mother said emotionally voiced.

I looked at my mom. She had on a pretty pink midi dress with a black three-quarter length blazer. My mother was brown skin, standing 5'3 my mom was so THICK about 250 lbs., full lips, pretty brown eyes. Her hair was in a razor cut bob with a side part down the middle. My mom was four years older than Aunt Deana but, she didn't look 49 years old. My mom put you in the mind of actress Tasha Smith. My mother Deborah was thick. She wasn't sloppy built. Her thickness was in the right spot. You could literally sit a glass on her ass.

"Chyna I just love Skylar." My mom said referring to Rasheeda daughter. She starts kindergarten on Monday. She is such a sweet child my mom said and smiled. "Mom I appreciate you taking care of Rasheeda daughter. While she locked up" I said peering over my shoulder; it had to be over 300 people at my welcome home party. My mother waved her hand at me.

"Chyna you know I love helping people. That's why I'm an Registered Nurse. I was sad about Rasheeda mom passing her service was beautiful. She left Rasheeda and Skylar some money in her Will but, I'll tell Rasheeda that when she come home." My mom said.

I hugged my mom again. "Stay outta trouble please baby girl. Let me ask you something Chyna. When you gon sit down and act like a lady and find a man?" My mom questioned me.

"Okay mom chill you throwing too many question at me. I can't promise you nothing. Can we talk about this another time I just…"

My mom cut me off. "I know Chyna you always get mad when I ask you about street shit and relationships. We will talk about this shit again, real soon." She angrily said to me and pointed her finger in my face. "I'm going to mingle with the crowd mom." I said slightly agitated.

"I'm going in the kitchen because I cooked all that food and they better serve it right." My mom said and walked around me. Mom went to the back where I'm assuming the kitchen was. I walked to the bar.

I was slapping hands with people, hugging people and having small talk by the time I got to the bar. I was over it; I ain't that social. That's Legend right there he love this type shit, me naw I rather get money. I appreciate the party. I'm just ready leave now.

I got to the bar and my cousin Nia was bartending. "Hey cuzzin." I said to Nia. "Hey cuzzin." She said all dry. "What the fuck is wrong with you? I see there is some shit going on with you? Shit I'm home now cuzzin. Talk to me. Who I gotta shoot?" I asked Nia serious as hell. "Nia give me get that new Crown Apple. I need two shots' first before you tell me what's up with you." Nia pour two shots in a glass and slid my drink to me.

I notice she lost a lot of weight. Nia was what you call high yellow she was 5'9. She used to be 180 lbs. now it look like she 150 lbs. She always wore her hair honey blonde in a short in a pixie cut, deep dimples and, green cat eyes, she got a gap between her teeth, but she was still cute as fuck. I noticed that Nia and, all the other four bartenders had on a black skater skirt's and a white fitted tee, black letters that read; ***A Hunnid Grand or More.***

Nia came from around the bar and sat next to me. I told the other bartender to hold Nia down until we get done talking. "Nia who made them shirts?" I seen some of the food servers with them shirts on too. Nia like the twentieth person I seen with this shirt on. "It was my idea Chyna to show you some love and niggas from your team and our family just followed suit."

"Chyna… Cortez been beating on me" Nia said changing

the subject. I knew something was up with her. She usually come visit me in jail every two months and about a year ago the visits just stopped. I looked at Nia and she had this look in her eyes; of shame and embarrassment.

"Nia who is Cortez?" I hope she ain't talking about the nigga Cortez. *"That nigga hates me and my team more than Mankind."* I thought to myself. "You remember Pretty ass Cortez?

I was tryna remember. I know exactly who Cortez was. His brother Jae and right-hand Freddy B man robbed my trap, We took over Cortez territory. Cortez went to jail, so his block was up for grabs. He got word that I took over his spot and sent Jae and Freddy B to rob the trap house and set it on fire. Hating ass nigga, I offered them niggas a job working for me.

When I found out from Jazzlyn the type shit they had going on I was livid. I hired two bitches Nevea and Kiyann to set them up. It was Winter 2010. I sent Kiyann and Nevea to the club; to get on Jae and Freddy B. Them dumb ass niggas took the bait. Niggas love a bad bitch both Nevia And Kiyann was strippers from Club Lex.

Nevea is five-feet seven-inches, little waist, Nevea had a

K. Michelle booty. Nevea was Black & Korean, she favored the actress Lashontae Heckard. Kiyann is five-foot-five inches, Kiyann got this milk chocolate complexion that is so pretty. Her chinky eyes gave her an exotic look. Thirty inches of Malaysian hair to her ass. Kiyann legs is so nice and tone, she so flexable niggas love her. That's why I put them on my team to seduce niggas.

I followed them out the club. I called Gunna, Ring ring this bitch don't never answer. I redialed Gunna number she answered on the second ring. "Get ready." Was all I said into the phone and hung up. Fifteen minutes later I got a text from Kiyann. Saying (Done). Nivea and Kiyann spiked them niggas drinks with GHB and now it was show time.

Long story short I tortured them niggas to death with a chain saw. I found out from Nevea that Cortez was due home on the fifteenth of November 2010. I cut Jae's head off with a chainsaw and mailed it to Cortez baby momma's house. When Cortez was released he was already mad at the world because, he couldn't find his brother. So, I sent the nigga the answers he was looking for.

I sent Cortez Jae's head in a box and, mail it to him; with a note attached: ***BRO I HEARD YOU WAS LOOKING FOR ME!*** Ever since then that nigga hated me. He didn't know for sure if I killed his brother, but the brutal way Jae died. He suspected me. *Fuck him though.* He laid low after that and I ain't seen or heard of him until today. Me and Gunna dumped the rest of Jae and Freddy B's body in the Schuylkill River.

"He the one we went to school with? I asked Nia? I was playing dumb because he got her so brain washed. I didn't want her to know the history of me and Cortez beef. Dick make bitches do stupid shit like go against the grain (family). "Yes Chyna." Nia replied and rolled her eyes up in her head. "How the fuck you hook up with him. I would've never thought he was a woman beater, nowadays you never know who into what."

"I seen him at the mall one day and the rest is history. He treated me like no other and, I fell in love with him." Nia said almost in tears. I put my hand around her shoulder. "I didn't wanna tell you Chyna because; I know how you get down" Nia said looking nervous. She was playing with her fingers I grabbed her hands, she was shaking at this point.

People kept walking past interrupting us by saying what's up and hugging me. After the fourth person hugged me. I turned my attention back to Nia. "Are you still with him?" She paused and looked away. I turned her head towards me. "Nia are you still with him?" I asked looking directly in her eyes?

"Yes, Chyna I am, I love him and, he takes care of me." Soooo, you gonna stay with a nigga just because he throwing money at you." I said giving her a '**BITCH WHAT**' look.

"You don't understand Chyna." Nia said frustrated. "I got a 2017 Mercedes Benz E-class, a condo fully furnished with the best decor, purses, shoes and designer clothes." Nia said in one breath. I cut this bitch off.

"See he gotchu where he want you. He throws money at you and, you continue take his beatings. He know you are not gon leave him because he think you need him. I bet he is the reason why you stop visiting me?" I said in an angry tone.

Nia got quiet. "Yea he said he didn't want me in no dirty ass jail visiting people." Nia said it like it made sense. He brain washed this bitch. "*CONTROL*!" I got up and screamed in Nia face.

I was mad, but I had to calm down or Nia would never confide in me again. Nia was my childhood favorite cousin. We always been tight. I hate a fuck nigga that put his hands on a female. HAND ME YOUR PHONE!" I demanded Nia. She got up off the bar stool. Nia went behind the bar and grabbed her phone. I stored my number in Nia phone.

"Tonight Chyna we just gon party. I'll come pass Legends house to talk to you some more." Nia said walking back behind the bar. "Oh, we going talk about this shit again. Aye and another thing your coming to move with me fuck that." Nia couldn't believe my last statement. I was serious too.

I'll give her a job, so she can have her own money. My Aunt Denise was Nia mom. She is strung out on heroin, pills and coke well shit pretty much whatever she can get her hands on. She never paid Nia no attention. Denise move to New Jersey when we was like fifteen. My mom and Aunt Deana raised Nia.

Nia lived with me, Legend and my mom or Aunt Deana off and on. When Denise lived in Philly. Denise would just disappear and be gone for days. Denise's lack of care and affection. Made Nia look for love elsewhere. Nia wanted to be love by a man. I know being with this lame ass nigga Cortez, probably filled a void in her life; from not having her mother really around.

Nia graduated from college. I don't know what happen. She had a good job as an Accountant. Matter fact Nia worked close with Bianca. They worked for the same company BRY Group INC. That's how Legend met Bianca through Nia. I walked around the party tryna find Legend. DJ Khaled song Wild Thoughts was playing:

"I don't know if you can take it, know you wanna me nakey, nakey, naked I wanna be baby, baby, baby. Spinning and it's wet just like it came from Maytag, white girl wasted on that brown liquor, when I get like this I can't be around you I'm too lit; dim down a notch cause I could name some thangs that I'm gon do." "Wild, wild, wild… wild, wild, wild thoughts… wild, wild, wild, when I'm with you, all I get is wild thoughts… wild, wild, wild!"

I bumped into somebody while I was dancing solo. I was enjoying drinking my long island ice tea. The smell of cologne hit me in my nose damn somebody smell good. I turned around to see who bumped me and my heart skipped a beat. It was Lucci smiling and looking down to my 5-foot frame. Lucci was looking me directly in my eyes. I turned my head to avoid eye contact.

"Chyna Doll you wearing the fuck outta that jumpsuit." Lucci said and looking at me like I was desert and undressing me with his eyes. "Hello to you Lucci and goodbye Lucci." I tried to slide pass him while sneaking a peek at his wardrobe. Gucci everything... t-shirt, Gucci dark denim jeans, Gucci belt and Gucci sneakers. *"DAMN!"* I thought to myself! He looked good. Around his neck was a gold chain and his wrist a watch that matched perfectly together.

This nigga even had some Gucci framed glasses. His beard was neatly trimmed, low haircut lined up perfectly. Lucci was perfect in my eyes. I think it's his confidence and swag. He look good to me. *"Jesus what you doing to me? I thought you loved me? You keep putting this man in my presence!"* I said in my head.

This nigga looked so good to me. I gotta get away from him and focus on. *"No niggas Chyna!"* I kept repeating in my head. I never had to do that. Usually I ignore niggas and keep it moving but not, this nigga Lucci.

"Chyna you gon be my wife one day." Lucci said and licked his lips. Lucci grabbed my hand. I snatched my hand away from him. "I know you just came home and you tryna get back to business but, in due time. You gone be mine Chyna Doll." Lucci said with confidence.

"Naw nigga I don't do relationships. I fuck em and leave em." I said like I wasn't just in a trance; when this nigga come around. "Yea ...Yea." Lucci said and waved his hand at me like I was spitting bullshit.

"Them rules don't apply to me." He said. Lucci bent down and kissed my neck. He had a strong grip on my waist. At this point my whole body was on fire. Lucci whispered in my ear. "I know your pussy wet or should I say my pussy. She soaking wet right now ain't she Chyna Doll don't lie?" Lucci said smiling.

His warm mint breath was turning me on. I'm sprung and Lucci ain't even touch me yet. I rolled my eyes and tried to walk again. "This ain't your pussy Lucci. I'm a single woman." I flirtatiously said. He finally let my waist go. "Yea you single for now." He said over his shoulder and I watched him walked through the crowd. I looked on the stage and there was Legend. No wonder I couldn't find him. I sat there and listen to Legend speech. I got a feeling it's gonna to be a long night!

Chapter 14

I KNOW A NIGGA COOL NOW

Legend

    I was so happy to see my twin. I can get back to my first love. My auto body shops. The drug game is getting old. Chyna coming home was a good ass feeling. Shit it was better than pussy. Naw a nigga trippin off the weed. This ain't better than pussy but, it's close to it. I'm high as fuck right now and, I need some pussy! I grabbed the mic from the DJ and went on stage.

    When I got up on stage. I seen Boss hog pushing through the crowd on his way up to the stage. Soon as I got on stage everybody at the party went wild. Like I was a celebrity or some shit. I was hood famous and, I wasn't even trying be. Boss hog loved this hood fame…. Shit… *Me too*. I looked at that nigga and he was cheesing hard like a beat was about to drop and, we about to spit 16 bars.

    "I'm glad everyone came out. Welcome home sis." I said loud into the mic. I made eye contact with Chyna and took a deep breath before I spoke. I wasn't emotional. Well fuck it. I ain't gon lie. Sometimes when it comes to Chyna I am. "I missed you so much over these past five years. Now that you home I know a nigga cool." I said and cleared my throat because, a nigga was getting too emotional. I hit my fist across my chest. "I love you Hunnid." I said emotionally.

Chyna blew a kiss to me. and I handed the mic over Boss hog. He started laughing and covered the mic with his hand. Boss hog looked at me and whispered. "Soft ass nigga!" I punched that nigga in the arm. He play way too much. He don't have no chill even in serious moments at times. I made my way off stage and thought about Bianca.

When I visited Bianca after she first arrived at the rehab center. She asked me. "Do you love me Legend?" Bianca's eyes cut into my soul. I saw pain behind them and it was killing me, that I couldn't take her pain away.

I looked at her like she was crazy. "Are you serious after all we been through?" I replied. "Legend you buy me things to show your love. I tell you time and time again that all I want is you." Bianca admitted.

Bianca was never materialistic. She was with me before the money and hood fame. When Chyna went to jail things change. I became the man because I took over Chyna's empire and, my twin made quite a name for herself in these streets. Bitches started flocking at my feet and niggas started to hate me. I did some dumb shit and cheated on her with some baddie name Shalissa.

I thought the bitch was bad. Shalissa robbed me while I was on a business trip in Pittsburgh. Shalissa and her boyfriend broke into my hide away spot I used to take Shalissa and went in my stash. They stole $57,000 from me. Her and her broke ass boyfriend Blue. I blame myself for not being on point and letting this Shalissa too close to me. I had my little nigga ATL take care of Shalissa permanently but, the nigga Blue went to jail. I can't wait until he get out. I got something for him.

My twin Chyna is a wild child. She do her shit out in the open. I do sneaky shit. Bianca wouldn't let me cheating on her go. Even with Shalissa not existing anymore. She wouldn't let us move on and be great.

I know a nigga ain't shit for cheating on a woman like Bianca but, a nigga love heaux. Sometimes that can be your downfall or your demise. Bianca calling my name brought me back to reality *"Legend... Legend" Bianca called my name. "Huh?" I said and looked into Bianca pretty hazel eyes. "Are you listening to anything, I'm saying?" Bianca asked me.*

"Yea I heard you." I said trying to convinced her. Bianca twisted her mouth up like I was lying but, she knew me all too well. I was lying. I ain't heard nothing. "Naw I didn't bae what you say?" She sighed deeply. "Legend I asked you do you think we can repair our relationship. Did the love you had for me go away?" Bianca cried silently, and I watch a lone tear slid down her beautiful face. I swallowed a lump in my throat before I spoke to her.

"The love never left. Bianca you got my heart. I love you Bianca I care about your well-being more than; I care about myself. I don't want you to ever feel like I don't love you." I said full of emotion. "I feel like I'm losing you babe." She said through tears.

"Bianca..." I softly held the side of her face. I pecked her lips. You are my world, I never felt the love I feel for with any woman I ever been with. We going through something right now but, we going bounce back." I looked at Bianca and waited

for a response but, she gestured me to come closer. Bianca kissed my lips so passionately. The kiss felt like it was good bye. She move back out of my grasp. "Legend I gotta go back I'll call you later tonight after dinner." She softly spoke.

I was 38 hot. She cut the visit short. I guess she just needed time to herself. I hug her "Bianca I love you remember that and I won't let you fight this shit by yourself." I whispered in her ear. She pecked my lips one last time. Bianca got up and I watched her until she rounded the corner. "Damn." I said to no one in particular. I put my head in my hands and prayed silently that we get through this shit.

Bianca was released from that program and was doing good but, she relapsed, and I had to re-enter her back in the program. I'm tired of this shit but no matter how tired I get of Bianca bullshit. I can't turn my back on her. I scanned the room as I listen to Boss hog cracking jokes and ripping on mutha fuckas in the crowd.

I saw my mom. I was on my way over to holla at her. I stopped mid stride. Everything was moving in slow motion "BIANCA!!!" What the fuck she doing here, outta rehab? I ran my hands down my face and walk straight over to them. My mom's eye grew big. She saw me coming in their direction.

I got fire in my eyes. Bianca turned around. She looked so beautiful and that white fitted dress, gold heels, hair all done up nice and her makeup was flawless. She got her weight up too, I strongly gripped her hand. Just because Bianca looked good as fuck. I was still mad that she left rehab without completing the program again.

"WHAT THE FUCK YOU DOING OUTTA REHAB?" I said with aggression and squeezed her hand. "Ouch Legend your hurting me." Bianca whined but I didn't care. My mom stepped in "Legend don't make me fuck you up." My mother voiced.

I eased up on her hand because my mom didn't play about Bianca and, I didn't want to disrespect my mom. My mom tapped me on my shoulder. "Chill son talk to her first and hear her out. I'll give you two time to talk. I'm going to go find crazy ass Ashanti." My mom said calling Gunna by her government.

I turned back to Bianca who looked nervous. "What the fuck you doing outta rehab? Your ninety days is not over yet!" I asked Bianca. "Legend they let me out for good behavior" Bianca quickly lied. "Bitch do I look stupid to you?" I said getting in Bianca face. Bianca never lied to me but, ever since she started getting high. She became a habitual liar. I really didn't want people to know about my woman being a fucking junkie. *"How am I supplying the whole city with the same shit my women smoking. I'm such a fucking hypocrite."* I thought to myself.

I seen Bianca doing a lot of talking but, I couldn't hear what she was saying, I zoned out of the conversation. Once the first lie came out her mouth. I wanted to smack her lying ass. I don't why she tried to tell me that weak ass lie. I grabbed Bianca by her waist. "Let's go somewhere else and talk. I pushed Bianca to the nearest bathroom which was the men's bathroom. Oh well fuck it. We going right in here. We got in the bathroom. I locked the door. "What are you doing Legend" Bianca asked, and her face turned beet red. "Shut the fuck up Bianca" I yelled in her face.

"You gon tell me what's going on. Before I call the fucking rehab center and start asking questions." I angrily said spit flying out my mouth. Bianca eyes turned glossy. She blinked her eyes and tears was just pouring. Makeup was running down her face.

"Baby I love you. I hate that my addiction tore this relationship up." Bianca said crying uncontrollable. I touched her chin with my thumb and index finger and lifted her chin. I looked in her eyes.

"What is going on I'm giving you this chance to tell me." I questioned. "Legend I've always had a little bit of an addiction. It's how I cope with things that happened to me in the past. Things I never got over. Meeting you was the best thing that happen to me. When we first met I did pills here and there like Percocet, Molly and Xanax." Bianca confessed. "Then you made me the most happiest bitch in this world. I had no want or need for the it." She admitted. I took my fingers off her chin and leaned against the bathroom wall with my hands across my chest.

"After about a year or so in the relationship I started noticing things like you not really answer your phone when I call. You coming in the house late at night or not at all. At first, I was giving you the benefit of the doubt. You did just take over Chyna's empire. Maybe he getting shit in order and just got alot on his plate. Then when you was in the house it was late night phone calls and text messages. I found condoms in your car. That's when

I knew you were cheating on me. I started slowly popping pills again. I remember one night. You was gone for two weeks. No phone calls from you no nothing. That shit hurt because; you never told me you was going out of town Gunna told me." Bianca said pointing her index finger into my chest.

"I started snorting lines to numb the pain." Bianca voice elevated with anger. She pointed her finger in my face. "You was fucking that bitch Shalissa. She had you wide open." Bianca said making her hands in a wide gesture. "You was mad as fuck when you found out she robbed you and was only entertaining you just for her nigga to rob you. Yeah your bitch ass thought I didn't know. Then after you found out the grass wasn't greener on the other side. You came back **HOME.**" Bianca bellows in my face.

Bianca was yelling so loud that Chyna came to the door to check on us. "Yo bro? sis? Ya'll cool in there." Chyna asked."

"Yea sis we cool." I calmly admitted through the door. I turned my attention back to Bianca. "I never knew you was such a weak ass woman to turn to drugs though."

The look in Bianca eyes showed she was hurt about what I just said. Right after I said it I immediately regretted saying that bullshit. Damn I dropped my head. Emotions will make a fool out of you at times. We do and say shit we don't mean. I said that ignorant shit. Now I can't even take it back. *"Fuck."* I thought to myself.

I tried to hug Bianca and she pushed me away. She tried to leave the bathroom but, I blocked her from opening up the door. I looked down at her ass in that dress. Damn I'm horny as fuck right now. *"Naw Legend it is not the time to be focusing on ass."* Bianca turned around and hugged me so tight. As if I was trying to leave. Bianca cried her eyes out.

"When I was sixteen. My uncle raped me and got me pregnant. My mom never believed me only my aunt did. Which is my uncle's wife." Bianca was shaking so bad while telling me this. story I was steaming hot. I took my thumb and wiped her tears and put my arms around lower back.

"I went to go live with my grandma because my mom was embarrassed about me being so young and pregnant. My grandma never knew who I was pregnant by. My mom made a liar out of me. She told my grandma I was just a young whore, having sex with all the guys in our neighborhood. Meanwhile my uncle took my virginity. What's even crazy is I started enjoying the sex with my uncle because he was manipulating my mind. My uncle had me thinking this type of shit is normal."

I raised my head thinking *"Normal this nigga is sick."* I thought myself trying to interrupt Bianca story.

"My aunt Kimbella called and told my grandma the truth. My uncle was arrested. After two years of going back and forth to court. My uncle was sentence to twenty years but died after only serving five years. He suffered from congestive heart failure."

"Why wouldn't your mom believe you?" I asked Bianca with a raised brow. "I was scared to hear why?" I thought to myself. My mother lied because she was having an affair with my uncle. CRAZY SHIT!" Bianca expressed. "My mom was fucking her sister's husband!" Bianca blurted out. "Hell yeah this some sick shit bae." I said to Bianca.

"My grandma don't believe in abortions. She made me have the baby." "Bianca blurted out. I was speechless. "Babe you got a baby by your uncle?" Bianca was crying hysterically. I could barely understand; what she was saying. She nodded her head up and down "Yes…" Bianca said in a low tone. I kissed her cheek.

"Where the baby at? I asked. "It's a boy Legend. I named him Dallas. He should be twenty-one years old. That's the thing Legend. I don't know where he is at. My grandma made me give him up for adoption. After years of trying to find him; the little bit of information my grandma gave me." Bianca said in a concerned tone.

"My search was unsuccessful. It kills me daily to not know if he okay or is he still alive? How am I supposed to find him? Huh Legend?" Bianca asked and buried her face in my stomach. "How am I suppose to tell my son your uncle is your dad." Bianca expressed. At this moment I looked at Bianca totally different. "She was raped and had a baby by her uncle and was forced to give him up for adoption. How am I supposed to fix this shit?" I said to myself. "Trust me babe we will find him." I whispered to Bianca. *"This situation is way deeper than I thought FUCK!!!!"*

Chapter 15

WHY WOULD HE INVITE HIS BITCH?

Chyna

Lucci didn't bother me for the rest of night. I don't know if I was mad or jealous that he was entertaining this pretty ass dark skin bitch. I'll give it to her. The bitch was bad, but my question is why would he bring her here; to my party? I was chilling in the corner of my party observing shit and smoking my fifth blunt. I noticed Bianca walked in. She was wearing a white bandage dress. That was backless, and gold Lust For Life cage heels. Bianca's hair was in big wand curls. Bianca didn't need weave bundles. Her jet black hair came almost to her butt.

Bianca was mixed with Korean and Black. Bianca mother was Black, but her father was Korean. She was older than me and Legend. Bianca was thirty seven years old. My sister looked good. I hope her, and Legend work shit out. I like her for my Legend because; she is about him and him only. Her loyalty to me and my family been tested on several occasions and she passed with flying colors.

We made eye contact Bianca waved at me and

showcasing the biggest smile on her face. Bianca rushed through the crowd to get to me and I met her half way. She hugged me with so much force. I pulled back from the hug. "Sister why you crying?" I questioned. "I missed you so much Chyna!" Bianca expressed.

She wiped her tears and I grabbed her a napkin off the bar. Bianca was dabbing the napkin on her face drying the tears. Trying save her makeup. "I'm so happy to see you Chyna." Bianca emotionally said. She shook her head looking disappointed.

"Bianca when did you get out of rehab?" Bianca slowly spun her head with a distressed look. Without words being said. I nodded my head up and down. I patted Bianca on her shoulder. "I knew Bianca long enough to know there was something wrong.

"Chyna I'm fighting this addiction and I'm fighting to keep my relationship with Legend together. He threatens to leave me, and it hurts so bad Chyna." Bianca said with so much emotion. Even my gangsta ass was almost in tears; I felt her pain. "Everything's gonna be good Bianca. I'm home now. Legend isn't going nowhere. You're his ride or die. Legend was just in his feelings." I simply stated.

Bianca shifted her weight from left to right and said, "I'm sorry this is your first night home and I'm on my bullshit. First all off bitch welcome home. You look good as fuck. Bitch you slayed that jumpsuit." Bianca said screaming in excitement. I waved my hand at her, "Bitch you family. I don't care what you need I gotchu." I seriously responded. "Thanks Chyna I see your mom over there I'm gon to talk to her real quick." Bianca quickly said and walked away!

I walked passed the bitch who was entertaining Lucci all night. Now ever since Lucci came to the jail to see me. He been out here in these streets telling people we're a couple. I leaned on the bar. "Yo let me get two shots of Henny" I told the bartender. "Welcome home Hunnid." Lucci's chick said while pulling the bar stool out and sitting down. "Thanks, but do I know you?" I asked her. I quickly drunk both of my shots of Henny. Slammed the glasses down on the bar.

"J... Ja'Onna..." She replied stuttering. "I'm Lucci's girlfriend." She said holding her hand out like I was going shake it. I looked down at her hand like it had shit on it. The bitch was smiling hard as fuck like she was Lucci's wife. I almost spit my fucking drink out, I grabbed that weed Gunna gave me earlier out my clutch purse. I acted like what this chick said didn't faze me. I needed to smoke ASAP. *"How this nigga keep sweating me but, got a whole bitch. Typical fucking niggas"* I thought to myself.

"Hunnid." The chick called my name. I lifted my head up after taking a puff on the weed I just rolled. My eyes met hers. Anticipating what she wanted now. She had a worried look on her face on her face. "Do you and Lucci fuck around?" I looked her up and down. "You better ask somebody about me. Before you be missing without a trace. I said and blew the weed smoke in her face."

I got up off the bar stool and walked away. The bitch looked scared. She regretted asking me anything. As she should, *"I don't answer to no one fuck."* I thought. I laughed to myself and started bouncing my head up and down to **Cardi B Bodak Yellow... Say lil bitch you can't fuck with me if you wanted to ohhh... these expensive these red bottoms, these is bloody shoes, ohh hit the store, I can get em both, I don't wanna choose, bah I'm quick, cut a nigga off, so don't get comfortable, look ooh.. I don't dance now, I make money**

moves aye say I don't gotta dance, I make money moves ooh, If I see you and I don't speak that means I don't fuck with you, imma a boss, you're a worker, bitch I make bloody moves!

Cardi B did it with this song and I can relate. I was really feeling this song. I walked through the crowd. Legend had the strippers on stage now. I went closer to the stage to get a better view. Yea I luv dem strippers, I seen Bianca and Legend headed towards the bathroom. "I hope they get past this shit and can move on" I thought. "Chyna!" I heard, and it sound like my mom. I turned around I was really too high and drunk to talk to my mom. I hope she saying goodnight. "I'm leaving baby. I gotta get up early to take Skylar to the doctor. Enjoy your party welcome home." She said and tightly hugged me. She pulled away from me.

"Can you stay your little cute black ass out of trouble?" My mother seriously questioned me with her index finger pointed in my face. My eyes red and low. I stepped back from my mom. She the only person that can talk to me like that and live to tell it. She will strike me too, she didn't care who I was in these streets. She will swing on me quick as fuck. As I threw my hands up in surrender stance. "I can't make no promises mommy but, I love you and respect you.

"Okay Chyna that time ain't knock no sense into you. Stop over the house tomorrow." Aite I will" I replied. I was on my way to ask the DJ; do he got the Pittsburgh rapper Asco100k mixtape Dabb Lord. I played this whole mixtape daily, while I was locked up. That's my shit, I ran right into my longtime friend Jazlynn.

She been addicted to crack and whatever else she can get her hands onto. For well over ten years. She used to be gorgeous. Standing at five feet six inches. She was about 150lbs. Now she only weighed 110lbs, she had long curly hair that she use to keep dyed Auburn. Now it's in its natural state and from years of not taking care of her hair. Just running the streets chasing her high. The shit is short and nappy It look like she took styling gel and tried to mold her hair down. Bottom line my childhood friend looked a mess. Her baby dad Mike started her getting high. He died of an overdose a couple years back. Jazlynn mother Ms. Kena got custody of her two kids. I thought by now she would of got her shit together but, I guess not. Jazlynn approached me.

"Chyna… **Hunnid!**" She said in her ghetto ass voice. She

leaned into me for a hug. She had on this black shirt that looked two sizes too big for her. She smiled at me and some of her teeth were rotten. Damn her teeth never looked like that. One thing about Jazzlyn. She never looked like an addict. I'm mad the five years I been gone nobody looked out for her. Gunna never liked her but, Jazlynn always had a special place in my heart. I couldn't help her get clean. I tried many times and she always left the rehab. On some real shit, I think that's what Bianca ass escaped the rehab joint too.

    I always looked out for Jazzlyn and her kids and made sure she ate and had clean clothes. Her mom didn't fuck with her for several reasons. The bullshit Jazlynn put Ms. Kena through over the years I understood but, I always told Ms. Kena I'll try my best to protect Jazlynn in these streets.

    I made Jazlynn my ear to the streets being that she ain't allowed to cop from areas that I run. She gotta go outskirts to cop her shit. I fired a nigga for serving her she off limits. "I'm glad your home Chyna." Jazlynn said. "I remember when you bailed my crackhead ass out of jail." Jazlynn start doing the crackhead dance. The dance they do when they can't sit still. She kept repeating the same shit over and over again. That's what Jazlyn was doing right now, and she was starting get on my fucking nerves already. She is way worse than what I thought. She never got on my nerves. I gotta come up with a plan to get her together. She in too deep and eventually; she gon end up like Mike.

"Yo… Jazlynn what the fuck you want? You fucking my high up bitch!" I said with an attitude. "Chyna you know out of all people I don't lie to you. That nigga y'all just put on the team he be on the Southside. His name is like that rapper Gucci…a… a Lucci. That's his name." Jazlynn said stuttering. "Yea what about him?"

"You know before y'all put him on the team. I was able to go cop over there. Since you don't let nobody serve me in your areas Chyna." Jazlynn said and rolled her eyes. "Bitch get to the point I know what the fuck I did and, this time you going get yourself together or I'm cutting you off. When the last time you seen your kids Jazz huh?" I angrily asked Jazzlyn. "About…well Chyna she don't let me. My mom said I gotta get clean all this rahh… rahhh bullshit." Jazzlyn said dryly.

"That's exactly what you gon do to." I told Jazlynn. She

rolled her eyes again. "Aye Jazz roll your eyes again I'm choke the fuck out of you. I love your ass like a sister but, don't get it fucked up!" I replied through clench teeth. "Okay Chyna let me finish my story. The nigga he supplying name is Nugget. I be coping from him. I was at one of Nuggets trap houses. I asked to use the bathroom. He must have forgot I was in there because; they was running they mouths like bitches do." Jazlynn said and pointed to my drink.

She was making a gesture to have some. I gave her my drink, I don't want it back because; all the love in the world I got for Jazz. I would never drink behind her she be on that Southside, sucking and fucking for that crack. Jazz tried to hand me the glass back. I threw my hands up.

"Naw I'm cool Jazz keep that shit." I said with a smirk on my face. Jaz shrugged her shoulders and finished the drink. She sat the glass down and continued her story. "They gon rob Lucci next Saturday night at the drop." Jazlyn said peering over her shoulder making sure nobody was listening to her. "You sure Jaz?" I popped up out my seat. "These niggas tryna rob me?" I asked furious. Jaz touched my shoulder "Shhhh... Chyna you loud as hell. You tryna get me killed!" I ignored her statement. "Are you sure?" I questioned.

"They said with Hunnid in jail it's much easier. Dude said once you get out they got be cautious because; you wild as fuck and you with the bullshit. Supposedly, that nigga Nia is fucking got something to do with it. They said his name too Chyna. Also, Nugget told them niggas. He seen you one day in broad daylight run up on a nigga with a AR. You made him strip ass naked. You took all his jewelry off and you took his BMW too." Jazz said side-eyeing. She knew how I got down but, still! "I don't remember that shit Jazz." I said through a laugh. "Of course, you don't Chyna. You never remember wild shit that you do." Jaz said and smiled. Funny thing is I do remember that shit. Nigga owed me thirty bands. He didn't pay me but, he was still out here tricking on these bitches. Stunting at the club. He brought a new BMW and didn't run me my fucking change. I'm fucking Hunnid, I make the rules. I remember Legend being mad at me that I did that shit to Ol' boy in broad daylight. The nigga was spending my money in broad daylight.

After I thought about what Jazz was saying there is a new

shipment coming in on Friday. I need all the names of these pussy ass niggas and a location. "I got you." Jazlynn said. "Write your number down so we can meet up somewhere."

"Aite." I said and asked the bartender for paper and a pen. I wrote my number down and hugged Jazlynn "Call me tomorrow." I said, and I walked away.

I walked to the bathroom. I noticed Bianca and Legend been in there for a minute. As I got closer to the door. I heard Bianca crying and a Legend hollering. I knocked on the door. "Y'all aite in there" I ask putting my ear to the door. It was quiet for a couple seconds then I heard Legend say, "Sis we cool."

"Okay" I replied. I went over to the bar and ask the bartender for another piece of paper and a marker. I wrote **DO NOT DISTURB** on the paper. "Let me get some tape." I demanded to the bartender. I walked back over to the door and taped the note on there. So, Bianca and Legend can have some privacy without people trying to come in.

I walked back to the bar in deep thought. *"Somebody tryna rob me. Bianca is all over the place. Jazlynn need help ASAP before she overdose."* I want to know how these niggas know that

I gotta shipment coming in. I can't wait until this meeting tomorrow with my team. I'm getting rid of all weak links in the chain! "HUNNID'S HOME !"

Chapter 16

FIGHTING MY DEMONS

September 2017

Bianca

I woke up early that morning, contemplating if I wanted to do the right thing and sign myself out this rehab center or, just fucking leave. If I try to sign myself out. They will call Legend and that's what I don't want. Gunna informed me that; Chyna coming home today and they having a party. I talked to Gunna last week, fuck it I'm leaving. I am not going to miss my sister's party!

I took a shower and got dressed. I put on black sweat-suit and tee from H&M with all black Huaraches. Group meetings started at 9 a.m. I got time to slip out before then. "Good Morning Bianca," this chick name Jessy said. She was a heroin addict. This bitch was a lawyer so; that just let me know anybody can fall victim to drugs. Rich or poor anybody can.

I waved at her, "Are you coming to group B?" Jessy asked me. Yea I'll be there I lied through my teeth. I looked at the wall clock it was 8:07 a.m.

I knew most of the staff was preparing for group and, the side door is the best way to escape. I watched how the camera angle wasn't directly on the door. If you stay close to the wall. It will be hard for them to see you. I walked down the hall looking around palms sweating. It felt like my stomach was doing summer sets. I had to shit, I was so nervous. I slipped out the side door and, stayed as close to the wall as possible. Looking at the parking lot I didn't see anybody. I speed walked through the parking lot with my hood over my head. I got passed the gates and walked down the street to the gas station to call Velvet to come get me.

45 minutes later

Velvet arrived at the gas station. I gave her this bullshit ass story about me needing some money. She repeatedly questioned me about Legend. I dodged every question fuck all that. I would not miss my sister's welcome home party. I had Velvet take me to get a white bandage dress from a little boutique in the hood. The girl knew Legend because her man cop from him. She gave me the dress half off and these bad ass *Lust for life* sandals too. "Thanks boo." I told the cashier. I left out the store excited. "Where to now Bianca?" Velvet asked me all nervous.

"Bitch you act like you the one that ran from the rehab center." I said to Velvet who was smoking a Newport and avoiding eye contact with me. "Bianca I'm tired of getting caught in your shenanigans. Legend is going to kill me when he finds out you left. Don't tell him I came and got you." Velvet stated. "Velvet chill Legend will forgive you later." I said through a laugh.

"You think everything is a joke. Why won't you just get yourself together. You got a good man. He got money, nice cars and nice home. You dumb ass fuck!" Velvet admitted. I guess she call her self-checking me. "Bitch first of all don't worry about what my man got and how good of a man he is to me. What you want Legend or something?" I asked Velvet cocking my head to the side.

"Take me to the dollar store please. I don't need no lecture. My fucking sisters home I'm good." I said with an attitude. Before Velvet could respond. I jumped out her car and slammed her door! "Jealous ass bitch!!" I said to myself. I went in the dollar store to get me some flexi-rods. I was really chancing it being in the hood.

I didn't want nobody to tell Legend. I was out of rehab without completing the program for the second time. I got in the dollar store and got two packs of flexi rods and some makeup. Cheap ass makeup, I'm so use to Mac and Rihanna's Fenty line of makeup.

I never got a chance to tell Legend what the fuck is really going on with me. I called Legend every day for a week straight to talk to him and, he never answered my calls. After several attempts of trying to get in touch with Legend. I gave up or should I say I think he gave up on me. That shit bother's the fuck out of me.

The last thing I wanted was for Legend to not want me. He was my everything. I swore to myself that after this. I will try my best to get myself together and, get serious about my relationship with Legend

I AM FIGHTING MY DEMONS! March 2017

My first rehab trip: I wasn't even there sixty days and I rolled. I was supposed to do ninety days, shit that wasn't happening. I was fed up, Legend was entertaining bitches and was getting too comfortable. I left rehab to see what Legend was up to.

I beat her ass too went to jail bitch press charges. I was released from jail. Well Legend bailed me out and paid the bitch to keep her mouth shut and don't press charges on me. Days after being released from jail I thought Legend was done with that bitch. Come to find he was still fucking with her. His excuse when I asked him about it. He wanted to make her believed he still fucked with her. So she won't press charges. Niggas say anything. My dumb ass believed him until, I overheard him on the phone with her.

"Baby you know I care about you. Naw, I'm just here to check on my house. I don't want her no more baby. I only want you." Legend said to the female on the phone. I didn't even question him about that conversation. I went straight to my car to ride to the other side of town, I grabbed my iPhone 7 out of my back pocket. I called up my cousin Velvet, I couldn't dare let somebody see me cop and embarrass Legend!

Ring...Ring "Hello... Velvet?" I said into the phone. "Yea!" Velvet said. "Come outside I need you to do something for me." I told Velvet. "Bianca I'm tired of being in the middle of your drug habit shit. Didn't you just get out of jail today you need to chill Bianca. Plus, Legend came over here yesterday questioning me. Asking me do you get high?" Velvet said in an irritated tone.

"What you tell him Velvet did you tell on me?" I nervously ask her. No I did not but, if you don't get yourself together I am. At first this was just a once in a blue type thing now your doing the shit more often. You go-..." I cut her ass off. "Fuck the lecture bitch come outside." I said with my eyes rolled up in my head.

"Bitch can't tell me what to do."

"Bianca this is the last time." Velvet said and hung up the phone. Velvet came out the house minutes later with a gray Victoria Secret sweat suit on.

We named her Velvet when she was little because, her skin was so smooth. Velvet's real name is Venecia. Velvet was bi-racial just like me. Her mother was white her father was my mom's sister. Velvet was only twenty-six. Velvet and I were raised together by our grandma. Velvet felt like she owed me. Our uncle was tryna do her like he did me.

I just convinced him to let Velvet be. He tried to come in

Velvet's room and I wasn't having it. I protected Velvet from him. Even if that meant me getting rape and abused. Velvet still until this day felt like she owes me for saving her from getting rape. I'm ain't gon lie. I used that as advantage to get her to cop that coke for me. She never really like copping for me. I had Velvet to cop me an Eight ball. I did damn near half of it in the car.

When I got home, Legend wasn't there. I should of just went to bed but, nooooo…. my dumb ass figured since he was gone. I'm leaving too I went to get in my car and noticed I had a flat. My high was fucking with my mental because, I stole Legend's drop top Benz coupe. Only driving less than fifteen minutes. I'm not sure if a bitch dozed off but, when I came to I tried to swerve to avoid the fire hydrant. I slammed my foot hard on the brake. It was too late. I crashed right into the fire hydrant.

I must've hit my head off the steering wheel and, blacked out. I looked around and realized I was on the Westside in fucking Legends territory fuck. The car was smoking. I looked to see if anybody was outside and there was a crowd down the street looking right at me.

I looked in the cracked-up driver side mirror. The crowd started approaching the car. "Think quick bitch." I tried the door to get out and it wouldn't open. Shit I shoulda drop the top. I climbed out the window the glass tore through my skin. Damn that shit burn. I gotta hurry up before this car catch on fire. All this smoke was coming from up under the hood, I looked down at my legs. I felt something wet. I was all cut up from the glass. I wiped the blood with my hand and wiped it on my shirt.

I looked left and took off running towards the crack house to hide. I didn't want anyone from that crowd outside to see me. One of Legends bitch ass flunkies gave me up. I open the backdoor to the crack house and looked around this house was fucked up. "Lawd please help me."

I gotta fight these demons, syringes, liquor bottles and, cigarettes butts everywhere. It smelled like urine in here but, this was the only place I had to hide at the time fuck it. I ran upstairs to hide. My last and only option because, all the rooms was dirty as fuck. Desperate measures force you to do some bullshit. You don't want to do.

I got underneath the broke down bed that's had so much

garbage under it. I felt like I was in the city dump. I was breathing so fast I know somebody seen me. I know somebody called Legend everybody knew his custom made, bright red drop top Benz, nobody in the hood had a car like him.

I don't know how long I was hiding under this bed. I was so high off that coke made me nod off. I heard voices I opened my eyes and tried my best to not moved. I heard footstep, one of the voices was Legend. "Joe when did you see her come in here?" Legend asked. "I swear to God Boss that she crashed your car and I seen her run in here. I called you ASAP I watched the house until you got here," the flunky said snitching on me. "Aite, we checking this house top to bottom. She still be in here then I heard Legend raspy voice say.

After hearing that I was scared shitless Legend going fuck me up. I wish I could blank and this all be a dream. He going really find out everything now. Oh lawd, please don't let me get bit by a roach or something worse like a rat. "Do roaches bite?" I questioned myself.

It smelled like ass and urine under here, I gotta get outta here quick as I heard footsteps getting closer. I said a silent prayer that Legend don't find me. If he do I pray he don't kill me.

"BIANCA…. BIANCA I know you in here." Legend's raspy voiced echoed through the crack house. "Come on baby, I'm not mad, I just wanna talk." Legend said pretending to sound sincere. I knew he was lying, niggas always say they ain't mad. Then fuck you up. My heart started pounding fast I think I'm having an anxiety attack!

BOOM...BOOM..BOOOOOM The door was being kicked in. It felt like the whole house was going cave in. This nigga Legend was mad because why else would he kicked that fucking door in. He could have opened the door. It didn't have a lock on it. I closed my eyes and braced myself for the storm that was brewing.

"OH MY GOD!" Legend lifted the whole bed up off the floor. When I turned around and looked in this man face I didn't recognize this man standing over top of me. Legend would never have murder in his eyes while looking at me. Legend looked at me like I wasn't shit there was no care, compassion or love in Legend's eyes.

Legend gripped me up by my hair. I started crying and squirming to get out of his grip. I know by the time all this is over I'm gon have to rock a Halle Berry short haircut because a bitch is most definitely gon be bald. Legend started choking me so hard that I was gasping for air. The man choking me is not the man I fell in love with. This was the street side of Legend. I'm convinced that I'm gon die today for sure.

In our six-year relationship, Legend never put his hands on me. It's like he was having an outer body experience. Legend choked me so hard I started getting light headed. Legend's 6 foot something 236 lbs. frame I couldn't do nothing with him at all. I was fighting him back at first but, the more I fought back the tighter his grip on my neck became tighter.

I started getting light headed and I blacked out. When I woke up I was in the hospital restrained to the bed. "What the fuck hey...hey… why the fuck am I tied to the bed?" Bianca stop all that damn hollering. It sounded like Mrs. Debbie, Legend's mom. She worked at this hospital. Damn was I her patient why would she let them tie me down to a bed the fuck.

"Mrs. Debbie why am I here?" I asked her. "You need

help baby. My son brought you in here two days ago. I promised him I would check on you. You was high off of coke and crashed Legends' car and stole money. Do you remember any of this?" She asked me.

Standing there in her all white nursing uniform with her hands on her hips. Mrs. Debbie was waiting for my answer. "No ma'am I do not." I said with my head hung low. I was embarrassed at this point of my actions. I hate person I become when I get high. Mrs. Debbie came close to bed and pushed the call button to alert the nurse. "Yes, may I help you?" Someone answered.

"Yes, can you send her nurse in here Jennifer?"

"Yes Mrs. Debbie." The girl answered. Mrs. Debbie touched my tied-up hand gently. "Baby Legend loves you. I got on him about putting his hands on you. I don't play that abusive bullshit son or not. He told me he was so mad that he choked you. I smack the shit out of him." Mrs. Debbie said in a sincere tone.

I smiled at Mrs. Debbie. "I been through so much. Legend does not know what I been through before I moved to Philly" I said while looking right into Mrs. Debbie's eyes. "Well baby," she said rubbing my back and kissing my cheek. "You got to tell him the truth so that he understands you more. I love you like a daughter and I want to help you, but you gotta be honest with me." Mrs. Debbie expressed with a stern look.

I nodded my head and heard the door open in walked the nurse. Legend came walking in behind the nurse. My heart was racing. He didn't speak he kissed his mom's cheek. "What's up mom?" He said sarcastically. Legend trying let it be known that; he ain't speaking to me petty is fuck why he here then. "Oh, nothing just came to check on my daughter!" Mrs. Debbie said just as sarcastic as Legend by calling me her daughter.

"My lunch is over. Hey Jennifer, call me on extension number 2389 about Bianca care." Mrs. Debbie said to my nurse. "Okay Debbie I sure will. You know I'll take good care of her." The nurse Jennifer said and winked her eye at Mrs. Debbie. As Mrs. Debbie exited the room. "I'll be back at the end of my shift Bianca." Mrs. Debbie said winking her eye at me. "Okay Momma D." I said nervously fixing my blankets. I didn't want to be left alone with Legend.

"Bianca I will get your vitals, release these restraints and order your food tray. We need to talk about the next step. Your drug levels was lethal. You need help honey." The nurse Jennifer said with concern voice. Here are some pamphlets about three different drug facilities you can go to. My opinion Green Leaf Rehabilitation is the best. Nurse Jennifer said pointed to her chest.

I looked over at Legend, he was just sitting there staring at me like I was a statue. "Excuse me nurse this is her second attempt of trying to get clean." Legend said. "Bianca needs aggressive rehab." Legend added. Nurse Jennifer looked at me waiting for a response. "I will go to Green Leaf." I said above a whisper and, my head hug low.

"Green Leaf is a very aggressive rehab. They have excellent reviews from people that completed the program. Green Leaf has made their life better. I'll be back with the paperwork for you to look over and sign" Nurse Jennifer said and exited the room.

Legends phone ring… ring… "Hello" his raspy voice answered. "Oh yea aite, bet I'm on my way." Legend said into the phone. I put my head down in my hands. How could he leave me in here; dealing with this shit by myself? He must be still mad about his drop top or the money they claim I stole. "Bianca I gotta go emergency at the trap house. I'll be right back." He said not even making eye contact with me.

He looked so good. He had on the new Air Jordan retro low UNC sneaks. Sky blue joggers dick print on swoll, white tee with the throwback picture of Michael Jordan in sky blue. No chain just a watch, beard on fleek. My babe look so good to me but, right now he was treating me like shit.

The nurse came in and took the restraints off. I'm so glad the nurse took them restraint off. Why was I tied down to a bed anyway? If they didn't take them off Momma D was going have to help me. Moments later the nurse came in and explained the rehab in details, gave me the paperwork and I signed them. She told me transportation will take 2-4 hours after paperwork is signed.

Dietary brought my food tray in. They gave me a turkey sandwich, ginger ale, milk and lemon cookies. I looked at it like it was foreign. A bitch like me, need some steak or chicken. "Wishful thinking." I said and shrugged my shoulders. I started eating the sandwich and my room door open up in walked Legend with a bag of Chick- Fil –A.

"Ohh... shit Legend. You just don't know," I started to say but Legend cut me off. "Yea I know." Legend said with a slight attitude.

"Shit probably taste like jail food. I thought your ass would want a decent meal before you go to Green Leaf." He said and took a seat. As soon he sat down. "Bianca can you tell me what fuck made you start getting high. Coke doe babe come on?" Legend question rubbing his hands over his waves.

"I have a lot to tell you that I shoulda revealed years ago but, I was embarrassed. Legend jumped out his seat. "Embarrassed bitch how the fuck you think I feel." He said raising his voice and my door opened. It was the transportation driver. Thank you God. The look Legend gave me, broke my heart into pieces. His look made me want to say fuck rehab.

I need to talk to my man but, how could I be with him right now. When the coke was my companion. I have to cut all ties with the coke and, then get my man. I looked up to the ceiling and said a silent prayer. "Hello Bianca, are you ready?" The nurse asked me. "Yes I am, let's go." I said getting off the bed. I know

God has a plan for me but, I just don't know what it is. I do know one thing I never had a man like Legend and for me to put my drug habit before everything is very selfish of me. Why couldn't I just tell Legend the truth about my past? If Legend ever give me a chance again to tell him my story I don't care where we are I'm going to talk.

September 2017

The car ride back to Velvet's apartment was quiet Velvet know how I get down. She tryna check me about my man. Just mind your fucking business. I looked over at Velvet and she was shaking her head. "What the fuck you shaking your head for?" I asked Velvet. "Because Bianca you're crazy as fuck. You escaped out of drug rehab twice. You went to jail and now you're about to crash a party. What is your job saying? Did you take a medical absence." Velvet said and pulled into her parking spot at her apartment.

"You know I never call off so, I had buku sick time." I simply told Velvet. I've worked for BRY Group INC as an Mutual Fund Accountant, for seven years as one of the top Accountant's.

After getting all my shit out Velvets car. I jogged to Velvet's apartment start getting ready for tonight. Velvet's little apartment was nice black and purple theme. Purple suede sectional, huge purple and black area rug, black oval glass tables, unique African artwork covering the walls and, a 70' inch Flat screen.

I took a long hot shower did my hair and makeup. It was now 6:45 pm time for me to get dress I looked in the mirror and was more than satisfied with my attire. "Bitch whettt" I said and twirled in front of the full-length mirror, I look like a model. I had Velvet order me an Uber.

I pulled up to the party shit was lit. That didn't surprise me Chyna always brought the whole city out. Let me get my fine ass in here in sixty days gone. I got my weight back up. I was thick as fuck my white bandage dress hug all my curves. My cheap ass gold jewelry was shining and looked beautiful against my tanned skin. The rehab center had a patio and the sun would shine so bright. I would just lay out there for hours and have a peace of mind.

I got inside the party was jumping. The first person I seen was Chyna in this pink bandage jumpsuit. Gat damn sissy got thick as fuck. That jail food got sis looking right. If I didn't know sis went to jail. I would think she went to Dr. Miami to get her body done. I pushed myself through the crowd to get to my sissy. Lawd I missed her so much.

I hugged her so tight. Chyna asked me how I get out of rehab early. I side eyed her I'm gon keep it a buck wit Chyna but, not right now I'm on a mission. "Chyna I'm fighting this addiction and my relationship with your brother. Legend threaten to leave me" I said through tears. Chyna waved me off "Legend just in his feelings. He ain't gon nowhere" Chyna said all nonchalant.

Chyna and I talked a little more and I seen her mom. "Aite, I'm about to holla at Momma Deb for a minute." I quickly told Chyna and walked away. Mrs. Debbie eyes grew big when she saw me. I tightly hugged her I love Mrs. Deb because; she was like a mother I never had. I yawned for a mother daughter bond with my own mother but, still until this day we have no relationship. It's like she hates me, and I don't know why! Mrs. Deb have that caring and compassion about her she listen to me. She don't judge me either.

"Hey baby." She said and looked me up and down. "Hey

Momma D."

"Hhm." Mrs. Debbie mumbled. "How did you get out of rehab so soon?" She questioned. I didn't wanna lie to her but then I did wanna lie because, she was gon be so disappointed in me. I avoided eye contact with her. "I left." I said in a disappointed tone. She put her hand on my chin to raise my head up.

"By the way you look beautiful just like the old Bianca. Your movement is a little shifty hunny." Mrs. Debbie said looking in my face. Mrs. Debbie eyes was not focused on me anymore. Her eyes were looking at something behind me. I turned around and me and Legend eyes met. I wanted to run to him and jump on Legend and kiss him all over his face. Common sense stopped me. I wasn't for sure if he was still mad at me. So I just stayed put. I was standing there like I was star struck!

Legend aggressively grabbed my arm. "What the fuck are you doing out of rehab. Your ninety days isn't up yet?" Legend whispered in my ear. I looked him right in his eyes and lied, "They let me out early." I said after swallowing a lump in my throat. I was still trying keep a straight face. "Legend are you listening to me?" I asked him. I notice he zoned out and was not paying attention. Legend grabbed me by my arm even tighter and, pushed through the crowd. I was so nervous. I didn't know what was going happen next.

We ended up in the men's bathroom that nigga pushed that bathroom door open so hard. I thought for sure it would come off the hinges. I started crying, Legend looked at me with pure hate. "Shut the fuck up, you gon tell me what's going on. Before I call the rehab and start asking questions. I took a deep breath and, begin to tell him what happened to me then, what's happening to me now. At this point I'm tired and ready to let my man know the person I really am. I wondering after hearing all this will Legend leave me?

Chapter 17

PARTY IS LIT

Chyna

The party was lit. Legend was on stage saying his little speech almost had me in tears. I seen Boss Hog on stage too, with his comedian ass always cracking jokes. "Chyna go to the end of the stage. I got something for you I think you gon like." Legend said with the biggest smile on his face.

I mean mugged the shit outta him. "Aye bro you know I'm over surprises for tonight. "Get your mean ass by the stage Chyna damn." Legend said through a laugh. I picked up my bottle of Henny and my blunt I just rolled. I probably didn't need no more weed tonight but, fuck aye it's a celebration. I approach the bar "Yo." I said to the bartender. She switched her manly looking ass over to me smiling. Bitch looked like Chris Rock. When he played Pookie. I laughed because she really look like Chris Rock with a wig on and lashes. *"Who hired her to bartend looking like that?"*

"Yes, Hunnid how may I help you?" She asked. Swear to god all I can think about while looking at her is Pookie the crackhead on New Jack City. "Scottie help me I'm gon die." Pookie got caught up in the Cartel being a snitch. That shit still funny til this day!

"Grabbed me two shot glasses and bring them to the end of the stage." I said to Chris Rock looking bartender, trying my best not to laugh. "Aite, I'm on it." The ugly bartender said. I got off the barstool and went to the front of the stage. I'm ready to get into some gangsta shit come on Legend.

"These niggas I'm about to bring to the stage. Me and Chyna met them a while back in Pittsburgh. They was doing a video shoot and she loved all of their rap style and flow. She loved their music so much she had me to get me a MP3 player while she was locked up. So she can download their music. I ran into one of them at the Gucci store in New York about a month ago. I told him you was coming home sis and, he said he would get all them together and, come through and show you some love" Legend's raspy voice screamed like he was an announcer. The lights went off and I heard the beat drop Asco100k runs out on stage.

Asco100k (Dabb Lord)

Go Dabb Lord…Go Dabb Lord…Go Dabb Lord

Rollie will cost you a verse, whoadie will pass a perc, before you hide them bricks, put pertroleum on them first, That's gon hide the scent, who that behind tent O-dog behind the benz.

Owey walks on stage and the beat change.

Owey (Brick Walk)

Sooo…what I got your bitch, got her boo'd up, you a basic nigga and, I'm souped up I got that Nike tech and I'm suited up what..what. Reese Youngn walks out on stage. The beat change again. Damn I really feel like I'm at a concert.

Reese Youngn (Thriller)

I got soo much money…I got soo much money…I got soo much money. Fuck a pussy nigga dog, I got too many guns, fuck a stripper bitch today I got too many one's, I heard them niggas looking, we gon shoot when they come… Stunna2fly runs out on stage dancing. Fuck ya gang..Fuck ya gang Pittsburgh in the mutha fucking building. What's up Philly? Welcome Hunnid Stunna2fly said into the mic.

Stunna2fly (Fuck ya Gang)

Fuck ya gang…fuck ya block…BANG

Fuck ya gang, you ain't in these streets, you still on the porch,

Fuck ya gang you ain't shooting shit shoulda stayed in sports.

Beat changes Shotta walk on stage.

Shotta So Savage (Know me now)

If you ain't know me then, bet you wann know me now, You know these hoes gonna choose, cuz I run this side of town, They be like that's my boo every time I come around.

When Asco100k ran out on stage wearing cut up damage jeans, Pittsburgh Pirates Jersey, Gucci belt and black and yellow Jordan 13 Retro and a gold chain. I looked over at Legend, he had the biggest smile on his face. I lift my glass up to salute Legend for this performance. I met him when he was just a young nigga rapping.

We did some business out in Pittsburgh and the nigga that we was doing business with was related to two of the rappers. He was shooting a video me, and Legend pulled up. I had to ask Ol' boy who that was rapping. He told me that Asco100k and Stunna2fly was his lil cousin's. I told Ol' boy damn they hard. After that day. I started listening to them. While I was on the streets and, when I was in jail. I had Legend to get me a MP3 player. Asco100k (Dabb Lord), Stuuna2fly (Confession to the streets), Owey (Forever Straight), Reese Youngn Ryder (The Apocalypse) Shotta So Savage (Feel me or Kill me).

Stunna2fly came over to me. We slap hands. Stunna had on some burgundy joggers S.O.G (Swag out Gang) logo on them and, matching burgundy jacket on his feet was burgundy Jordan's. Stunna2fly had this nice ass fucking gold watch. "Welcome home Hunnid." Reese Youngn screamed through the mic. He had on a red leather jacket, t-shirt that had a picture of somebody and it said Ryder, biker jeans and some red and white Jordan's on his feet. The gold chain he had around his neck, was a picture of the same person he had on his t-shirt."I was locked up too on some bullshit but it's all good! Stunna2fly said smiling. "What you drinking?" Shotta So Savage asked me still with the mic in one hand. Shotta had on royal blue Nike joggers, with the jacket to match and some all royal blue Labron 15 on his feet. Shotta had this thick ass Cuban gold chain around his neck. Shotta's had the styrofoam double cup's in the other hand. "Henny." I screamed in his ear. I pulled him some in his cup and pass him the blunt I was smoking. Stunna2fly took couple puffs of it. "Aye this some fire ass weed." Stunna2fly said putting the mic up to his mouth. "Come see me after the show Stunna." Gunna yelled all excited. Gunna was posted up in the corner with her new boo Phoenix.

I hope Phoenix tame that ass. Gunna always with a different groupie that shit is dangerous. It was cool to see all the Pittsburgh rapper's from the same city; rapping together and getting along that's what's up they show each other love. They all had crazy different rap styles too.

After all of them performed The Race remix that featured all five of them. The Race is a song originally by a rapper name Tay K 47. The crowd went wild. The crowd loved them shit, it felt like I was at a concert. The Pittsburgh rapper's entourage was getting plenty entertainment from the strippers. After the Pittsburgh rappers was done with their performance. We all went backstage including Legend and Gunna bust it up small talk.

"I had a good time out here. Welcome home again Hunnid. Ya bro told me you just did five years. Damn, there is niggas that can't even do five days. I respect your gangsta." Owey said and slapped hands with me. Owey wardrobed consisted of; nice ass hunter green jacket that had all these different patches on it, dark denim jeans, a Gucci t-shirt and on his feet was some wheat color Timberland. "It's all good, I'm getting back to the money now." I said and took a sip of my drink.

"I feel you that's what it's all about. Getting this money. I'm about to get outta here doe. I got Legend's number. If I come through do a show or some shit. I'll holla at y'all. Send y'all some tickets or something." Owey said while snapping pics with Gunna. "Aite." I said to Owey. I was giving him a hug. Asco100k looked at me. "Damn, I can't believe ya lil pretty ass is really about that life. Oh, yea my cousin schooled me about you." Stunna2fly said showing all his gold fronts. "I can see this music shit gon take y'all far. Stay focus."

"Always!" Shotta So Savage said and slapped hands with Legend and Gunna. Reese Youngn gave me a hug and slap hands with Gunna and Legend. Him and his entourage left out the back exit. What a night. I was ready to go now. The bartender already did last call on drinks. I'm out. Let me go tell Legend and the crew I'm out. **THE PARTY WAS LIT!**

Chapter 18

I JUST WANNA LAY NEXT TO HER

Lucci

Chyna left her party early; talking bout she gon see us tomorrow at 9 a.m. for a meeting. I went to go find J'Onna I don't know what I was thinking. I'm tryna make Chyna my wife and do this dumb ass shit. Mannn...us niggas do dumb shit daily, fuck it it's already done. I seen her talking to some chick by the door. I walked over there she tried to show me off. "Baby you ready to go." J'Onna said sounding real confident. I'm bout to knock this confidence right off her shoulder. "Baby? Bitch we just fucking. I ain't your baby." I said and grilled the shit outta J'Onna.

"It's time for you to get dropped off. You getting too clingy." I said while searching my pockets for my phone to call

Chyna. J'Onna face turn so red with embarrassment in front of this skinny chick she was talking to. "Jay I'll call you tomorrow." The girl said while laughing at J'Onna and walked away.

"You wasn't saying that when I was sucking your dick." J'Onna said. I pushed her through the exit and hit my alarm and started my car. We got in the car and this bitch was still talking. "Lucci you told me I was the best you ever had." J'Onna expressed. "Let me explain something to you. I always enjoy your head but, me telling you that you are the best. Ma wasn't a marriage proposal. Now shut the fuck up talking stupid to me before you be Ubering it home."

J'Onna knew I wasn't playing. The whole ride to her house she was silent. I was in my zone listening to that Jay-z 4:44. I was thinking about Chyna sexy chocolate ass. This is the first time in my thirty-two years a female had me speechless. Chyna was so beautiful and gangsta. Damn that shit turn me on. I saw how people loved her at the party tonight. She did a lot for the community also, she definitely gave back. If I play my cards right, naw fuck that I am gon play my cards right. Chyna will be my wife!

I love being a whore though. *"Could Chyna be the one to tame me?"* I questioned myself. J'Onna calling my name snapped me out of my daydream. I was pulling up to her house. "Huh, yea why you fucking hollering?" I said to J'Onna loud annoying ass. "Lucci I asked you are you coming in or you going back to the party to fuck with that bitch Hunnid?" J'Onna salty ass said and turned to look at me. I was so close to smacking her but, I don't hit women so it's best for her to get away from me. "Bitch don't ever disrespect my man's sister. I'll forget you a female and smack sense into your dumbass." I said through clenched teeth.

J'Onna started looking nervous and was rushing to gather her shit. She looked at me with tears in her eyes. "I'm sorry Lucci." J'Onna said. "Don't be sorry be careful. You will get yourself hurt saying the wrong shit." I seriously warned J'Onna.

J'Onna opened the door to get out. She paused and lowered her head in the car. "I love you Lucci. I know you don't love me back but, I'm willing to wait for you. I also seen the way you look at Hunnid. You like her, don't you?" J'Onna asked me.

I just looked up from my phone. I was checking my messages and searching for Chyna's number. I looked up from my phone. "Goodnight J'Onna close my fucking door." I said in an irritated tone. J'Onna sucked her teeth and close my door. I didn't even wait for her to get in the house before I pulled off.

I was going to go home but I made a U-turn. Enroute to Legends crib. I knew Chyna was staying there. I just wanted to see her. Twenty-seven minutes later I pulled up to Legends crib. I parked right beside his Benz. Aww shit to my surprise him and Bianca was exiting the car. Legend gave me a head nod. He knew what it was, I wanted his sister. Plus, he trust me because I'm a real ass nigga. "Bro where you coming from?" Bianca asked me. "I had to drop shawty off. She was getting on my nerves." I responded. "Lucci that girl was not getting on your nerves. You think you slick; you want my sister bad, don't you?" Bianca asked me.

As we all walked in the house. I smiled at Bianca she knew what was up. Bianca looked good she got her weight back. I hope her, and Legend get it together. "Go home Lucci." Legend said while walking up the stairs with Bianca behind him. She smacked his arm. "Stop cock blocking." Bianca said to Legend.

"Nigga ain't fucking in my crib either." Legend said and,

I heard a door shut. I reached in my pocket I pulled my iPhone 7 out unlocked it. I went to my contacts and stopped at Wife. I tapped it and waited for the phone to ring... ring. "Hello." she said outta breath and it sound like she was in the middle of something. Aww hell naw I hope she wasn't giving my pussy away. Five years I know that pussy tight. "Chyna don't play with me. You fucking another nigga?" I asked very aggressive. "Who the fuck is this?" Chyna asked.

It sound like a car door shut and a car starting up. "It's your man." I said with so much confidence shit I was believing the shit myself. "Lucci why are you bothering me? What do you want?" Chyna said sounding gangsta as fuck. "Lower your tone Chyna I'm not no lil nigga. I work with you not for you." I said mad that she tried to talk down on me like I was a lil nigga.

"Whatever Lucci get off my fucking line." Chyna said. CLICK! I heard the phone beep which told me that she hung up on me. Damn this task is gon be harder than I thought. Fuck it I ain't doing nothing else. I'll wait right here for her. I went to my car, popped the trunk and grabbed some clothes. Yup a nigga stayed with extra clothes on me. Never know what the night may bring. She gon be shock when she get here.

I went back in the house and got a bottled of water out the fridge. I went up the stairs taking the steps two at a time. I found the guest room Chyna was staying in. I rolled a blunt and took a quick shower. Twenty minutes later Chyna still wasn't there. Good I can smoke my blunt solo. I knew I had to be high to deal with her feisty ass. I heard the door shut and heels clicking.

"She's here." I thought. I turned on demand on to see Golden State Warrior beat on the Cavs. Chyna entered the room calm as hell. Fuck she so thick. Got my dick getting excited. She glanced at me. "Lucci why the fuck you in my room. Don't you got somewhere to be?" She asked with her hands on her hip looking sexy as ever. "Stop looking at me like that Lucci." Chyna said and gave me a side smile.

The way she smiled at me while saying stop looking at her I knew she liked a nigga. "Hmmm...all that chocolate." I lustfully said. That jumpsuit was fitting her so perfect that ass was sitting just right. Make a nigga wanna jump behind it. *"Damn she fine."* I thought to myself. I didn't wanna scare her off. So, I kept my thoughts to myself for now.

"Don't you got somewhere to be?" Chyna asked me for the second time. "You are so fucking pretty Ma." I said peeking at my vibrating phone. It was a long ass text message from J'Onna. Bitch is weird. I deleted it and looked up at Chyna. "To answer your question naw I don't have nowhere to be. I wanted to spend some time with you." I told her licking my lips.

"NIGGAAA!" Chyna screamed in my face. Our stare off was interrupted by moaning coming from the other room. Legend and Bianca was getting it smackin over there. Damn listening to that shit was making me horny. "What you smiling for nigga? You ain't getting no pussy." Chyna said. I looked at her with my face in a scowl. "Baby if I wanted pussy I coulda stayed over J'Onna house." I seriously said with my mouth twisted.

"Go there Lucci speaking of J'Onna...J'Onna that's her name? The bitch you had with you at my party, right?" Chyna asked me and was pulling her clothes out the bags. "Yea what about her?" I asked with raised brow and licked my blunt. I just rolled sealing it off.

"You better let your lil hoes know." Chyna said and made her hand like a gun. I laughed because she sooo...gangsta. "Are you listening Lucci?"

"Yes," I said. I puffed the blunt. My eyes was low, and a nigga was sleepy. I passed her the blunt and grabbed her by her waist. "I know Legend and Boss hog told you how I get down, I'm not beefing with these weird ass bitches about you; for what you ain't even my man." Chyna said and shrugged her shoulders.

"So, if you want shawty to live I suggest you tell her to stay in her lane. Don't be crossing in lanes if she can't keep up with the speed." Chyna said, invading my personal space, looking me straight in my eyes. "My aim is good." She informed me. She moved my hands off of her waist.

I felt like shit. I thought I had her. My dick was so hard I thought it would explode. The way Chyna was in my personal space; had me super excited. Chyna blew the smoke out. "J'Onna is just something to do. I don..." I was about to say but, Chyna cut me off. "I don't care what she is to you. Just keep your animals in the zoo. Goodnight Lucci let yourself out. Oh, yea remember everybody gotta meet me at the apartment tomorrow morning at 9 a.m. for a meeting. I gotta re-introduce myself. Just in case mutha fuckas forgot who I am!" She said grabbing her towel and night clothes off the dresser; going into the bathroom.

Shit I ain't leaving a nigga going to sleep. I got under Chyna's comforter and got comfortable. I threw the comforter over my head and dozed off!

Chapter 19

I'M NEW TO THIS SHIT

Gunna

After taking Phoenix home from the Club Lex that night. Phoenix was so drunk. I didn't wanna leave her there and niggas take advantage of her. Crazy thing is me and her been inseparable since that night. I was tryna fight the feelings I had for her but, I lost the battle. We just got in from Chyna coming home party that shit was lit. Pittsburgh niggas came through showed Chyna some love. Them nigga's is cool as hell too. "Baby you want something to eat?" Phoenix asked me? "Naw bae I'm cool I'm ready to lay it down.

You know Chyna want us at that meeting early as hell tomorrow. I said, I took my clothes off and got some basketball shorts and a wife beater to sleep in. My phone started ringing. I looked at the screen and it said Bestie. "Yo what you doing?" Chyna asked me. "Shit about to lay down. I'm tired as fuck Chyna." I said through a yawn. "I just wanna say I am so glad you and Phoenix got together. That's the kinda bitch you need. She been tryna get with you way before I got locked up. She been chasing you for six years." Chyna said. "Yea I know Chyna but, a relationship doe I'm new to this shit. I ain't use to fucking with one bitch doe." I honestly stated.

"Hold the fuck up, you giving me advice nigga? You in a whole relationship with Lucci." I said and crossed my arms my chest; while holding my phone to my ear with my shoulder.

"Naw matter of fact that's what I called you for; you know this nigga was here in my room, in my bed when I got here?" Chyna fussed.

"Oh yea? Chyna I'm gon be honest I like Lucci for you. He a thoroughbred and you a female version of him. I can't fuck with no nigga right now bestie. I'm having flashbacks of the bullshit I went through with all these fuck niggas." Chyna said sounding irritated. "I know just give him a chance." I replied. "Give him a chance." Chyna screamed. "The nigga brought a bitch to my welcome home party, that raised red flags with me." Chyna said. "Yea but where he at now doe?" I said trying make a point.

"I hope he took his black ass home. Naw that nigga still here." Chyna admitted.

"He smoked hella blunts with me and, he was drunk off

that Patron. He really like you too." I said reminiscing about the party. "I can't believe this nigga still here" I heard Chyna say. "Lucci I thought I told you to go home. I heard Chyna say. "Goodnight bestie." I said and hung up. I don't wanna hear them arguing.

Phoenix came in my bedroom with these lil ass cotton boy short if I had a dick it would be bricked up right now. I patted the bed signal her to come lay with me. "I would love to baby." Phoenix said and jumped in the bed right in my arms. I gotta prepare myself mentally for the meeting tomorrow. Bitch ass nigga Mankind will have his day. That lil nigga Dallas, I got the info on Dallas. Mankind's grandma adopted Dallas. When Dallas was a baby. Mankind got two baby mommas one of them live not too far from the low trap house and Jazzlyn informed me his other baby's mom is in jail. Jazlynn didn't have the name of the baby mom that's in jail name. Plus there some new niggas that we hired. Chyna don't know about, I can just hear her mouth now "who the fuck is these niggas?" I thought.

"What you thinking about bae?" Phoenix sweet voice ask me. "Just street shit but I'm focus on you now. "What's up" I said and licked my lips. I wrapped my arms around Phoenix soft ass body. Phoenix always smelled so damn good. That Juicy Couture fragrance hmmmm…. had a nigga horny. Phoenix laid her head on my chest. "Phoenix I need you to do me a solid." I said holding Phoenix tighter in my arms. "Anything babe, you know I got you," She said as she sat up and pecked my lips.

"Look into Chyna's case for me. Some shit ain't right." I said. "I'll start on it sometime this week. I just need her name and date of birth." Phoenix said. "Aite bet." My doorbell rang. "Who the fuck ringing my doorbell this time of night. Bae get up real quick. While I go see who the fuck this is." I said moving Phoenix off me.

I looked at my security system monitor. I saw fucking Kylah standing at my door with her hands on her hip. Smoking a cigarette. *"How this bitch know where I live? I never brought her here."* I question myself. "Who is it Gunna?" Phoenix asked. "Kylah a bitch I used to fuck with. "So why the fuck is she here at 3 a.m. Gunna huh?" Phoenix asked with an attitude. Phoenix looked so sexy when she's mad. "I don't know I ain't talk to her in weeks. Ever since me and you been kicking it." I replied honestly.

Ding dong ding dong… The bitch wouldn't lay off the doorbell. I grabbed my gun off the dresser and screwed the silencer on. "Gunna you really think you need that?" Phoenix asked. "Bae the type of lifestyle I live. I always got to prepare myself for whatever. This bitch might have niggas in the cut waiting to off me. I gotta be quicker than that." I said. "Gunna you got a point I'm coming downstairs with you." Phoenix said and hopped up out the bed. I stop dead in my tracks. "No, you're not. That will make shit worse. Stay your pretty ass up here." I whispered.

Phoenix crossed her arms across her chest and, shifted her weight to one side. "Gunna I'm not stupid." Phoenix said. "Bae please stay here." I said in an irritated tone. I pushed her back on the bed and climbed between her legs. Forgetting that I still had the gun in my hand. Funny thing was little sweet and innocent ass Phoenix wasn't even scared. I kissed her lips, kissing her neck down to her collar bone. Phoenix's moans was getting me so aroused and ready to taste her sweet pussy. I took the gun and rubbed the tip of the silencer; repeatedly over her clit.

"Ohhh... damn... Gunna you so freaky I love it bae." Phoenix sexy voice said. Ding dong... "The fucking doorbell shit I almost forgot. I'll be back." I said and kissed Phoenix lips one more time. I ran down the stairs and unlocked the door. I opened the door and, came face to face with Kylah. "So, this is where you live huh Gunna?" Kaylah yelled at me, like I was her nigga or some shit. "I wasn't good enough to be welcome to your home. You had me at a fucking hotel huh?" Kylah started huffing and puffing. Here come them wack ass tears cascading down her face. I was so cold hearted. Her tears didn't give me an ounce of concern. Fuck these hoes.

"Bitch if you don't get off my doorstep with that bullshit. Your dumb ass gon make the five o'clock news." I said in a malicious tone. "You ain't shit...FUCK YOU Gunna I'm not good enough for you, but that stripper bitch is?" She screamed at me. "Good bitch the feelings is mutual." I told her weird ass.

Kylah tried to lunged at me and missed. She ran right into the wall on my front porch. I just shook my head. These hoes is goofy as hell. She hit her head hard. I tried to refrain from laughing; the shit was hysterical. Kylah rubbed her head and stood there. "You gon get yours Gunna I promise that." I tried to punch her in the face but, she ran. I pointed my gun at her and, let off one shot to her leg. She fell "Bitch don't ever threaten me. Now that was a warning shot next time it won't be." I warned her. Kylah was limping to her car I hope my neighbors don't call the police. "Fuck!" I scream out in anger. Let me go in the house before the police come.

Thank the Trap Lords for the silencers. The Trap Lords are who we buy all our guns off. They sell us heavy artillery. I went back in the house and washed my hands and went upstairs to cuddle with my girl.

When I opened the bedroom door Phoenix was sitting Indian style on my King I8 Sleep Number bed. "I didn't come down there because I knew you had hoes. Matter fact you are a hoe. I knew that when I got with you. I'm giving you time to get rid of your hoes. I know that will take time. I hope not too much time because I'm not gon keep getting interrupted. When I'm spending time with you because bitches are in their feelings. Furthermore, I'm in law school. Before law school I used to knock bitches out for even looking at me wrong. I've changed myself."

Phoenix said all in one breathe and, got up off the bed. She walked up on me and put her arms around my neck. "Gunna if I have to come out of retirement. Then I will, I don't do the disrespect shit." Phoenix schooled me.

"I know all this, you have to give me a minute bae, to let these hoes know what's up. I blocked them from calling me. Their using other people's phones. They showing up at my trap houses, at the bars and clubs I be at. Shit a bitch showed up here uninvited. On the real you the first women I ever brought to my crib. This relationship shit… **I'M NEW TO THIS SHIT!"**

Chapter 20

THE MAYOR'S WIFE

Kristen Weiss

Summer 2009

I walked into the police department with an evil grin spread across my face. My twenty-year-old son just revealed to me that Deana Jackson, a drug Queen Pen, conceived a child with my husband. He is the Mayor of Philadelphia. My son followed his father for several weeks and every time. He was acquainted by a well dress nigger bitch. After my little investigation and the private investigator I hired. I learned that they been having affair, for some time now. So, what is a wife like me to do? I will stop at nothing to tear Deana's empire down.

Anybody who is in my way will get destroyed too. I got the information that I needed on Deana's people she had working for her. Well not all of them just a few. I lucked up when I ran background checks on a few of those guys. They had warrants. "What's the name again?" Officer Zelowski asked me. I was trying to get information on Deana's workers Raymond Jones. Officer Zelowski typed the information into the computer database. "Damn Kristen, he definitely has a warrant." Officer Zelowski said with excitement. "Good...good." I said smiling hard.

"Print all that information for me. Come on we are taking a ride." I said jumping out of my seat. "Where are we going?" He asked looking confused?

"We are going to pick this bastard up." I replied grabbing my Chanel purse Off of Zelowski's desk. "You the one with the badge and uniform on. He will not take me seriously. Hurry up I'll be in the car." I responded. Zelowski didn't object He know I would cut him off and probably get him fired. He didn't want to jeopardize his job. Moments later Officer Zelowski came out the building with a bag. He waved his hand signaling me to follow behind him, in the marked police car. I followed him to a rest stop ten miles later.

He pulled on the side of me at the rest stop. Zelowski gave me Raymond Jones information. I just called my informant and he informed me; that Raymond be hiding out at this address" Officer Zelowski said. Raymond Jones forty five-year old man. That worked for Deana for over fifteen years. "Here's the address I got from my informant Kristen. Now what do I get?" Zelowski ask peering at me with those ice blue eyes. "What do you get?" I repeated like I really didn't quite understand the question. "Yes, Kristen for my services today?" Zelowski questioned and he was serious too. "You get to keep your job." I said showcasing a smirk and I pulled off.

We got to the house in Blue Bell PA, Raymond lived in the Suburban area of Philadelphia. I pulled up first and waited for Officer Zelowski to arrive. I parked two blocks down from the address. About four minutes later Zelowski arrived. We approached the house and ring the doorbell twice.

This voluptuous ghetto women answered the door. It was dressed in this red lingerie underwear and teddy. The things the attire was so tight and small. I'm confused on how it was able to get in the lingerie. Her breast was sitting up so high. They were looking directly at me not to mention she was well over six foot tall.

I was a bit intimidated by this thing. Well I'm not for sure the sex on this dinosaur. This Thing had this blonde color wig on, Bright lime green color long nails, super long lashes. This thang had the strongest face features. As if it was a man in its former life.

I cleared my throat and look over at Zelowski, who was trying his best not to laugh. Zelowski had this smirk on his face. I'm pretty sure he is wondering; what the hell this thing was in front of us. "Don't just stand there and stare at my beauty." The thing said and rubbed its hand up and down its body in a sexual manner. "What the fuck y'all white people want?" Thing said popping the gum It had in its mouth? I spoke up "Hmm... Is Raymond Jones here?" I asked politely.

"What y'all need with Ray?" Thing asked hand on its hip. "Sir I mean Ma'am." I corrected myself, trying my best not to laugh. "This is a legal matter!" I told the thing. "OHH! Thing said looking surprised. Zelowski pushed passed It and entered the home. It smelled like sex, liquor and cigarettes. "Oh God!" I said holding my nose. Zelowski was waving his hand trying to clear the smoke.

We heard sniffing come from the kitchen area. We entered the kitchen and there was a black older lighter complexion man. Sitting at the kitchen table sniffing a white substance off a mirror. Zelowski walked right up to this guy and tapped him on the shoulder.

"Are you Raymond Jones?" This guy was so high off of whatever he was putting up his nose. This is actually the first time I seen someone do drugs. The guy laughed, then lifted his head from the mirror. "What you want with me white boy?" The guy said. "I have a warrant for your arrest." Zelowski said flashing a paper in the guy's face.

"Oh Wow!" He laughed eyes low. He was high outta his mind. Why would this be funny. You have two strangers in your house; while he snorted drugs up his nose. This guy didn't seem to be a bit worried of his legal issues. Wait until I tell him this. "Mr. Jones you are facing fifteen years for a drug case." I informed him. Zelowski gave him the paperwork.

"Damn I fucked up." He said reading the warrant. "She gon kill me." He mumbled under his breath. "Please stand up." I told him. It seem like Raymond sobered up real quick after that. "Hold up." He said with his hands up. "Maybe I can help y'all if y'all help me." He said putting his hands behind his back.

Zelowski handcuffed him. The thing that answered the

door came into the kitchen. Now it/she was fully dressed. "What happen Raymond?" I fucked up that's what happen." Raymond admitted. "Hmmm!" The thing said and mumbled something under Its breath.

"Deana gon kill you."

"What you say?" I asked thing.

"Whyyyy... mind your business, little white lady before; I steal those Christian Louboutin heels off your feet hunny!" She said bobbing her head from left to right. Like the little ghetto shit I hate! *"Niggers ughhh."* I thought to myself.

I wouldn't dare say that to thing, It, looked dangerous. "Miss he's going to jail" Zelowski told thing.

"Don't touch him." Thing screamed and Zelowski gripped thing up. I was appalled. When I saw the thing got out of Zelowski's hold and slammed Zelowski to the floor.

Raymond Jones was handcuffed. Just leaning against the wall screaming. "Sugar don't do that Sugar." Raymond yelled out in frustration. "Why you make this harder than it need to be." Raymond cried. This grown ass thug was literally crying. The thing ran out the house nervous. Thing put hands on an Officer.

Thing jumped in a little white Honda and pulled off.

"See I knew that was a man." I said to Zelowski as he getting up off the floor. He gave me a stern look. Technically we couldn't do anything because this arrest was not real. We are going take him to a secluded area. Scare the life out of him. Zelowski walked Raymond Jones to his marked police car. Zelowski put him in the backseat.

"Follow me." I demanded. "Wait Kristen" Zelowski said stopping me in my tracks. I spun around "Yes Zelowski." I said. "You owe me big time for this bullshit. That was most definitely a man." He said laughing. Zelowski went to the driver side of his police car and, got in.

I got in my car and pulled off behind him. Twenty minutes later we were at the secluded area. A ran down warehouse in inner city of Philly. Zelowski got Raymond Jones out of the police car and walked him in the abandon building. "What the fuck this ain't no precinct! Raymond yelled. "Wow you, black people do have some knowledge huh." I sarcastically said. "White bitch shut the fuck up. Don't I know your ugly ass from somewhere." Raymond squinted his eyes and asked me?

"No, you do not but; considering your ass is in the hot seat. Your about to get to know me tough guy." I said. I watched Zelowski sit him a dusty chair. That sat in the middle of the old warehouse. I got real close to him. Raymond was a skinny, frail, thin, black man standing about 5'11.

"Listen you are going give us Deana Jackson or go to jail for fifteen years. You see all these charges on you. Maybe we can tell Deana; you not only got pulled over. You got caught. I bet you didn't tell her either. About your long list of legal trouble. You've been getting in these last past seven to eight months." I said with confidence and a sneaky grin

Raymond Jones drop his head in his hands and started crying. "It's up to you Raymond either give us what we want. You'll be a free man." I dryly said.

"I will tell you what you need to know but, it's not going to be easy tryna get Deana." He grinned. I clapped my hands.

"That's all I needed to know. Now let's get this plan into motion." I said peering over my shoulder at Zelowski. *"Black bitch is going to wish she never fucked with my family."* I thought to myself.

Officer Zelowski and I been having an affair for about six months. I have my needs and he fulfills all of them. He isn't like my old ass husband of twenty years. Mayor just sticks to missionary style. I'm tired of the same old sex. Zelowski is young thirty-five years old. He is so muscular and handsome. Then he has those sexy ice blue eyes. Hmmm he introduce me to Dontae who is also a rookie cop. Now with my help; he got promoted to be an undercover cop about two weeks ago.

Zelowski and Dontae was in some trouble. When I first started having an affair with Zelowski. I believe it was January of 2009. I can't remember the date. Well I should remember the date it was all over the news for months. About a nineteen-year-old black boy that was shot and killed on his way back to his college campus dorm. He was unarmed Dontae and Zelowski was on patrol around the area.

January 28, 2009

"Where you going boy?" Dontae asked the boy. The boy ignored them not on purpose. The boy headphones was on his ear. When the boy seen the cop car pull on the side of him: he

took his headphones off. "Can I help you officer's?" The boy innocently asked. "I go to school down here at Thomas Jefferson University." The boy answered and pointed down the street.

"What's your name?" Zelowski and Dontae both asked him at the same time. while getting out the police car. "Nasir Stanley." The boy nervously answered.

"You got Identification on you." Zelowski questioned. Nasir was a black man walking around at night with a hoodie on. Hmmm...not such a smart idea being that two nervous rookie cops just stop you. Nasir went to reach for his school I.D. Zelowski pulled his weapon and shot Zasir in the chest.

Nasir held his chest and dropped to the ground but, he wasn't dead. Nasir was gasping for air. "Help me...please." He said struggling to breathe. Dontae got on the ground. "Fuck man. Why you do that? I'm gon call for help!" Dontae nervously yelled.

Zelowski aimed his weapon at Donate. "Come on what you doing?" Dontae fearfully asked Zelowski. "Look we gon have to kill this boy. I am not losing my job because of this punk kid." Zelowski replied in a low tone; gun still aimed at Dontae.

"What we gonna do?" Dontae asked with the most frightening look appearing on his face. This the moment in his life, he wish he did the right thing and, saved this kid life but, Dontae didn't. He let him die. As Donate cradle the boy head and, the boy looked Dontae straight in his eyes. "Please help me." The boy mumbled. Blood was oozing out the side of his mouth. The boy took his last breath.

"Fuck now what we do?" Dontae asked frantically looking around. Nobody was outside it was 2 a.m. in the morning. They searched the kid's pockets. He had his school I.D., his phone and a work badge to the J&J Pizza.

"Damn hold on, I know who to call." Zelowski said. That's when Zelowski called me to get them out of this trouble. I got there in no time and, some weeks back. My husband did a keep the guns off the street day in the inner city. One of the venders that was there to destroy the guns. I paid him $20,000 to give me ten dirty guns. I was trying to use them for that Deana bitch but, I needed these two dummies Dontae and Zelowski. I will use this against them to gain trust.

"Hmmm.... smart huh? I know." I gave the gun to

Zelowski put it in Nasir Stanley hand and call for backup. "Tell them he was running with the gun and, shooting at you guys. "Dontae say you just found his body. Justice system don't do nothing about these kinda cases anyway." I said and walked away got in my car and left.

Nobody really questioned the scene. They just believed the kid was armed and tried to kill two cops. The gun we placed on him was not clean. Come to find out the gun had two bodies on it. The media said he was a college kid by day street thug by night. I loved it! The only thing is his mother don't believe her son was such a bad kid. The black bitch is still trying to have the whole case investigated again. I hope they keep denying her because, somebody going to jail, and it will not be me. I laughed to myself!

Chapter 21

SHE GOTTA SPECIAL PLACE IN MY HEART

Boss Hog

I woke up thinking about Rasheeda fine ass. My dick was so hard right now. I talk to her on the phone like every couple days. After that visit at the jail. I was intrigued by Rasheeda. Talking to her on the regular calms me. I never met a female and their conversation was interesting enough for me to pay them attention: better yet a conversation that didn't involve sex. Before Chyna was released I talked to her once a week. Legend was supposed to go get Rasheeda daughter Skylar but, he was busy doing some errands for his auto body shop, he called me.

Ring...Ring "Yoooo what's up bro?

"What you doing?" Legend asked me.

"About to go see my mom and go to the mall"

"Oh yea? I need you to do me a solid" He said slowly like he wasn't for sure if he wanted to ask me.

"I gotchu." I said before even knowing what shit he needed me to do.

"I told my mom I would give her a break and get Skylar."

Legend started saying and, I cut him off.

"Hold the fuck up! You called me to fucking babysit. Nigga you trippin!" I said mad he even called my phone with the babysitter club bullshit.

"Nigga Rasheeda is your women anyways so it really ain't babysitting because, Skylar is your step-daughter. Might as well bond with her." Legend raspy ass voice said. Nigga always sound like he need a throat lozenge.

"Come on bro my mom need a break and, she gotta work too." Legend expressed. "Damn!" I said and rubbed my hands down my face. "Why me doe? Aite I'll call Ma Duke and grabbed her." I simply said to Legend. What I really was thinking… *"Why the fuck Mrs. Deb take Skylar's ass."* Then they gon put me in the middle babysitting, I don't even do kids. THE FUCK!!!

That day I got her daughter Skylar from Mrs. Deb. Just my fucking luck. Mrs. Deb end up getting mandated at work. I had Skylar for two days. I couldn't believe it. What surprised me is how well-mannered Skylar is and how pretty she is. Skylar looked just like her mom. In those two days with Skylar I ended up bonding with the five year old. She is just so full of life. After that

I started getting Skylar every week. I even took Skylar to meet my mom and Dad they love her.

I know Rasheeda really ain't got nobody. I don't even know why I'm even doing that shit. I never really cared about a female or dey kids. Plusss... I had to emphasis plus because, shawty still in jail. She got like two weeks left which is cool. I was on my way to this meeting Chyna wanted to have. I know what baby sis was doing. She was letting nigga's know she was home. I got up outta bed and took a shower. I got dressed in gray Champion sweat suit, all white Nike Composite. I grabbed my keys, turned off my television and hopped in my money green 2016 Chevy Impala.

I made it to the location where Chyna wanted to meet. It's an old apartment building. She had me and Gunna purchased to switch shit up. I pulled up and seen a whole bunch of cars but, niggas was in their everyday cars, not they foreign shit. I parked and got out took the stairs to the 2nd floor. I hope Chyna ignorant ass got some breakfast in here waking niggas up early as fuck to talk.

I entered the room. "What's up y'all!" I said slapping

hands with Gunna, Lucci, Legend, and ATL. I hugged Chyna. Sis was looking right in her red off the shoulder Gucci tee, distressed ripped jeans, custom made Gucci sneakers. I ain't never seen them Gucci sneakers in stores. Come on Chyna. She didn't learn nothing from those five years she just did. She had Gucci gun holster and two Glock 19 resting.

"Good Morning everyone." Chyna said.

"Welcome home Hunnid!" A couple niggas screamed. "You know shits about to change. A bitch home now so it's on, I'm not saying my family didn't do a good job but, I had time to think about a lot of shit. All week I'll be going to each trap house to see how shit is really run. There is a couple lieutenant's that I never met." Chyna said then stop talking and, her eyes was on Trapo.

"Aye yo! You right there in the all black." She pointed to one of the new lieutenants his name was Trapo. He turned his head around and pointed to his chest

"Who me?"

"Yea what's your name?" Chyna asked walking towards Trapo. "Trapo!" He said looking Chyna right in the eyes.

"What side you work? Chyna questioned.

Lucci interrupted. "Bae he work for me. What's up?" Chyna spun around. "Yeah well you need to tell your workers that at these meetings. When I'm talking nobody talks." Chyna said with an attitude. Trapo didn't looked nervous but this lil nigga don't know how Chyna really get down. "

"Yea." he started to say something else and I shook my head. No, no, no to Trapo. He better take heed to the shit and shut up. "Come here!" Chyna demanded. He walked over to Chyna and she got all in his face. You must be too young to know but, Lucci just saved your ass right now. "You would be in the Delaware river; talking while I'm talking at a fucking meeting."

"I apologize Hunnid my fault to be honest; when niggas talk about you in the street (Legend's twin) I thought you was a nigga. I'm shocked as hell to find out you are a bi-, a female I meant." Trapo said.

"How long you been lieutenant?" Chyna asked Trapo. Like three months Trapo said "Yea you still got some shit to learn." Chyna said looking around the room at faces. "Lucci if Ol' boy don't check out as a standup nigga. That's your ass and the nigga getting demoted."

"Wifey don't worry I only fuck with thoroughbreds!" Lucci said and threw his hands up. Wow I ain't never seen Chyna spare a niggas life. Chyna must be fucking Lucci. If that lil nigga fuck up anything that's gon be on Lucci hands.

"Every month the pre-paid phones will be replaced with new ones. "We will be meeting up once a month to ensure safety and money count is on point." Chyna said still looking at everybody. She was remembering faces. Chyna always been like that. It didn't matter if you was a low-level runner of hers. She knew your name and everything about you.

Chyna talked to every worker individual. Just to get to know them better, I liked that about her She is evil but at the same time got a good heart. After all the lieutenants from each trap house left. Chyna told us to stay put. "I want y'all to give as much information on the people; y'all got working at the trap houses, cooking dope, bagging dope, and the runners." Chyna announced. I knew it. That's Chyna for you. My cousin Lucci didn't know he about to find out.

"What you need that for?" Lucci asked. I turned around

and mean mugged the fuck outta this nigga. Chyna grabbed her phone and keys. "I'll see y'all later I'm gon go see my mom." Chyna said in irritated tone. She looked Lucci up and down. Chyna laughed at him. Lucci was looking at Chyna like she was crazy. Soon as Chyna left the room.

"What nigga?" Lucci asked me. Cuz you in love with my sis huh?" I questioned Lucci with raise brow. "Naw not yet but soon." Lucci said rubbing his hands together and smiling.

I looked across the room for Legend and Gunna. Legend was on the phone arguing with Bianca and, Gunna was on facetime with Phoenix. "First thing you need to learn about sis is there is a rhyme and reason for everything she do. She don't like answering questions and she want all that info because, there is a snitch around us." I informed Lucci.

My phone ring and I looked at the screen it was Rasheeda calling. "Hello...you have a collect call from Rasheed. From SCI Muncy, to accept the call press 1. Beeepp. "Hello." I said into the phone. "What are you doing?" Rasheeda sweet voice said through the phone. I love her voice it calms a nigga swear. "Just handling business. What's good Sheeda?"

"Nothing just called to check on you. I'm ready to leave this place." Rasheeda said sounding sad. "Be patient your time's coming."

"Shit patient!!! I've been patient for almost six years." She said through a slight chuckle.

I'm going to get Skylar later, when I leave here take her to McDonalds and to the mall. She love the build-a-bear store."

"Aww your so sweet Raheim. I don't know how to ever repay you." "Hmmm... I know how!" I said just to fuck with her. "Raheim your mind is always in the wrong places." Rasheeda whined. "You been locked up damn there six years. Your mind should be there too. I know me. I'm just a freak. I love to fuck." I spoke honestly. Rasheeda laughed, "Well thanks for telling me you're a whore." Rasheed sarcastically replied.

"Well tame me then." I flirtatiously said. Rasheeda can call me anytime but, she just called me once a week. I laughed at how me and her got cool. Mrs. Debbie was talking to her on the phone. When me and Legend was over there for Sunday dinner. Legend was talking to her and Rasheeda asked who that in the background. I yelled, "A real nigga is in the background. Get on my team I'll upgrade your life."

Rasheeda's come back was, "If I was to ever give you a chance there wouldn't be a team. I'm a solo act baby. What a bitch like me; look like being on a team with some basic bitches? I think not. I was in a long-term relationship. How do these bitches go from being wifey to being a side chick. Damn niggas cold in 2017. They be demoting bitches out they spot. Fuck with me ain't no room for another." I was speechless after she got done talking.

Ever since then I liked her feisty ass even more. "Calm down killa" I said laughing. Pulling a blunt outta my pocket breaking the weed down. I looked up and everybody were staring at me. "What the fuck y'all lookin at?" I said sealing the blunt tightly. "I think somebody found they match." Gunna said pointing at me.

"Fuck you Gunna we ain't seen you much, since Phoenix came around! "What nigga you ain't allowed outside. Your ass definitely ain't been bar hopping in a couple weeks." Gunna waved me off she knew I wasn't lying. "Raheim leave Gunna alone she in love chill." Rasheeda said.

You have one minute to talk.

"Damn Raheim I hate that; I gotta hang up but, I'll call you next week." Rasheeda said in a low sad tone. "Babe why you be doing that doe?" I asked Rasheeda, It just seems like Rasheeda really feeling me but, most times play it off.

I know her past relationship with her baby dad got her guard up. I'm not him even if I am out here still on some whore shit. We ain't together to be honest. I don't know what me and Rasheeda doing.

"What Raheim?"

"Call me back babe. We need to talk about this shit, you hiding behind." I voiced. "Hiding?" Rasheeda said sounding clueless. "Raheim I'm gon try..." Beep, beep. The phone up. *"Damn! I hope she calls back later. I wanted to hear what she had to say!"*

"What's wrong nigga?" Gunna asked. "Shawty ain't feeling you or some shit. You look like you just got rejected." Legend jumped in.

"Naw bro the phone hung up." Legend busted out laughing. "My nigga you sprung off the jail bitch" Legend laughed hysterically. "Don't go there Legend. I love Bianca but, talking about my bitch I will embarrass you. The shit you gon through with her. You ain't got no room to talk." Legend grabbed his keys and stormed out the apartment.

"Why you do that Boss?" Gunna asked me. "Nigga always tryna clown somebody. When his bitch out here doing the most. Nigga wanna clown me?" I said passing the blunt to ATL. He puffed it twice and passed it back. "I'm out y'all. I gotta go see what's cracking at the trap house. I don't want to hear Hunnid's mouth. About shit being unorganized and niggas slacking. I might have to get rid of a couple niggas. Hunnid stern ass will find something wrong"

"I remember Hunnid being hell before she got locked up. Back then I was just a runner. Nigga I ain't forget how; Hunnid used to hop out her old school with a mink coat on and, some timberlands. Shot gun in her hand. Raising hell in the trap. When shit wasn't right. I watched her off a couple niggas just because; money came up short. She will tell you before she let you work for her. If you thinking about stealing from her be ready to die. Boss that's a cold ass woman." ATL seriously said.

"Who you telling, I grew up with her ass. Chyna always

been thrown off. Fighting all the time she wasn't like a troublemaker but, bitches was always jealous of her. First they thought she was just a pretty girl. Until she started laying hands on bitches." I said blowing smoke out my mouth.

"I'm out Boss." ATL said cutting me off. "I gotta go nigga we can go down memory lane another day but, right now my life and job is on the line." He said and left.

I looked down at my phone wishing Rasheeda would call back. My phone ringed...I looked at my screen it was Mrs. Debbie "Hello?"

"Hey baby it's Mrs. Debbie. I gotta get to the hospital my cousin is very ill. The reason for my call is Skylar is running a fever and she need to go to the doctors. Can you take her for me? I'll call the doctor and give you permission to take her?" Mrs. Debbie said in a hurry. "Yes Mrs. Debbie. I think Chyna is on her way over there to see you." I tried to explain.

"Well Chyna going have to come with me to see my cousin because, her black ass was supposed to be here over an hour ago for breakfast. Chyna had me cook all this shit." Mrs. Debbie said." OHHHH...yea you cooked breakfast? I'm hungry as he-, I mean I'm super hungry." I said rubbing my stomach. "Baby you know your welcomed" She said. "I'm on my way Mrs. Deb"

"Okay Raheim." She replied.

I left out the apartment. I was supposed to check the trap house but, dad duties call. Dad duties...what the fuck I'm not Skylar dad! I called Gunna "Talk to me." Gunna said into the phone sounding just like a nigga.

"Gunna can you spot check me?"

"Yea I gotchu Boss what's up?" Gunna questioned. "I gotta take Skylar to the doctors." "Dad duties" Gunna said giggling. "This shit funny to you nigga?" I asked Gunna.

"Hell, yea I never took you to be the dad type. Boss you growing up on me."

"Fuck you Gunna just make sure you do a thorough walk thru and, I hung up on her.

Ten minutes later I pulled up to Mrs. Debbie house. I saw Chyna G-Wagon in the driveway. I parked on the side of Chyna's G-Wagon. I got out my truck and went to ring Mrs. Deb doorbell and the door swung open. Chyna had a pleasant smile on her face. "Playing daddy huh? I love it bro." She said still smiling. I brushed her off and walked passed her. I notice she had the phone on her ear. "Leave me alone Chyna. Where is Skylar?" I asked and looked around the living room.

When I looked up Mrs. Deb came walking towards me with a pale Skylar in her arms. Skylar's face lit up. When she saw me she reached for me. "Raheim." Skylar's little hoarse voice said. "My baby is sick." I said taking her outta Mrs. Deb arms. Skylar nodded her head. Chyna came over to me and handed me the phone. "Who on here? I don't got time to talk Chyna." I told Gunna to handle that. While I take Skylar to the hospital." Boss hog I know just put the phone to your ear." Chyna demanded. I looked at the phone and, put the phone to my ear. "Yo who this?"

"Raheim I just want to kiss all on you so much!" Rasheeda sweet voice said. "Hello Sheeda."

"Yes, I appreciate you so much for everything that you do for my daughter." She said excited and joyful. "It's cool Sheeda I told you, I got y'all." I heard Rasheeda start sniffling sounds like she was crying. "Don.t cry Sheeda!"

"Naw Raheim these are tears of joy." She said. "I hope our friendship remains the same when I come home." Rasheeda said. "Huh the same?" I asked Rasheeda.

"You want us to remain friends and nothing more I asked her? Nevermind don't answer that, call me later. I gotta get to the doctors Skylar burning up." I hurried off the phone.

Rasheeda was still talking when I hand the phone back to Chyna. Chyna covered the speaker of her phone with her hand. "Boss hog Rasheeda really want to be more than friends with you. She just scared. I mean look at the fucking situation. She's in jail. You a fine ass nigga with money. You got a lot of bitches entertaining you but, you also chose to entertain her and her daughter. That shits rare bro." Chyna explained. "I ain't worried about it." I waved Chyna off. "Yes, you are." She said, and I left out the door.

Chyna came outside this time. She wasn't on the phone. "Call me and let me know how Skylar is doing. I'm about to go to the hospital with my mom. Then go take care of that business shit from earlier." She stated. "Aite." I said as I put Skylar in her booster seat. Yea a nigga had a booster seat for Skylar in my trunk. I strapped Skylar down. She wasn't her bubbly self today. She definitely was sick, I backed out Mrs. Deb driveway.

When I pulled up to the doctor's office I picked Skylar up out the booster seat. I carried her in the doctor's. The intake chick at the doctors was all in my fucking face; staring instead of doing her fucking job. "Yoo are you just gon stare or check me my daughter in." I said in an ignorant and loud tone. She was so shocked I said that shit. It made her a little nervous. She started typing away on her computer. "What's the patient's name?" The secretary asked me. "Skylar Connell." I replied.

The chick's eyes grew big. She was getting antsy in her seat all of a sudden. I'm not for sure why. "Is there a problem?" I questioned. "Oh no my computer is just acting weird. What brings her in today?" She got a fever of 102. "Okay let me print her a wrist band. Are you Raheim? "Yea why?" Oh nothing I see in here her grandmother Deborah Jackson gave you consent, to have her seen by the doctor." The goofy bitch told me the shit I already knew.

"Yea that correct." I replied. "Here is her wrist band. Follow me to room three for the nurse to get vitals. The nurse came in and took Skylar vitals. I was sitting on the hospital bed cradling Skylar little body. The door was cracked a little bit. I don't know if my eyes was playing tricks on me but, I looked up I coulda swore I seen Mankind walk pass. Naw nigga not while I got my daughter." I said to myself. I got up off the bed and laid Skylar down.

"No Raheim don't leave me. I don't feel good." Skylar little voice said. "Baby I'll never leave you I'm just shutting the door okay." Skylar nodded her head. I shut the door but, not before peeking out into the waiting area.

I knew I seen that Mankind. His back was turned, and he was talking to the intake bitch. "What the fuck is going on?" I thought. I know this nigga ain't gon try nothing slick, while I got Skylar with me. His life will never be the same; if this nigga try some shit with me while I got Skylar. I seen a lady with a lab jacket on her way towards the room. I closed the door and sat back on the bed. Covering Skylar with the blanket.

The lady knocked. "Hello." The lady greeted me. She came in washed her hands and sat down at the computer. "My name is Chastity. I'm the student doctor assisting Dr. Manuel today. I will ask some questions about the reason for your visit today." The lady explained. The lady took her vitals. Skylar pulse was a little high. Which can be elevated by a fever or pain the lady explained to me.

"Are you dad?" she asked. I sat there and pondered on whether or not I should say yea. I also didn't wanna overstep boundaries. "Yes, he is my daddy." Skylar little voice said. "Daddy is tired from work." Skylar said like we rehearsed the shit in the car. I smiled and said. "Yes I'm her dad." I said with the confidence that Skylar gave me.

"Well dad I will report all the vitals to the Dr. Manuel. When did this fever start?" she asked. "Last night around midnight. Her grandma gave her some Tylenol. The fever went down to 98.3 but when she woke up in this morning it was over 102." I said sounding like a proud father that did the right thing.

"Okay let me check your ear sweety." she said to Skylar. She looked in both Skylar ears. "Sweety do your ears hurt?" Skylar said yes. "Dad we have two ear infections here. I cannot confirm it, but I can see there is something going on. The doctor will come in and look her over to confirm."

She gave me these more papers to sign for consent again. Like I just didn't sign shit in the waiting area. *"DAMN"*. The doctor came in and was talking. I swear I was paying attention but, then I wasn't. I prayed that this bitch ass nigga wasn't waiting on me outside. The doctor check Skylar ears and determined both her ears were infected.

"Doc what kind of meds you give for ear infection?" I'm going to write you a prescription for Amoxicillin twice daily for seven days or, until medication is completely gone. Make sure she takes the whole medication because; if not the ear infection will come back. I'll also give her some Amoxicillin and Motrin while she here. Oh, I'll give prescription for Motrin give it every six hours for pain." Doc explained all the details to me I felt like a proud dad on a mission.

The doctor shook my hand and exited the room. I pulled out my phone and called Hunnid. What's good Boss? How's my godchild?" Chyna asked sounding all outta breath. "She got an ear infection. They gave her some antibiotics for seven days. I got some shit I wanna run pass you. When me and Skylar first got here, I told the check-in bitch Skylar name and her eyes grew big. She started acting funny. Then when I was waiting on the doctor I saw the check in bitch talking to Mankind. What's the odds of him just showing up here? While I'm here with Skylar." I said anxiously. "That shit interesting." Chyna said like she was plotting. "Where he at now? He still there?" Chyna asked.

"I don't know Hunnid; I'm not about to chance it with this nigga trying catch me off guard. While I got my daughter and shit." I said getting angry at the thought of this nigga hurting Skylar. "Your daughter huh?" I see you Chyna said. She thought I didn't pay attention to what the fuck she was saying, trying throw shade. Yea I caught it but right now ain't the time. "Say no more bro. I'm on my way. I'm going see if that nigga still at the hospital!"

"Naw get your business done Hunnid. I'll call Lucci." I said. "We on our way." Hunnid said and hung up. I looked at the phone and wondered who is we? I laid Skylar head on my chest while I waited for the nurse. Skylar looked so miserable. I waited for the nurse to come give Skylar a dose of Motrin and Amoxicillin. Ten minutes later the nurse came back in and gave Skylar the medicine. I was getting Skylar dressed. The nurse brought in the prescriptions and I signed the discharged papers. "Have a good day." The nurse said. "Yea you too I said over my shoulder."

This is why I didn't want no kids. If I didn't have Skylar with me I woulda been left this fucking hospital. I would've followed that nigga outta here and put my gun in his mouth. I looked into Skylar sleepy eyes. The medicine was taking effect. I just wanted to get her home and lay her down. "Raheim?" Skylar called my name when I looked up from my phone. She was looking directly into my eyes. "Yes baby?"

"You don't want to be my daddy?" She asked in the sweetest voice. "I would love to, but this is a talk I need to have with your mom." I said softly, trying not to hurt Skylar's feelings. "Her won't mind. Her likes you." Skylar sleepy voice said. "How you know Skylar?" I asked curiously.

"Mommy told Auntie Chyna that she loves you because of the way you take time out with me and, how you treat me. See Raheim only daddies do that!" I was speechless that this five-year-old was telling me all of this; she was so smart.

"I have to talk to your mom first." I reiterated in a low tone. Skylar pouted and I ain't gon lie a nigga felt like shit. I kissed her on her cheek. "Skylar baby I am your dad." She looked to me and gave me a faint smile. I think the drugs was starting to work.

My phone buzzed. That must mean Chyna and whoever are here. I struggled to get my phone out my pocket. I still had Skylar laying on me. She didn't want me to put her down. I finally got my phone out and, it was some bitch name Jillian. I her to voicemail. My phone ringed again and, I answered without looking at it. "Who this and it better be important." I spat into the phone.

"Damn Boss Hog why you mad at me? It is important I miss you!" She said. "I'll call you later Jillian." I tried to rush her off the phone. "What you doing Boss?" Jillian ask me. I switch the phone to the other ear.

"Daddy is it time to go yet?" Skylar asked with her eyes still closed. "Daddy" Jillian screamed. "Boss when did you have a fucking baby huh?"

"Aye stop yelling; my daughter is tryna sleep I'm gon call you back."

"I'm confused I." Jillian started to say, and I hung up on her. My phone buzzed again, and it was Hunnid calling. "Come outside I'm parked by your car. I ain't see Ol' boy out here."

Chyna, informed me. "Tell that nigga to come on. I'm hungry as fuck." I heard Lucci ass in the background. "Oh, that's who we is huh Hunnid? Y'all ain't slick!" I laughed.

I left the hospital room and the check-in bitch was staring at me. I made a mental note of her face. I had a feeling this wouldn't be the last time I saw her. I had Skylar in my arms, I didn't let her walk because she of all them meds. I went to the parking lot. I look left and right. Chyna walked up on me. I love to see Hunnid in war mode. Lucci was standing behind. Chyna walked in front of me. I didn't see nobody out here. You can never be too cautious. I got to my whip and put Skylar in her car seat. I decided to take Skylar home with me, instead of taking her back to Mrs. Deb.

Mrs. Deb was dealing with her own family shit. This will give her a break. I started my car up and pulled off. Chyna and Lucci followed behind me the whole time. Fifteen minutes later I was home. Chyna and Lucci got out the car. They came in my house. I carried Skylar in the house. I put Skylar down on the sofa and, got a blanket from my closet in the hallway. This was a sofa bed. I pulled it out and made it comfy for Skylar. Chyna and Lucci watch me from across the room.

"Boss hog I ain't never seen you this soft." Lucci stated. "Yeah bro I take my hat off to you for taking on somebody's responsibility." Chyna voiced.

"On some real shit Chyna. I love Skylar. You know today she asked me could I be her dad. What kinda shit is that huh? I wanted to talk to Rasheeda about it first, before I sign up for fatherhood. Looking Skylar in her eyes, I couldn't tell her no. These past months with Skylar being in my life; has brought my gangsta ass some calm. I'll admit that." I said laying Skylar on the sofa bed. Then I pulled the blanket over Skylar.

I turned on the Disney channel. Skylar loved the Disney channel. "Daddy can I have some ginger ale?"

"Yes Skylar." I went to the kitchen and realize I didn't have any. I had to fill her prescription. I gotta make a store run. I'll ask if the love birds would stay here and watch Skylar. "Lucci I need to run to the store. I don't have no ginger ale or her medicine here." I said while putting my jacket back on.

"We'll sit with her." Lucci said. I walked pass the living room and Chyna was lying in the sofa bed with Skylar. "When we around Skylar I guess. We all get soft." I laughed to myself. I got in my car and went to Walmart. I listen to NBA young boy (No Smoke) lil nigga got bars. Twenty minutes later I pulled up to Walmart. I found a parking spot quick as hell. Yea... In and out is what I'm tryna do. I gotta get back to Skylar.

My phone ringed. I looked at it. Damn its Mrs. Deb. I forgot to call her at the hospital. After seeing Mankind that shit threw me off. "Hello... Raheim I understand you think Skylar is your daughter and, you taking care of shit but when was grandma getting a call huh?" She laughed.

"I'm sorry Mrs. Deb I was so focus on getting her home. I had to run to Walmart to get her prescriptions." I replied. "Huh uhhh" Mrs. Deb mumble.

"It's all good baby I understand. I know you have a bond with her. I love that too You stepped up. You been the male figure in her life; with no strings attached. I know your crazy ass is a good man. Are you bringing her home later? What they say was wrong?" Mrs. Deb questioned.

"She got an ear infection in both ears. They gave her antibiotics but, naw Mrs. Deb I'm gon keep her until she gets better. You schooled me so much over these past couple months on parenting. I feel like I can do anything for Skylar!" I said through a slight laughed."

"Alright then Raheim. I'll call later to check on y'all" Mrs. Deb said. "Bye Mrs. Deb."

When I hung the phone up. I looked around. It's crowded in here. I was now standing in line to drop off Skylar prescription. It was my turn, I gave the pharmacist all the information. Whoa outta the corner off my eye. I saw the chick from Skylar Doctors office, walking down the aisle. I went to get a shopping cart and started shopping. I need some Pedialyte, thermometer, ginger ale, crackers and soup. I was looking at all the different flavors of Pedialyte. Strawberry is Skylar's favorite flavor.

I got two bottles of Pedialyte and two boxes of freeze pop Pedialyte. I put the shit in the cart I heard a voice behind me. "I didn't know you had a baby Boss Hog." I turned around and was face to face with Mankind. "It ain't for you to know my business nigga. What the fuck you want? Let me find out you following me." I said displaying murder in my eyes.

This nigga had a hidden motive. "You ain't that important

Boss hog. Following you? Naw I ain't one of your bitches." Mankind said still looking in my shopping cart.

"I ain't forgot that shit at the club either nigga." Mankind said. "I'm glad you didn't, so when I kill your dumb ass. You will know why. Broke miserable ass nigga get money, stop wasting your time tryna bully niggas!" I said. The check-in bitch walked up. "Babe lets go." She said to Mankind. I looked in my shopping cart again to make sure I had everything I needed from this aisle. Mankind looked me right in my eyes "Nigga that ain't your daughter!" He spat with venom.

Chapter 22

THIS NIGGA JUST SNATCHED MY SOUL

Chyna

When I got out the shower this nigga Lucci was laid in the bed covered up in my comforter. I smiled inside. I didn't want to admit the shit to Lucci but, this was a lovely sight. I told Lucci to go home. He doesn't listen. Lucci looked so good in that wife beater. Them chocolate muscular arms, all tatted up and, his neatly trimmed beard. Hmm…hmm. Damn just looking at his ass laid out in my bed sleep. The sight was making my pussy so wet. I act like I was getting clothes out the drawer.

From the dresser mirror I had a clear view of Lucci. "Chyna Doll." Lucci said. *"I thought he was sleep."*

"You don't have to stand there and stare at me Ma." Lucci said laying down not even looking in my direction. "Come lay with me. You can stare all you want. You don't have to sneak and do it." He laughed. I looked up at Lucci from the mirror and cocked my head to the side.

"Lucci ain't nobody worried about your black ass." I said. Lucci swung the covers over his body and jumped outta bed. He wrapped his arms around my waist and kissed my neck. He smelled so good Dolce and Gabbana light blue was invading my nostrils. "Hmmm." A moan slipped out.

"Lawd I didn't want that to happen." I forgot that quick I was supposed to play hard to get with Lucci but, right now he was making me feel so good. This felt so right. I close my eyes and imagine Lucci deep inside of me. A bitch been deprived of penetration for too long. My moans became louder as I felt Lucci hands caressing my whole body.

"Aww… shit Chyna Doll you feel so good in my arms." Lucci whispered in my ear. Lucci untied my robe from behind. His finger found my throbbing clit. He rubbed his thumb over my clit in slow motion. I swear to God I was ready to cum. That shit felt so good. He slipped his index and middle finger in my warm wetness and started finger fucking me slow. I was in pure ecstasy. All a sudden, I felt Lucci's tongue on my clit. "Fuck you taste so sweet." Lucci said lustfully, licking my clit and finger fucking me at the same time.

This nigga was like a Pussyologist. He knew exactly where and how to eat pussy. I was holding on the dresser but, I was losing my balance. Lucci head game was the best I ever had. Lucci was moving his tongue in and out of my pussy, like a dick. Gat damn I'm losing control of myself. "Ohhhhh…. shit Lucci damn." I screamed. "Hmmm... mmmm… oh shit." I yelled out in passion biting my lip.

Lucci shouldn't be single. What dumb bitch let him go. This is the type of head game that; have a bitch go nigga dumb. You don't see shit he do, you don't hear shit he do. This nigga is a saint in your eyes because, his head game clouds your thinking. I came all in Lucci's mouth. He stood up licked his lips. Lucci smiled at me. I stood there staring at Lucci still tryna catch my breath. This nigga just snatched my soul. I'm light headed. I laughed to myself. As I slowly come down off cloud nine, reality set in what the fuck just happen. I can't mix business with pleasure. Niggas ain't shit, my smile turned into a frown.

Lucci noticed it too! "What's wrong?" Chyna Doll he asked going in the bathroom. I heard water. It sound like he was brushing his teeth. He came out the bathroom and I looked down at his hard dick poking out his basketball shorts. "I can't do this Lucci" I said. "Do what fuck me?" He asked with his brows raised.

"I don't wanna fuck you anyways. I want to get to know you. I just got acquainted with your pussy so that's a start." Lucci sarcastically replied.

I continued to look down at his hard dick. "Ahh... don't worry about him. He just a little excited to be in your presence." Lucci said looking down and tapping his dick. "Naw you don't get it. I can't mess with you. We are business partners." I said through clench teeth. I was getting irritated. Lucci didn't get it clearly. I don't even know why I let him lick the pussy. Well not really that shit was too good to regret it.

I need to quit lying to myself. "Lucci mixing business with pleasure is messy." I informed him. I tried to tell myself every day to not like Lucci. *"That pep talk didn't work clearly."* I thought to myself. "Chyna… Chyna!" Lucci called out my name, trying to reason with me.

"Just go home please!"

"Chyna!" Lucci called me and, I walked away from him. I wasn't trying to hear what he said. I needed to hop back in the shower seventeen minutes later. I got out the shower dressed in pajamas pants and wife beater. Lucci was sleep, I heard him snoring. I thought I told his ass to go home. "Chyna doll come lay down. We got a big day ahead of us tomorrow." Lucci said patted the bed. For some reason I listened. I was a little tipsy still. Fuck it me and him will talk about this shit tomorrow when both of us is sober!

7:38 a.m. In The Morning

I woke up to the smell of bacon. I knew it was Bianca cooking. That bitch can throw down. I got up outta bed and realized Lucci was gone. He could at least have told me he was leaving. Oh well he ain't my nigga. I got outta bed, brushed my teeth and, washed my face. I looked in the walk -in closet to for something to put on.

I saw this off the shoulder red Gucci tee, crazy distressed jeans and, yo these custom made Gucci sneakers that were made just for me. The style of the shoe was like leather Converse. Gold chain around the outside of the shoe. A lion and diamonds on the side. Red and green Gucci symbol on the tongue of the shoe. Whoever made these got crazy style. I peered it up with my Gucci gun holster fuck it up and match the artillery.

That bitch Shay picked out some nice shit for me. She

organized all my shit in my closet by colors. Warm colors to cool colors and black, gray and white. My shoes was the same way but, ugggh I wish my house was done I need Shay to do my closet in my own house. I don't understand how the shit ain't ready yet. Legend gotta give me the information to the Forman. I'll call him and see what's up. I need my own space. Living with Legend was not in my plans. Especially when I got money to live wherever the fuck I want.

Over the last five years I made like $230,000 in jail off of Molly's, Percocet and K-2. I supplied inmates and people's on the outside with pills. I made a deal with them 60/40. Oh well take it or leave it. That's what I told them. Aye them pills is the root of all evil and everybody wanted them. You gotta pay the price. I wasn't stupid I knew no other inmate wasn't bringing that type of quality and quantity of drug in.

The warden of the jail was obsessed with Rasheeda. She came up with the perfect plan to include him into our smuggling operation. That shit worked. C.O. Brown would go meet the driver and get the shipment. It was handed over to the warden then Joe from the kitchen. Joe would sneak the drugs in with the daily food delivery. I always made sure Rasheeda got a cut to; send it home for her mom and Skylar to live comfortably. Before getting my drug smuggling business off the ground. I would have Legend to send me double money. I could split it with Rasheeda.

I always had a weird fashion sense. Today I played it safe. I pulled out the Gucci attire and, my gun holster and laid it on the bed. I shower with my Victoria Secret Pink shower fresh body wash. This body wash smell so fucking good. I told Gunna make sure she get me some good smelling body wash. I think the bitch went to every store that had Victoria Secret, Bath & Bodywork's, Juicy Couture body wash, Summer Dove, Amazing Grace and O'lay.

As I was in the shower washing, my mind drifted back to last night. Lucci mouth game was crazy but, I ain't fucking with him. I got big moves today. I washed and exited the shower. I dried off and lotion up with Pink Shower Fresh lotion. I got dressed within three minutes. I had these damn flat irons and wand curlers. I don't know how to use the wand, but a bitch can flat iron her ass off. About twelve minutes later my hair was flat iron so nice. I love this hair. It's so soft. I grabbed my Gucci bag and, put my keys and extra gun in my bag. I made my bed up and went to the kitchen.

Bianca was in there dancing and pouring juice into a glass for somebody. I couldn't see the person she was pouring the juice for. It couldn't have been Legend. He just walked past me on the phone. I got to entrance of the kitchen. Lucci was sitting at the table eating breakfast and reading the newspaper like this nigga live here. "Good morning sister." Bianca said with the biggest smile spread across her face.

"What's up sis?" I said and Lucci moved the corner of the newspaper and looked over at me. "Good morning Chyna Doll." He said putting a spoonful of eggs in his mouth. "Aww he got a nickname for you sis, already I love it." Bianca said.

"I heard somebody moaning last night. Get it sis!" Bianca said winking her green eyes at me. "Bitch you was the one making all that noise that wasn't me." I bashfully said. "I will admit my man did have me screaming his name last night." Bianca kissed my cheek. "You look cute boo." Bianca said preparing my plate. She sat my plate down in front of me. "I know it's been a long time since you had real food; I gave your extra sis." Bianca simply said.

I tried to eat my food. Lucci kept staring at me. I hurried up and ate my breakfast. I put my dish in the dishwasher. When I turned around Lucci was staring directly at me. He look so good. Sporting black Nike joggers, island green Nike tee that matched perfectly with the island Green Foamposite sneakers. He had on a gold chain and watch.

Did this nigga go home? He fly as hell. "Chyna stop playing hard to get, you want a nigga, don't you?" Lucci arrogant ass said. I looked at him like he was stupid. "Nigga I don't want you, I want this money. Now hurry up so we don't be late to this meeting.

"It's cool." Lucci said. Lucci stood up out his seat. "I'm not gon beg you to give me a chance and I'm definitely not gon chase you. Even doe." He paused, last night I had you screaming my name. You wanted me then. You agreed to talk to me today about the shit. Now you don't wanna talk? You full of shit Chyna!" Lucci said angrily and walked out the kitchen.

"Fuck you Lucci you mad huh!" I screamed after him.

When I got outside to my car. Lucci's car was gone, damn

that nigga must really been mad. He gone already. As I was about to get in the car I saw Legend come out. He still had the phone glued to his ear. Who the fuck is this nigga talking too. "Chyna follow me" Legend cover his phone receiver up and said.

I had Legend purchase this building where the meetings will be held. I read about this shit in the newspaper while I was upstate. I wasn't for sure where it was. I know the area is quiet. I had Legend look in to all that, make sure there was no cops that lived close by. Furthermore; I won't have no drugs in there just hold meetings. I didn't want it to be in the hood. I got in my car and followed behind legend.

I was listening to **Tammy Rivera All These Kisses... Day so hard, so much stress, life won't let up, boy just rest, lay down and let me cover you in all these kisses!**

I pulled up to the building, this use to be a building that held plumbing supplies they went outta business last year, Legend informed me. I got out the car went inside there was about fifty people in here. Some faces I knew very well like Bad Ass and ATL. I wonder where Geno was.

When I went to jail Geno and ATL was young niggas.

They were runners then now; today they are lieutenants in my Empire. They earned that shit doe and, I know I can depend on them.

"Welcome home Hunnid." A couple niggas said to me. "Good Morning y'all. I know y'all wondering why I got y'all up here early in the morning. Shit is about to change. A bitch home now. I'm not saying my family didn't do a good job but, I had over five years to think. I gotta think smarter than how we been moving.

All week I plan on visiting all ten trap houses. I want to see how shit really ranned. The meeting was quick. I dismissed everybody accept the Lieutenants. Every month we will be meeting once a month.

"I need information on all the people working for me. Runners the bitches cooking & bagging that work up. Matter fact Bianca needs her old job back. I don't know or trust this bitch Legend hired to be our accountant. After that shit with Dontae I'm a lil weary about who I have around me." I admitted to Lucci. "Yea I feel you. You gotta cross all your T's dot all ya mutha fucking I's in this game. Ain't too much loyalty wifey." Lucci said smiling at me showing off them damn dimples.

I listened to Lucci spit that real shit to me. My phone ringed it was my mom. At that moment I realize that it was just me and Lucci in the damn warehouse. Everybody left, Gunna had to go handle business. Legend went to his auto body shop. He done with the drug game. I'm a little mad but, hey lil brother want to go straight and narrow and I gotta respect it. He the business side of me.

"Aite Lucci I'm out. My mom calling me again."

"Okay I'm following you then." Lucci stated. I whipped my head around, "for what?" I asked Lucci. "Naw I'm just kidding." He said getting in his car and he pulled off. I stood there thinking to myself. *"If this nigga don't' stop playing with me."*

I pulled up to my mother's house, I got out my car and went in the house. As soon I got in there I ran right into Boss hog. He was in there talking to my mom. My phone ringed, it was a jail call my cell bestie Rasheeda.

I got excited I pushed 1 to accepted the call. "What's up bestie." I said into the phone. Nothing just bored as fuck, checking on you. I can't wait to get out of here. Chyna how was your party?"

Rasheeda asked. "Raheim told me it was littttt." Rasheeda screamed. "Yea Legend and crew did dat!" I replied sitting plopping down on my mother's couch. "Anyways I know Skylar got a fever and, Raheim is taking her to the doctors. That man is a gift from God!" Rasheeda said smiling.

"Here he is. Tell him." I said giving the phone to Boss hog. I put Boss Hog on the Phone and all I heard was Rasheeda say. "I just want to kiss all over you." I heard Rasheeda say. After I heard that I exited the room. I let them talk in peace. I went to see Skylar laying on the bed. I laid next to her. "Hi Auntie baby." Skylar eyes lit up. "Auntie Chyna I'm sick." Skylar responded in the sweetest tone. "I know baby Raheim is taking you to." I was cut of mid-sentence.

Boss Hog was handing me the phone back. I heard Rasheeda still talking but, Boss Hog had the phone down. He was not listening to Rasheeda. "What the fuck going on?" I asked him. Boss hog just gave me the phone. I covered the speaker. "Rasheeda really want to be more than friends. "She just scared bro, look at y'all situation, put yourself in her shoes. Brooo she in jail, you a fine ass nigga with money. You got a lot of bitches your entertaining that's not in jail. You also chose to entertain her and her daughter the most. That shit rare nigga" I voiced.

"I ain't worried about it Chyna" Boss Hog replied and waved me off. I left it alone Mom are you ready to go to the hospital?" I yelled up the steps to my mother. "Yes, let me grab my purse." My mother replied. Mom called me earlier and, told me Cousin Joyce was admitted to the Hospital of the University of Pennsylvania.

Cousin Joyce was my mom's first cousin. She was in her late fifties. She was crazy as hell too, she is a retired Paramedic. After she retired she lost her mind. My mom informed me that; she got cancer and, she is refusing treatment. My mom is one of her emergency contact. I told my mom we had to ride in different cars because, I had shit to do after this.

When I got to the Saint John's hospital. I parked my car and waited in the front lobby of the hospital for my mom. My mom came in the hospital switching. She had her dark denim's jeans on, a fuchsia pink chiffon long sleeve top, silver flats and her silver Michael Kors bag. I laughed at my mom, she still looked young doe.

"Come on Chyna. You know I wanted you over the house today. So, me and you can have breakfast Joyce doctor called me earlier; she refusing to get Chemo treatment and, if she don't get it the cancer is going to get worse. My mom informed me with a worried look on her face.

"I just wanted you to come with me. I missed you baby. No matter how busy you was in them streets you always made time for me." My mom said with a warm smile. I hugged her. "Mom I'm back we good, I know you miss me. We getting back to this mother daughter thing. Like I never left." I said smiling hard. "I know baby." My mom said as we got on the elevator. "What floor?" I asked my mom. "Seven," she said. I pressed the button. When we got off the elevator. There was a big sign that said, "The Cancer Center" we went through the doors.

"Hello what room is Joyce Loffen in?" My mom asked the receptionist. The lady looked Cousin Joyce up on the computer. "She is in room 304." The receptionist replied. "Okay thank you." I said. We got to Joyce room. I looked at Cousin Joyce laying in that hospital bed. This is not how I remember her, before I went to jail. She was thick well over 250lbs. Now she only look like she weighs 150lbs her face was sunk in. Damn... "Fuck Cancer!"

"Joyce," my mother called her name. Joyce sat up in the bed, "Hey Deb," she said voice crackling. "OMG Chyna come here!" Joyce said. "How are you baby? You look good!" Joyce said. I hugged her, and she kissed my cheek. "Damn you thick Joyce said. "Who was you fucking in jail. I ain't never seen nobody come home looking like that. Shit make me wanna go to jail." Joyce laughed and me and my mom did too.

"Why didn't you call me and tell me you was back in the hospital? Why you refusing Chemo treatment?" My mom questioned getting straight to the point. "I know your upset, I didn't call you Deb but, I know you be busy with your new granddaughter. I didn't want to be a burden." Joyce sarcastically admitted.

Joyce ain't changed. She throwing shade at my mom for taking in Rasheeda daughter. She always got something to say. My mom told me she said, "What are you doing Deb taking that jailbird baby. What you running a group home. Chyna going meet somebody else and, send their kids with you too. You stupid that couldn't be me." Blahhh...blahhh. All this negative shit!

"Skylar has nothing to do with this. Your own daughter doesn't even know what's going on. She driving up here from South Carolina today." My mom said getting frustrated. "Deb, I didn't want my daughter to find out about this." Joyce said. "I told her Joyce. It's not right for your daughter to walk in to this blind." My mom expressed. "I'm sorry Deb, I didn't want Chemo because…" Joyce stop talking. She broke down and started crying. I am in the 2nd stage of Ovarian Cancer, I rather just let them give me Morphine. Let me die, I don't wanna live like this Deb. Look at me my hair coming out. I lost over 150lbs." Joyce emotionally wept.

My mom and I hugged Joyce while she cried. "Just please explore your options to survive! Wait until your daughter come to make a final decision, then go from there. Joyce there is always a chance of survival. You fight Joyce. You just giving up!" My mom said through tears. I consoled my mother. Tears was just cascading down my mother's face.

My phone ringed, I stepped out the room to answer. It was Boss Hog telling me Mankind was snooping around Children's hospital. That shit ain't sitting right with me. My phone beep it was my other line. I looked at my phone it was Lucci. "Say no more, we on my way!" I told Boss Hog.

I clicked over it was Lucci. "Yes, Luciano" I said like he been calling me all morning long? "What you doing wifey?" He questioned like I was really his woman! "Boss hog called me. He said the nigga Mankind was down at the hospital lurking!"

"Oh, yea I'll meet you down there. What hospital he at?" "Hospital of University of Pennsylvania" I said through the phone pulling my car keys out. "Cool" Lucci said and hung up.

I went back in the room, I gave Cousin Joyce and My mom a hug. Mom I'll be at your house later! I ran to the elevator. I hurried and pushed the button to the lobby. It seems like the fucking elevators always take their time; when you need to get somewhere quick. I ran off the elevator to my car. The hospital was like twenty minutes away. I swear it took me ten minutes.

I pulled in the parking lot of the hospital. Lucci was already parked there. Lucci exited his car and came to stand by my car. Both of us looked around. We didn't see anybody out of the ordinary nurses and doctors in the parking lot. I called Boss

Hog. Ring... Ring "Sis you outside?"

"Yup bro." I said staring at this all black BMW riding pass. "I'm hungry as fuck." Lucci said. "Hunnid that's who (we was huh) y'all ain't slick." Boss Hog said chuckling.

Boss hog came out the lobby doors with a sleeping Skylar in his hands. I smiled this is a beautiful sight. "I didn't see nobody out here" I said to Boss hog while admiring how pretty Skylar was. Skylar could really pass for Boss hog daughter too. She had his complexion but Rasheeda looks.

Boss Hog put Skylar in the car. While Lucci watched his back and, I watched the front of the car. "We going to follow him to the crib." Lucci said to me. Then told Boss hog to pull off after he did. Lucci led the front Boss Hog in the middle. I was in the back driving to Boss Hog crib.

We got to Boss Hog's condo downtown. We all parked in the garage, Boss hog's condo was laid out. His whole house was Blue and silver Blue four-piece leather sofa, loveseat, chair and chaise. Glass accent silver tables with, fish tank in the cocktail table. I ain't never seen no shit like that, his dining room table was mirror, this shit was laid out.

This is nice Boss Hog." I said still looking around in awe. "Thanks sis." Boss hog said. Boss hog put a sleeping Skylar down on the chaise. He went to the sofa and, pulled the bed out. He put sheets and blankets on the bed. Boss hog picked Skylar up and tucked her neatly in the bed.

The way Boss hog is so caring and his interaction with her had me and Lucci shocked. "I ain't never seen this soft side of you." Lucci said. "Yea Boss I have the utmost respect for you taking on somebody else's responsibility" I said to Boss Hog. "On some real shit Chyna, I love Skylar. You know today she asked me can I be her dad! At first, I wanted to talk to Rasheeda about it. Before I sign up for fatherhood but, how could I look in Skylar eyes and tell her no!"

"Skylar calms me." Boss hog said beating his fist on his chest. "Daddy can I have something to drink? You got ginger ale?" Skylar sweet voice said to Boss Hog. When Boss hog came back from the kitchen. Can you two love birds sit here with Skylar real quick. I don't got no apple juice or ginger ale. Aww shit I need to get her prescription filled" Boss asked us sounding like a frustrated father.

Forty-five minutes later Boss Hog came back telling me. He ran into the bitch from the hospital and Mankind at Walmart. "What he say?" I asked Boss hog. I looked over at Lucci he was rubbing his hands down his face waiting to hear what happen. "That nigga said Skylar ain't my baby after he was searching hard in my cart." Boss hog said displaying a puzzled look on his face. "Wait that nigga know Skylar's name?" Lucci questioned. "Naw cuz he just said that ain't your daughter" Boss Hog said pacing the floor.

Damn I think this nigga know something we don't, what is Rasheeda baby dads name?" Lucci asked me. "Ummm…I think It's Malik, yea that's his name. Rasheeda told me he from New York doe. "Could Malik and Mankind be the same person." Boss Hog questioned. I shrugged my shoulders "She never called him Mankind doe. I gotta rap to her about this shit. When she call me." I told Boss Hog and Lucci.

"If he is he ain't never did shit for Skylar. When her mom got sick, she reached out to the nigga. He never came to check on his daughter. So why now?" I questioned. "I don't know Chyna but, some shit ain't right" Boss hog said putting soup in the bowl for Skylar.

"Fuck that nigga he bleed like the rest! Come on Chyna lets go get something to eat! "Boss I'm out" Lucci said and, slap hands with Boss Hog.

I hugged him, and we hopped in our cars I pulled on the side of Lucci in the parking garage. I gotta go handle some business Lucci. I can't go get nothing to eat with you. He looked sad I'll catch you later" I said quickly and pulled off before he could say anything. I was listening to Dej Loaf Desire ...*I don't ask no questions, I just handle business, I don't ask for favors, I don't ask for niggas, who the fuck asked you nigga?*

I had ten trap houses #1 low house #2 high house #3 Red house #4 Greenhouse #5 Bella #6 Greg #7 Mass #8 General #9 Flower #10 Fierce. I know what y'all thinking I must of been high. When I named these house, I never really thought hard on the names. I just name the shit to separate them fuck a name. I pulled up to the lower house Gunna ran this spot and the higher house too.

I seen Gunna Jeep parked in the back. I exited my car. "What's up Hunnid." Some lil nigga said to me while opening the door to the trap house. I remember him from the meeting this morning "What's up? What's your name again?" I asked him? "Carlos but, the streets call me LO or Loso." He said, and we entered the trap house.

I was looking around. There was a man at the door and, four bitches at the table weighting the weed and bagging it. They all looked at me, "Hi Hunnid!" They said in unison. "What's up y'all where Gunna at" I asked them. "She in her office upstairs". The light skin one said. I went up the steps not before looking around the house, it was clean.

Niggas were in the kitchen smoking weed but, it wasn't a whole bunch of them. Just three including the nigga LO. They was putting money through the money machine. "What's up Hunnid." All the niggas said. "Yo what's y'all two names? Why weren't y'all at the meeting this morning?" I asked with an authority in my voice. "Legend never told us about it but, my name is Gutta." He said and put his hand out for me to shake.

I shook his hand, Gutta was chubby short nigga. Standing at 5foot 9 inches, brown skin nigga with gap between his teeth. He had short blonde dreads in his hair. I looked at the other nigga.

"My name is Caesar." He said giving me a brotherly hug. Caesar was tall skinny 6foot 2inches dark skin with a box. Bottom gold grillz. "Listen I don't like mutha fuckas missing meetings. Make this y'all last time missing one and, I'm gon talk to my twin about not communicating that with y'all." "Aite Hunnid we won't." They said in unison.

I went upstairs and Gunna was in her office on the phone. "You said Wednesday, now it's Friday? I don't play games like that nigga. About my fucking money either. I want my money, or I want the product. If I don't shits about to get real. Aite tomorrow at noon I need a date and time!" Gunna said and hung up the burner phone.

"What's up bestie how is business?"

"It's boomin." Gunna said smiling. "These fucking niggas I get the weed off! They on some bullshit. That shipment is supposed to have been here days ago." Gunna said frustrated. Why you copping off them niggas? I asked. Forgetting that my Godfather Fontell had to fall back for a little bit and, let shit die down.

"Never mind God dad was outta commission for a few."

I said looking down at my phone. "Yea Hunnid I had to do what I had to do." Gunna said taking her Philly 76ers fitted off and turning to the back. "If the nigga don't call tomorrow, we need that change back ASAP!" I said.

"You fucking right, I'm laying niggas down, If I don't get my change or my product" Gunna expressed.

"Have he ever been on some bullshit like this before?" I question. "Naw he is a stand-up dude. He said he'll throw something extra for my troubles." Gunna said. "Aite we gon see then Fontell ain't fucking with the weed shit foreal huh?" I asked Gunna.

"Naw he starting to fall back on a lot of shit. He getting old Chyna." Gunna voiced. "Yea I know he said he wanted to talk to me about some shit. When I touchdown, Fontell was at the party but, you know him he don't say much in public. I'm going go holla at him." I said.

"What's up with them bitches, you got working for you downstairs? I asked Gunna. "Kaylin is my little cousin you remember her right? Gunna asked me. "Ohh I remember damn she grew up" I said. "The other two is her best friends. Did you fuck any of them?" I asked Gunna smiling knowing Gunna she fucked one of them.

"Naw Hunnid." Gunna said with her mouth twisted up. "Don't naw Hunnid me I know you." I said side-eyeing Gunna. "Naw they young. I ain't fuck none of them but, they one friend Nicole. I fucked. She used to work here. Until she started acting all clingy and, showing her ass. I can't have that shit in my trap." Gunna said with an ugly scowl on her face. I nodded my head in agreement. "What was wrong with you earlier at the meeting you looked mad?" I questioned Gunna. "Naw nothing really just observing the meeting you know how I be. I say less and look and listen more street nigga shit."

I stood up and gave Gunna a brotherly hug. "Damn bestie I feel like we ain't one like we used to be." Gunna said. I mean mugged Gunna "Bitch you know you my heart but, when I'm in these streets. On a mission I'm all in. I only been home twenty-four hours.

"We will bust it up soon. I'm out I kissed Gunna lips, something I always did since, we was younger. Gunna that's my heart. It was never a sexual kiss. I just loved her so much. Gunna pulled back wiping my Fenty Beauty Lip gloss by Rihanna off her lips. "Don't do that shit in front of Phoenix." Gunna said with a serious look. "Damn...you must really be into her bestie."

"You ain't never tell me not to kiss you in front of a bitch, hmmmm.... somebody finally tamed your whore ass." I said and left out the door.

I went and checked all the trap houses except for Lucci's. I pulled up to Lucci first trap house. I was exhausted and hungry. I did manage to change my cloths doe. I was sporting white/black Nike Leggings, matching Nike white/black tee and some white/black Nike slides. I put my hair in two French braid, laid my edges down, gold door knocker earrings and, hot pink lipstick.

Yea I was real cute and comfortable. I end up switching rides too. I never stay in the same ride all day. I was now riding in my all White Benz G-wagon. I remember when I purchased this right before I got locked up. I'm so proud to have a brother that is an Auto Mechanic. He kept my G-wagon up for me. My G-wagon is six years old and, it still look and runs nice.

I pulled up to Lucci trap house. I seen a Red Cadillac Escalade Truck. That had to be a 2017. It was parked in front. I parked in the back of the red Escalade. There was a lot of people on the porch. Niggas and bitches they was looking inside my truck. Legend put presidential tent and it was bullet proof. I opened the door and bitches mouth drop. Shocked… yea a bitch home.

I was so little I had to like jump down out my truck. I shut the door and walked up on the porch. "Damn Hunnid you home. I ain't even know." Boss hog cousin Chris yelled.

"What's up Chris?" I said slapping hands with Boss Hog cousin. Chris was a tattoo artist and he hustle pills on the side. Chris was a aite nigga. I didn't know the rest of these people on the steps. Lil light skin nigga kept eyeing me. He was fine as fuck too! This nigga had green eyes. He had to be like 6'4, damn he tall athlete body, dark denim jeans, plain white tee, Giuseppe sneakers doe. Red framed glasses. He looked so delicious damn.

"Aye Lucci in there?" I asked Chris. "Yea but he in his office upstairs. I'll go grab him! Chris said getting up out his chair. "Naw nigga I don't need you to escort me in this bitch. I ain't company!" I said, Chris stepped back "Hunnid I was just gon show you where the office is calm down." Chris nervously said.

"I'm always calm." I said grilling the fuck outta everybody and went in the house. I heard somebody ask Chris. "Who dat Chris?" A by stander asked. "You don't know? That's Hunnid!" Chris expressed. "Damn foreal why didn't you introduce me to her nigga?" I laughed and proceeded to walk through the house.

It was a basic crib, one room the door was shut. I opened the door and, walked in. Lucci was sitting at his desk with his dick out moaning. "Damn bitch suck that dick yea like that." Lucci whispered. I seen fire engine red hair, balled up in his hands. Lucci was pushing her head up and down on his dick. He was so into it that; he didn't see me standing there. I purposely slammed the door shut BOOM! Lucci jumped up grabbing his gun that, was laying on the desk.

The chick that was sucking his dick looked at me. "Damn you don't you know how to knock? The ratchet chick said. "Luciano you better call an exterminator to get this rats outta here. I laughed reciting a comment Brooke Valentine from Love & Hip-Hop Hollywood. "What's up wifey?" Lucci peering over at me, putting his big black dick in his jeans and, pulled his jeans up.

"What's up wifey?" He asked for the second time. Like he

wasn't just in here getting head from another bitch, "Naw nigga if I was your wife, you wouldn't be stupid enough to be this comfortable entertaining another bitch. Getting your little dick suck in your office or anywhere else. Both of y'all woulda been dead by now! Don't you think?" I asked Lucci with a sinister grin on my face.

Lucci laughed at me. "Wifey ain't nothing little about my dick and you know it." Lucci said with confidence." I saw your mouth watering, when I was putting him up Lucci said. "Lucci why are you treating me like this? You was just at my house last night." The chick said and started fixing her clothes and combing that cheap ass weave she was rocking. I knew this bitch was lying because, Lucci spent the night with me. Furthermore, this ain't the same bitch he brought to my party! *"Hmmm...interesting he doing way too much."* I thought.

This is why I didn't wanna fuck with him. Fucking around with Lucci, I would just be killing hoes off like a serial killer. He got hoe-tendencies I see. I whipped my head around and looked this bitch straight in the face.

"Just stop boo please you look dumb!" I told red head

ratchet. "I look dumb?" She questioned pointing at her chest. "Who are you? Oh, your Hunnid I remember you. Why you even messing with this bitch Lucci? She just like a nigga!" Red head ratchet said. "She more hood than you. That's like messing with yourself!" she voiced.

"You know she kisses Gunna in the mouth. A bitch she claim is her best friend but, Gunna is a lesbian. That don't add up Lucci, I always thought they was fucking." She said still talking shit. I walked towards her. I hit her with three good punches to the face. She dropped to the floor. She was now laying on the floor snoring. I grabbed this weird ass bitch by her hair.

She still didn't wake up! "Chyna… Chyna." Lucci called me but, I ignored him. He shoulda check this bitch. I don't got this fuck shit to do; with these niggas and bitches. "Chyna let that girl go." Lucci said. "Fuck no." I pulled the bitch up by her hair. She finally opened her eyes tryna fight. She swung and hit me in the mouth.

"Damn that shit hurt." Lucci tried to break it up. He pulled me by the back of my leggings. Making me loose a gripped on her hair. I had a handful of synthetic red hair. I'm not sure why. This nigga wouldn't just grip me up. Even with Lucci hold on to my back of my leggings. On the side of my waistband was my Pink baby (Glock 19)!

I got loose from Lucci. I gripped this bitch up by her hair again. I pull my gun out and put it right to her head. "Bitch you think it's a game out here, shoulda kept your mouth closed." "Ughhhh please don't shoot me. Hunnid I'll keep my mouth shut please!" She yelled out in pain. "Chyna let her go, what the fuck. You making my trap house hot damn." Lucci said with anger in his voice. I let the bitches hair go.

The girl got up off the floor so quick. She tried to fix her hair and disheveled clothes. She looked relieved, like she just overcame the worse shit that happened to her. "Wifey sit down you came here for business." Lucci said sitting back in his chair behind his desk. I acted like I was putting my gun up. I slightly turned around because, the bitch was to my right. Pow pow I shot her right in her thigh and calf. She dropped down to the floor and, started screaming!

"Ohh… why Hunnid?" Lucci looked at me and shook his head. He pointed at me. "Lucci peered over his desk. Your outta pocket for that shit wifey. Your a fucking bully!" He said still never moving out his seat to check on the bitch. I shrugged my shoulders. Putting my gun behind me in my waistband. "Naw Lucci you better take notes. She was doing too much talking." I said and sat down in the chair across from Lucci desk. "Chyna you ain't gon help me get the girl to the car." Lucci asked with his hands pointing at the chick. Her annoying ass was screaming help!

"Hell, naw I don't shoot a bitch then help them. Shit this is called life lessons, this lesson is called keep your mouth shut 101!" I said through a laugh. "Ughhhh...Ohhhh its burning!" The chick was still screaming. Are we going talk business here Luciano or, are we gon play The Good Doctor?" I questioned.

Knock… knock. "Who is it?" Lucci asked while giving the girl a towel to wrap her leg with. Now there was blood everywhere. I got up to pour Lucci's Patron he had on his desk; in a glass of ice I got from his mini-fridge. "It's Chris Lucci you good?" Chris asked. Lucci opened the door for Chris. "What the fuck happened to her?" Chris asked with his hand on his hips, shaking his head.

"She… she shot me." The girl screamed out and pointing

to me. Chris looked at me and shook his head too. "What"? I said looking at Chris and sipped my drink of Patron. "Damn not only is the bitch annoying she a snitch too." I said pulling out my gun again and pointed it at her. "Chill Hunnid, you wildin babe." Lucci said.

Naw it's the principle, if you let mutha fuckas slide. They will get comfortable and start ice skating. I'm the fuck outta here I'm hungry and I still got more of my spots to look at." I said annoyed at Lucci dumb ass.

"Chyna hold up." I heard Lucci say. I turned around and looked him up and down. "Luciano I'm beyond mad" I said over my shoulder on my way out his little office. "Chyna hold up, I know you mad. Let me make it up to you." Lucci pleaded. I kept walking, I ain't even been home forty-eight hours yet and, I shot a non-factor, heaux ass bitch." I thought to myself.

Bitch tried it talking stupid to me like I'm a regular basic bitch. As I walked towards the crowd on the porch. People was talking, when I approach the porch. Everybody stop talking. It was like my presence put everybody on mute! I walked down the steps. I was about to get in my G-wagon when some chick out the crowd said, "Welp Hunnid home!" I don't know why bitches be testing her. She crazy!" I laughed and got in my G-wagon!

Dej Loaf and Jacquees mixtape Fuck A Friend Zone blast through my speakers! "**Make You Fall In Love...** *I just feel like my pussy better than all them bitches you been with, (all them bitches) take his ass on a field trip, you know me I like to build with 'em, he gone feel the difference? I'm take the pain? I'm bust down, no prescription (hold on, wait) You and me could be you and me but together shit that's your decision I'm cool where I'm at (I'm chillin) why you teasing me ? why you doing all that? I wrote your name in the sand baby, you got me drunk as hell"*

I pulled off, my phone lit up and it was Lucci. I pushed ignore. I gotta call Gunna check Lucci monthly gross. I gotta fall back from him. Lucci called back again. I silenced my phone. I was going go get something to eat, real quick. I head to the south side to check Boss hog trap house out.

I knew he wasn't there because, he had Skylar. I wonder if Ms. Tootsie Soul Food Cafe is open, good ass soul food spot in Philly. I drove there I pulled up. They were open too. Good my mouth was watering for; some fried wings, collard greens and

Macaroni. I think I want five breaded butterfly shrimps too! I found a parking spot. While I was ordered my food some random spoke to me. "Hey Hunnid, I didn't know you was home." The hood heaux Aubrey said while approach me. I looked up from my phone. "Yea what's up Aubrey?" I replied. "Nothing some Ol shit Hunnid. You know me all about my money boo!" Aubrey said and started twerking. I laughed. "Damn Aubrey you ain't change." I said laughing.

Aubrey was pretty ass dark skin chick. She was short like me. Her body was crazy. She always wore her hair long even before inches came out. Right now, she had at least forty inches of hair part down the middle. Shit almost come to her thighs, that's ridiculous hey to each its own. She love fucking niggas for money. She love being the center of attention. She love being messy typical hood bitch with no goals.

As I'm sitting there talking to her. I see the chick J'Onna that Lucci brought to my party walk up on Aubrey. "Are you ready?" She asked Aubrey. "Yea hold on." Aubrey said. "Oh, hey Hunnid. How you doing?" I ignored her bitch acting like we friends or some shit.

"Hmm." She mumbled some shit under her breath. "Y'all know each other?" Aubrey asked pointing between me and the J'Onna. "I don't know her bestie but my boyfriend Lucci took me to her party last night." J'Onna said. I rolled my eyes up in my head because, here we go again Lucci's heaux's. Lawd today been wild! She made sure she said she was Lucci girlfriend. "Oh, yea well me and Hunnid go way back to elementary." Aubrey said.

I was about to address J'Onna. God saved me from me fucking somebody up for the second time today. The waitress came

over with my food. "Here you go Hunnid." Thanks babe. I looked Lucci's chick up and down and said bye to Aubrey. "See you girl be safe out here." Aubrey said. I turned around "I love trouble." I said with the biggest smile. Audrey laughed and nodded her head.

I ate my food while I drove to the trap house on the Southside. I got out with my food. Geno was outside. "What's up nigga?" I said with a slight smile. Aawww shit my nigga Hunnid over here." He joked. We slapped hands and I went inside. There wasn't anybody in the living room area. I walked in the kitchen, there was one bitch in there bagging up work. "Damn Geno why she here by herself?"

"Hunnid she was late today like forty-five minutes and, I already paid her for this week. Fuck that, you know I hate a muthafucka; that can't be on time for their job. Time is everything to me. "I agree. You was like that when you was a youngin! You would be the first nigga on the block and, the last nigga to leave. You made me more money than all the niggas I had working for me on that corner." I said reminiscing. "Yeaaaaa." Geno said smiling.

"Hunnid I'm even better now." Geno said. Rubbing his hands together. "I know nigga I got updates every month about; how you and ATL was doing! I said while eating my chicken. "I remember when I first heard of you. I ain't gon say met because, we hadn't meet yet. Anyways Geno said rolling up his blunt up and, lighting it. I never thought you was as thorough as muthafuckas said you was. I'm thinking she a female she only like 4'9 or 5ft at the most and, she running shit, she dangerous. Naw I don't believe it but, you proved my young ass wrong." Geno said blowing smoke outta his mouth.

"That night I robbed that nigga Raymond." Me and Geno

both said in unison. "I was down bad; my mom left the crib like she always does. We ain't have no food, soap to wash our ass and no toothpaste. Shit we didn't even have toilet paper to wipe our ass. Bitch left me and my little sister to fend for ourselves. I was only sixteen I tried to work this job. When I got paid I only had enough money to pay the rent. Since the rent was past due. That took my whole check. We didn't have money for food or toiletries. That's the night I started robbing niggas. I ain't know the nigga worked for you Geno looked in my eyes and said.

"On some real shit I was in survival mode. I didn't give a fuck who money it was. Me and my little sister had to eat. That same day I robbed that nigga Cortez. He sent them niggas to off me. You killed both of them. I didn't even know them niggas was waiting outside my building.

"Hunnid your Rambo ass was hiding in that damn tree! How you get up there yo?" Geno asked grinning and, started coughing off the weed. Geno tapped the blunt letting the ashes fall in the ashtray. "Geno my short ass tried to do it from the roof but them project walls is high. That tree by your building was close so close together. There was a thick ass branch. I climbed on the branch not even thinking I could fall." I explained to Geno.

"Them niggas ain't see that shit coming. Why you do that?" Geno asked. "I don't like Cortez anyways fucking way. I seen something in you and, it wasn't a jack boy. I had people watching you too. I knew what you were up too. I know how your mom got down. That shit with Raymond, I handled that too. You worked that shit off. If I knew what I knew now. I woulda said fuck that nigga." I admitted.

"He a snitch Geno! He the reason why Auntie Deana locked up. All that shit Aunt Deana did for Raymond. I hate shit like that, niggas always bite the hand that feed them. He gon get his doe Geno said. "You know what Hunnid?" Geno asked looking in the opposite direction. I know he had something to tell me. It's just seem funny. He all grown up now. "Geno you know you can holla at me about anything." I said staring into his brown eyes.

Geno looked at the blunt and then looked me in my eyes. "This bitch was crazy! "Geno blurted out. I didn't know where this conversation was going. "What bitch Geno?" I asked him. "My mom Hunnid; she would try to have sex with me!" Geno's voice elevated. "She tried to give me head, her own son." Geno said with anger and so much emotion.

"I had to choke the shit outta her one day for; coming in my room while I was sleep. She put her mouth on my joint." Geno said pointed to his dick. "You know what she told me while I was choking her? She said she will suck my dick for twenty dollars. That shit crazy." Geno said blowing smoke outta his mouth.

"Only thing stop me from not killing her ass was, my little sister entering the room. Calling my name." My mouth dropped when Geno told me that! "You and Tayla is the only people who know that story. That's why I hustle so hard out here. I had to get me and my little sister outta there."

"Hold up nigga" I said interrupting Geno. "Tayla? Boss hog lil sister Tayla? Whoa she a good girl Geno treat her as such!" I said in a serious tone. '

I'm seriously tryna wife Tayla she special to me." Geno sincerely said. "Anyways damn what was I saying before you interrupted me Chyna?" I shrugged my shoulders. I was still stuck on him and Tayla getting together. As over protective Boss hog is about his lil sis, he better not fuck up!

"Oh, yea that's what it was... Damn I gotta lay off the weed." Geno said chuckling! "If it wasn't for you putting me on. I wouldn't have that house. My little sister wouldn't be going to that private school. I wouldn't have shit Hunnid." He said beating his fist across his chest. "What did I tell you? What I say I wanted outta you in return Geno huh? All I asked for is what?" questioning looking in his eyes.

"LOYALTY and I'll lay my life on the line for you Hunnid. You did more shit for me and my sister, than my mother ever did." Geno said and slapped hands with me.

"How many girls you normally have working?" I asked Geno putting a fork full of Collard Greens in my mouth. "I have four females working 8:00am-3:30pm and 4:00pm-11:30pm. Nobody have access to these doors but, me and Boss Hog. I pay my workers every week. I always switch up the times and day for distribution to the corner boys. I never keep shit the same, I always got a nigga at the door for security and I'm here most of the time." Geno said letting me know he got shit handle.

Geno had shit organized and my intuition was right about him since he was like 16. I finished my food and went to the rest of my trap houses. By the time I got done it was like 10 p.m. I was ready to lay it down. I wanna spend some time with my mom tomorrow and, go see Fontella. I looked at my phone and had several missed calls from Legend and Bianca. I hope they ain't fighting. This dumb ass nigga Legend left me a voicemail:

"Sis It's me... me and Bianca been tryna reach your hard-headed ass all day. I already know what you up to Because, niggas called me STAY THE FUCK OUTTA TROUBLE DAMN! Me and Bianca taking a vacation for a week. We need this time to reconnect with each other. We'll call you when we land!" "I love you sister" I heard Bianca say in the background!

I just smiled and hung up. I'm happy for them doe. *"Please work that shit out bro."* I said to myself. I pulled up at Legend's house. I couldn't fucking believe whose car was there. This nigga don't get it.

Chapter 23

I WANT THAT OLD THING BACK

Legend

I left Chyna's party a little early me and Bianca. I'm tryna figure out how I didn't know from the beginning Bianca was getting high, popping pills and shit. I bet you Chyna's ass knew. She would never tell me though! Chyna loved Bianca. Then to find out my girl got a twenty-year-old son is mind blowing damn! She was raped too and, the baby is her uncle's. I can't even imagine the demons she fighting. How embarrassing that was to tell me but, I still love her the same. She had no control over that shit. She was a kid.

Now I gotta call Jeff and see if he can find out anything about Bianca son. She can meet him. Jeff was a private investigator and computer genius. We pulled up to our house. I got out and went to the passenger side to let Bianca out. Yea I still treated her like royalty. I opened doors for my bitch. We were walking up to the house.

When I saw Lucci pull up. I don't know what this nigga wants because; he better get it together. Lucci got out the car and

I gave him a head nod. "Bro where are you coming from?" Bianca asked Lucci.

"I had to drop shawty off. She was getting on my nerves!" Lucci said. I'm thinking in my head, *"Lying ass nigga!"*

"Lucci that girl was not getting on your nerves. You think you slick. You want my sister real bad, don't you?" Bianca ask Lucci as we all walked in my house. I was walking up the stairs. "Lucci go home." Bianca smacked me on my arm. "Stop cock blocking." Bianca said. "Ain't no fucking in my crib nigga" I said shutting my bedroom door.

"Babe why don't you want Lucci and Chyna to hook up?" Bianca asked me. I ignored her questioned. I wanted to know why she can't complete rehab? "Bianca we ain't gonna worry about Chyna and Lucci hooking up! I need to know why the fuck you keep leaving rehab and not finishing the program?" I questioned her with madness in my voice. "Legend I finish two moths last time and two months this time! Together that four months" she said like I was a slow nigga who couldn't add or some shit. "You hear yourself? You sound real dumb neither program was completed. "What you think this shit like school credits rollover, naw you gotta start over! "I'm scared of losing you Legend. When I was in the rehab center the last time. You act like I never exist. I would call you and, you never answer you didn't visit me. That's why I left this time" Bianca said through tears. I want to be clean, I do Legend but, please don't make me go back there It's making me crazy" she voiced.

"When we get back from wherever we are going, you gotta promise me you will at least do daily outpatient treatment Bianca?" I promise baby!" Bianca said kissing me softly on the lips. You ain't in this alone and, I'm sorry you felt that way. I shoulda did better with the way I handled it. I will go with you every day to outpatient rehab...I love you so much!" I sincerely said. "You will Legend oh my god thank you baby!" Bianca jumped up on me with excitement and, wrapped her hands around my neck. She pecked my lips and, went in the bathroom to shower. I heard the water running. I undressed and joined Bianca in the shower. I saw her silhouette. When I opened the bathroom door. When I had this house build from the ground up. I made sure every bedroom had its own bathroom. I slid the shower door back. I Just stood there admiring Bianca slowly lather her wash cloth. I watched Bianca wash her arms and breast.

My man stood at attention in seconds. "Hmmm...mmm you just gon stand there and watch me?" Bianca asked in a sexual manner! "Yea just for a second, just pretend I ain't in here. Bianca was tryna be funny to a nigga. She started putting on a show, she lathered her whole body. The way the soap was just running down her body had a me on edge. I ain't gon lie, how could I just leave this woman alone. She's beautiful inside out and, most important, she has my heart and been down for me since day one. Bianca put one foot up on ledge of the shower, turned her body slightly towards my direction. She inserted her finger in her sweet box, she played with her box like, I wasn't standing there, I took my man out my boxer's. I started stroking him and enjoying the show. Bianca took her finger out her sweetness.

The water was just running down her body damnn... I'm blessed. Bianca put her finger in her mouth so seductively. She looked at me with love in her eyes. She gestured me to come here no words was said. I got right in the shower with her. Furthermore, my mans was about to explode watching her entertain herself! I started kissing her, I aggressively grabbed her ass and ran my hands up and down her backside. I turned her around and enter her from the back, while pulling on her wet hair. "Fuck throw that ass back babe" I said holding on to Bianca waist giving her long deep strokes. I pulled out and opened the bathroom door.

I was ready to take this shit to the bedroom. When we got to the bedroom, I pushed Bianca down on the bed. "Bae you know I like it rough" Bianca said. I spread her legs wide. I stepped back admiring her sweet box. "It's been a minute missed you" I said crawling up on the bed. I started rubbing Bianca clit gently. Mmm… she was so wet. I looked up at Bianca she was playing with her 38c's and looking me straight in my eyes. I kissed her inner thigh, still rubbing her clit. I kiss her navel moving up to her 38c's. I slurped and licked them. Her nipples were so hard. I kissed her neck. I pecked her lips then move to her ear. "I love you so much. Ain't no other women can get my dick as hard as it is right now. Baby please believe me. I'm in love with you" I whispered in Bianca ear. "Oh yes talk to me papi." Bianca screamed.

After putting her one leg up in the air behind my head. I slid my ten inches into her warm box. Bianca pushed back her facial expression change. "I'm sorry baby. It's been a minute. She will adjust." Bianca said. I started to move in slow circular motion, to widen her goodness. I was in pure ecstasy, once she started moaning. I was side stroking her with so much force she was moaning loud, hanging off the bed. "Damn Bianca this pussy is so good." I moan. "Ohhh mmmm. I'm cumming babe." Bianca said.

I switch positions, I stood up picked Bianca up and, slid her right down on my ten inch pole. I was holding on to her waist, she was taking this shit like a G too. Bianca sex was always amazing and fun. She loves trying new things and so do I. Bianca kiss was so wet and sloppy. I flipped her over and sat down on the bed. Bianca rode me reverse cowgirl. While I rubbed on her clit, juices were running down my sandbags. Bianca was rubbing my sandbags and bouncing on my pole. "Ughhh… shit babe." I said. I slid out putting her leg over me in a squat position. Bianca gave me the ride of my life.

This moment was like a new chapter in my life. This moment felt like we were starting over. Yea the pussy was that good. You ever have sex with someone after y'all argue, the pussy so good it gives you hope. Well this is exactly how a nigga felt right now. I know after this Bianca will most likely be pregnant.

We usually used protection but, I skipped that step. I missed her fuck a condom! "Legend. Ohhhhh Legend you feel so good." Bianca screamed outta breath. *I bet the neighbors know my name I heard Trey Songz*! Song was in my head. I giggled to myself.

Lucci and Chyna definitely heard us. I know one thing I bet not hear them. "Ughhh, Bianca I'm cumming move." I said grunting. Bianca laughed at me and kept riding me! I tried to move her but, the box was feeling so good. It was as if the cum was being fucked outta me. After I bust the biggest nut in my life. Bianca got off me. We laid up just holding each other. "Bianca...Bianca I whispered tapping her on the shoulder! She was dozing off." yes Legend she answered. "We will find your son, I need all the information you got on him" I told Bianca.

"Babe I'm nervous about finding Dallas" she admitted. "Hold up" I said and sat up in the bed you said his name is Dallas?" I asked with a raised brow. *"This could be the same Dallas that be with Mankind."* I thought to myself. I didn't want to tell Bianca. I met him already. I needed all my facts straight. "Yes babe." She said and sat up in the bed. "What's wrong Legend? Don't lie to me." Bianca voiced. I looked Bianca in her eyes and lied! "Aww...nothing I just thought with a name like Dallas, he won't be hard to find." I said stuttering. "Naw Legend you know something don't you?" Bianca asked. "Naw I don't know anything" I said. "Bianca baby let's go on vacation?" I tried to change the subject. "Don't change the subject." Bianca replied. "I just told you. I don't know nothing yet. He young as hell. He wouldn't be in the places I go." I tried to clean it up. "You promise; if you find anything out good or bad Legend you will tell me?" Bianca asked me with her head down. "Yea I promise. Now where do you wanna go?" I said lifting her chin, so she can look me in my eyes.

"I trust you so I'm just gon let this go. **Jamaica.**" Bianca said screaming from excitement! "Aite Jamaica it is. We need some alone time. Chyna home so now I got time to focus on, what's really important." I said making Bianca lay back down and, squeezing her tighter in my arms! "What's that?" Bianca asked side-eyeing me? I smiled and said YOU!!

Chapter 24

ON MY G SHYT

Chyna

Later on, that night when I got home. I mean Legend's house. Lucci was waiting there for me. He asked me was I still mad at him. He brought me dinner from Capital Grill. NY strip steak, Lobster tail, creamed spinach and lobster mac n cheese. Damn he must of talk to Bianca. How the fuck he knows that my favorite place to eat is Capital Grille? "I already ate." I said tryna hide my smile. "Chyna Doll stop playing with me. I know people that know people. That food you were eating earlier from, Ms. Tootsie's Soul Food Café. The food good but, you been gone almost six years."

"I know you was tweeking for some steak from your favorite restaurant." Lucci said holding the bag up teasing me. "I wanted to take you out to eat but, you fucked that up." He said walking towards me. He changed his clothes, Lucci was looking so good right now. Red Levi 501 jeans, Vintage T-shirt with the whole cast of hit show Martin, red and white Nike Huaraches, no chain just his earrings and bracelet. He smelled so good a bitch was getting horny. Just smelling his scent, he licked his and looked down at my small frame. He looked me in my eyes. It was like he was looking in my soul. "Come on Chyna Doll, you ruined my moment with my side chick. I was just about to nut. When you slammed the door." He smiled, leaning against Legend's porch.

I was just trying to get my food off him and go in the house. He leaned up off the porch and put his hand around my waist. "Niggas only have a side chick; when they got a woman. I thought you was single Lucci huh?" I asked moving his hand off of my waist? "What...you my women stop playing with me" Lucci said so seriously. "Nigga trust me, If I was your woman that bitch woulda been dead and, you wouldn't have no balls. I woulda shot them off." I said threaten him.

"If you would give me a chance. I can't be cutting my bitches off for you. Just to chase you and, you don't plan on taking shit to that next level. A man got needs ma." He said.

"Can we go in the house and, talk about this? Your food is getting cold. I know for a fact all the shit me and you did in these streets. We don't need to be out in the open like this. That's how you get caught off guard." Lucci said. *"Tell me something I don't know he talking to me like I'm a beginner in these streets Lucci got a point doe!"* I said to myself. I unlocked the door. We went in and I took the bag from him and sat down at the kitchen table to eat. Lucci was right I didn't need to be out in the opening.

Lucci sat across from me just staring at me. "What?" I asked him. "Why you are staring at me?" I question with a little attitude. "Damn I ain't allowed to just stare at my wife? I'm Tryna picture what our kids would look like." Lucci said cheesing hard. "Shitttt... kids I ain't having no fucking kids! I don't even like kids Lucci. Furthermore, I run the streets too much that would just slow me down Lucci. I ain't no damn housewife!" I said cutting my 12 oz steak up.

Lucci look at me like I just crushed his world. He need to get to know me because, being a mother is something that never crossed my mind. I don't ever want it to cross my mind. "Now at this moment this is not Chyna Doll talking, this is Hunnid talking. Bae what I do notice is you have two different sides, just like me. When I'm in these streets doing whatever to survive I'm Lucci but; when It's about my mom my family I'm Luciano that have a soft side" Lucci admitted.

"I get it, but your tough exterior doesn't scare me. I love it because you are strong enough to run a drug empire but, you are also compassionated enough to help woman like Rasheeda. That you barely knew. You made sure her daughter would be taking care of until she gets out of jail. I also know that you do a lot of shit for the hood. You also terrorize the hood too, your reckless, the shit I would hear about what you did to niggas out here, is shit most niggas wouldn't even do.

"I'm intrigued by you doe for some reason. I want you, I love the fight in you. You take risks just like me." Lucci said. I was speechless this nigga just read me like a book. My face had a blank expression. Lucci's phone ring, Lucci silenced it. From that day on me and Lucci was together every day. I'm saying it like weeks and months went pass. It's been a week, I finally moved in to my house. Which was like four blocks from Legend. Legend and Bianca called me later that night and told me they will be in Jamaica for two weeks.

Lucci and I still didn't have sex and I was cool with that. Naw I'm lying like shit, I was so horny and, when he would go to sleep. I go in the bathroom and masturbate. I couldn't lay next to him without getting horny. After two days of masturbating, the pleasing myself got old. We were going over business shit and. counting money.

We both fell asleep on the couch. Me and Lucci been running the streets all week taking care of business. I woke up to Lucci eating my snatch like it was the last meal. I didn't stop him, I moved his head, pushing him back made him sit up on the couch. He went in his jean pocket for a condom. I snatched the condom out his hand, sliding it down his rock hard donga.

Lucci eyes rolled in the back of his head. I had my hands around his neck, kissing him. I was going buck wild on the dick. He felt so good. Lucci kissed my perky breast. Biting me on my neck! "Damn Chyna Doll I knew this pussy was good." I tried my best to hold in my moan but, he was starting to fuck me back. hitting my spot. I squirted all over Lucci large donga and pelvic area. "Damn I love that shit." Lucci said flipping me over, with my legs apart giving me deep strokes. "Damn babe I'm cumming already. You got one on me. I never cum this quick." Lucci said tryna catch his breath. Sweat pouring down his face.

Ring… Ring… I jumped up hearing my phone ringing. I

looked over on the sofa Lucci was knocked out sleep with his mouth open fully dressed. I looked down at my snatch and notice I'm still fully dressed and so Is Lucci. I put my hands down my Gucci Jacquard jogging pants. My snatch didn't even feel loose. "What the fuck. I was dreaming." I whispered to myself.

Me and Lucci didn't have sex *"what!"* I was so confused. "Did you just smell your pussy?" Lucci asked me through a yawn. Lucci sat up on the couch, wiping his eyes. "Huh?" I asked sounding clueless ass fuck. "What you looking for down there?" Lucci asked. "On some real shit Luciano, you gon crack up. I had a dream that we fucked!" I said embarrassed. Lucci bust out and started laughing.

"That shit can be arranged, you ready for this dick Chyna Doll?" I waved him off getting up off my couch. When I turned around Lucci was standing behind me, putting his hands around my waist. I reached in my back pocket of my Gucci joggers to retrieve my phone. I looked in my missed calls.

"It bet not be no nigga calling you." Lucci said looking down at my phone. "Whatever Luciano. I think it's time for you to go!" I said trying to not look Lucci in the face. I kept my face and attention in my phone. "Oh, now you can't look in my eye when you talking to me." Lucci stated with his eyebrows raised waiting for my answer.

"Naw it's not that. I just need some space right now." Truth be told my ass was nervous to let him in. He doesn't need to know that.

"I'm going to get us something to eat. You hungry? what you want to eat?" Lucci asked me going in the bathroom. "I just want a steak hoagie and fries." I said. Lucci came outta the bathroom. He was putting his shoes on and grabbed his Moschino hoodie. "I'll be right back Chyna Doll." Lucci said walking out my door.

That was at 7 p.m. It's now 12:39 a.m. This nigga didn't call or bring my food. I called his phone. it went straight to voicemail *"Fuck him!"* I thought to myself. I smoked a blunt, went in the kitchen, made me a sandwich and went to bed. This is why I don't never get my feeling caught up in a nigga. They always tryna run game. Two days later, I was at Gunna house. I needed help sorting these birds out for delivery. Me and Gunna couldn't do it by ourselves.

Boss hog was busy with Skylar. Legend still in Jamaica, ATL and Geno I had handling the Pill shipment. I got last night I tried to call Lucci several times today. Lucci's phone went straight to the voicemail. I know his black ass is alive because, Gunna seen him at the club last night. Pussy ass nigga. We been hanging tight up until two days ago. Me and Gunna agreed to meet up later and finish sorting the birds, so they be delivered to all the trap houses.

I looked at my ringing phone, it was my cousin Nia. "Hello cutie you on your way?" Nia ask me.

"Yes, Nia I'm pulling up now!"

"Okay." Nia said and hung up. Me and Nia went to get lunch to Hibachi Japanese Steakhouse & Sushi Bar on Columbus Boulevard. I parked, and we got out my 2017 black Porsche Panamera.

"What's been up with you bitch?" Nia asked.

"Nothing just trying to get back to where I was before I got locked up." I said looking over the menu on the wall. Hello welcome to Hibachi Japanese Steakhouse table for two?" The Petite Japanese ladies asked. "Yes," I said. The Petite Japanese ladies seated us. I looked in my phone and dialed J'Onna number.

If anybody know where Lucci is that bitch do. She wanna be important in his life so bad I'm about to bring her down to earth, right now.

Ring, Ring. "Hello." Her wanna be sexy voice came through the phone. "What's up J'Onna?" I said like we cool. Meanwhile the bitch hated me. Ever since she found out, Lucci was entertaining me. Lucci started falling back from her, to be around me. "You seen Lucci?"

"Who is this?" She asked me.

"J'Onna you know who this is!" J'Onna sucked her teeth. She sounded mad as fuck.

"Hunnid why are you calling me?" J'Onna asked nervously. "Are you gon answer my question or not?" I ask J'Onna through a laugh. "Well since you ain't telling me where he at just have him to call me." I said chuckling which made her even madder.

"I'm not telling him shit Hunnid! You think your short black ass run shit!" J'Onna said screaming through the phone. J'Onna was screaming so loud. It made Nia look at me.

"What the fuck is going on?" Nia asked she had this

puzzle look on her face. "I'm not telling Lucci shit." J'Onna repeated. Her voice was cracking. It now sounds like she had tears falling.

"Lucci supposed to be your hubby you find him yourself." J'Onna said getting hyped like she had won this argument. I laughed. "Bitch you are going to tell him I called because, your mad as fuck right now!" I said pushing the end button. Nia laughed so hard. "Cousin why you do that?" Nia asked.

"Fuck that bitch Nia. I was really looking for Lucci." We both bust out and started laughing. "You a whole fool for that shit." My phone ringed. I looked at the phone It was Lucci. "I told you cousin she was going tell him." I said sliding my finger across my iPhone. "Yo" I answered. "Ain't no yo why you bully people huh Chyna Doll?" Lucci asked me. I can tell he was smiling.

"I didn't bully nobody. If she woulda just answer my question instead of being smart. Then I wouldn't of hurt her feelings. You sure do know how to pick them don't you?" I said giving the Chef my order. "Chicken and steak, brown rice and a blueberry long island iced tea."

"Where you at?" Lucci ask me. "Oh no nigga you don't

have the right to question me. I need your help doe." I said seriously. "Aite Chyna Doll say less." Lucci said hanging up.

Me and Nia finished our meal. She talked my head off about Cortez punk ass beating on her, for coming in late from doctor appointment. When she was just stuck in traffic because, of an accident on I-95. "I hope that doctor's appointment doesn't got nothing to do with you being pregnant. If so you might as well get an abortion or prepare to be a single mother because, I'm killing his ass." I said with malice in my voice.

"Nia who was quiet now because, she was still stuck on the part I said get an abortion.

"When you coming to stay with me Nia?" I asked. I started packing my stuff but, at the same time I don't want him to catch me. I gotta move cautious Chyna!" Nia said with a scared expression on her face.

"Fuck him I'll come over there and shut shit down!" I said mad pounding on the table. "No, no I got this Chyna please I'll handle it." Nia said. I paid the bill and Nia tipped the waiter. Me and Nia left the restaurant ten minutes later. I told her to be safe. She refused to leave him and that is scary because he's beating on her daily for no reason.

I met Lucci and Gunna at the warehouse. So we can go and sort out this shipment of drugs. Lucci pulled up thirty minutes later. He still didn't tell me about the meeting he had with his cousin and, I didn't mention that I would be there either. Jazzlyn told me 10:00 p.m. tonight. Lucci left the warehouse lying talking about, he had some shit to do. The meet up time was 10 p.m. Jazzlyn told me old warehouse on 11th Street. Damn Lucci own cousin setting him up.

In this street shit when money is involved niggas don't care. They will betray their own family about some money. My Aunt Deana's son Keon tried to set her up. So he can take over her empire. Aunt Deana killed Keon. Why would you set your own mom up to be killed that's cold?

"Aite Chyna Doll and Gunna. I'm out." I watched him walk out the warehouse. I turned around and Gunna was looking me right in my face, grinning with a side smile.

"Bestie just marry the nigga, shit y'all already having arguments. You shooting bitches about him. What is all this for y'all to be business partners?" Gunna deep voice said, I laughed at her dumb ass. "I don't want him!" I told Gunna. I'm really trying to convince my damn self that I don't want Lucci. Gunna know me. She knew I wanted this man. "Yea, yea!!! He left didn't call, answer his phone or was it that he didn't bring you nothing to eat. I get it Chyna." Gunna said.

"You a street bitch you know how shit is. Stop giving him a hard time. Did you or did you not. Tell him to leave?" Gunna questioned. I had no comeback for Gunna.

"I hate that you know me so well. You just tryna give my nigga a hard time." Gunna said hugging me and I kissed her on the lips. Gunna got in her black Volvo S60 and pulled off.

I locked up the warehouse and got in my Chevy Impala. Instead of driving a car to the meeting. I decided to get my motorcycle all black Kawasaki Ninja H2R. I went in the house and change clothes. All black catsuit, black thigh high combat boots and, black leather gloves and ski mask.

I wanted to get there early to scope the scene out. It was a deserted area. This warehouse ain't been used in like twenty years. I used to love riding my bike, I felt so free. I remember Legend showing me how to ride, when I was like eighteen. I always said when I really start getting money. I'll cop one. I arrived at the warehouse like Twenty-nine minutes later.

I hit all the back streets to the warehouse. I parked my bike behind a tree, by the back door of the warehouse. For me to make a quick exit. I tried the door. Damn its locked. I tried the second door and it opened. *"Good."* I thought. If it was locked that would put a big damper in my plan. I looked around the room it was dark and dusty as hell.

I looked around to see where the steps are to get upper level of the building. I seen the steps and run upstairs to set up. I pulled my black mask over my face. I took my backpack off and set up my Assault Rifle on the kickstand. The Assault Rifle had a strap to it. I can wear it like a purse, straight army shit. There was a table I moved the table closer to the window. I sat my gun down. Yea I wasn't playing. I was getting all excited. This is how I be when I'm in killer mode. I don't play bout my money or my team. It's either kill or be killed. The windows were already busted out. I was just waiting for my target to pull up.

I was looking through my binoculars to my surprise. Lucci pulled in first looking around. I watched closely five minutes later. A white truck pulled up with three niggas inside. I guess Lucci trusted this shit because, he was solo. He didn't even bring Boss Hog with him. The passenger got out and had a duffle bag in his hand. They trying to play him my palms was itching. I can't wait to kill these niggas. I hate sucka shit like this. Words was exchange I see the passenger try to swing on Lucci! "Yea bitch ass niggas. It's showtime!" I said out loud to myself. Lucci punched the passengers in the face. The nigga in the driver side got out the truck with his gun in hand. I already had the beam on his arm, that he held the gun in POW...POW...POW...POW!

I shot him in both his arms and legs first, so he would have no mobility to do anything else. I hit his ass up! His mouth was wide open screaming in pain he dropped his gun. The other two niggas were looking around with their guns drawn. Lucci now had his gun drawled. He was hiding behind a tree. I shot both of them in their arms and legs too. POW... POW... POW... POW making them drop!

Lucci was still hiding behind the tree, looking around wondering where the shot was coming from; with his gun in his hand. I took my Assault Rifle off the kickstand and threw it around my neck. I put my Louis Vuitton backpack on. I ran down the steps exited the back door. I ran to my bike and cranked it up. I rode around to the side of the building where Lucci and these three pussy ass niggas is. When I got to the side of the building. Lucci had his gun aimed at me, shielding his self behind that tree.

I pulled right up on him. We just stared at each other neither one of us said anything. I think he knew because he lowered his gun. I heard one of the niggas on the ground moaning and crying like a little bitch. The driver of the truck looked at me and was holding his arm that was bleeding really bad, I got that nigga good.

Lucci quickly walked over and kicked the two guns them niggas had outta of their reach. How is there three niggas but two guns. Y'all deserve to die for stupidity!"

"Hunnid!" The driver said still in pain. How the fuck you get out. I thought you had ten years. I tried to kill this nigga before you came ho…" He tried to say but, his body collapsed!

Me and Lucci looked at each other and start laughing. Lucci. He had a blank expression on his face. He turned to me. "Wife! How the fuck did you know I was here?" Lucci questioned me? I blew Lucci a kiss and took my Assault Rifle shot all three of them niggas up. Smoke was coming from their bodies OVERKILL burn in hell pussies. Lucci walked over to me and took my mask off and kissed my lips. "Thanks, wifey." Lucci said smiling. "How…" Lucci started to ask me how I know he was here.

I cut him off. "Let's go." I searched their pockets for their cell phones. I got all six cell phones. I put them in my Louis Vuitton backpack bag. I'm ready to go get my gas can. "Hold up wifey you gotta knife?" Lucci ask.

"Yea." I said handing him a knife out my backpack. I gave him my pocket knife. He went over to the passenger and, cut his thumb off, blood was gushing everywhere. "Damn this nigga is mentally disturbed, just like my ass." I thought.

"What the fuck you do that for?" I ask Lucci. Lucci gave me the you don't know face. "Damn I forgot wifey you been gone five years technology change. That nigga got an iPhone sometimes you need a fingerprint to unlock that shit." Lucci said. I nodded my head and went over to my bike and got my gasoline can.

I soaked all three of their bodies with gasoline. I lit a piece of cloth and threw it on them niggas. All three of their bodies was on fire. Lucci and I stood there and watch they ass burn. Lucci tapped me on my ass. "Come on wifey. Let's get outta here. You sick in the head foreal. You standing here and watching these niggas burn. I don't wanna smell that shit." Lucci said covering his nose with his t-shirt.

I laughed, "I'm just trying to make sure they dead." I said. Lucci came close to my body and bent down to my short ass frame. He whispered. "Wifey them niggas been dead? What you about to do check the pulse? Baby girl they flesh burning. You don't smell that shit?" Lucci said smacking me on my ass.

"Let's go. I'm following you to your house." Lucci said. We left the warehouse. When we got to my house I put my bike in my garage. I went upstairs to let Lucci in. He was leaning on my door frame with the dead niggas finger in the bag. In his other hand was his overnight bag. I guess he was staying the night huh.

Lucci had blood on his shirt. "Luciano you a fool." I said leaving the door open. So he can come in. "You don't wanna use this finger to play with your clit." Lucci said laughing. I spun around on my heels and stuck my middle finger up. "Shit wifey that can be arranged." Lucci said with his tongue sticking out.

I ignored him and went to take a shower. Fifteen minutes later I returned to my living room I had on black legging and a fitted white Tee that says: **A Hunnid Different Ways**. Lucci was just now coming down the stairs with a towel around his neck, gray sweatpants, a wife beater and, Dolce & Gabbana slides. He was dressed so simple but, he looked so good to me. I had to cross my legs to control her down there. "Chyna Doll you got latex gloves?" Lucci ask me.

"Yup!" I replied. I went in the hallway closet and grabbed box off latex gloves. I handed him the latex gloves. Lucci went in the kitchen and laid down a garbage bag. Then took all the phones. We got off those niggas and lined them up. There were three phones. I put on a pair of latex gloves. I know this is an iPhone but, what kinda phone is this?" I asked picking up the big silver phone.

"Oh that's a Galaxy s7. Them are easy to get into." Lucci said putting his cousin thumb he cut off on the iPhone, so it can unlock. We were both quiet while we look in these phones. "What the fuck?" Lucci asked in shocked. "What you find?" I asked Lucci.

"I'm looking through his contacts to see what storage it is. I tapped it to see what the number was and, it's a whole bunch of numbers." Lucci said confused.

"Oh yea shit what storage is that? It's going to be hard to figure out." I told Lucci. "Wifey we got all night." Lucci explained to me. Lucci googled storage near me and, like ten storage places popped up. "Damn it's gon be a long night." Lucci said. "I'll drive." Lucci said over his shoulder picking his keys up walking out the door.

Two hours later and we went to four storage places already. We went to look for the numbers he had; in his notes. The storage number 9 combination 32-28-12 but, none of the four storage places, we went to was the right storage. We still had six more to go. We pulled up to E-Z storage on State Road. We pulled up to the storage and, rode around the storage parking lot until we found storage number 9. We both jumped out the car. I put the code into the combination lock, being that we been at this for hours. I knew the number by heart, plus I'm good with numbers.

It opened I looked at Lucci. "Wifey move so I can open it. I'm anxious to find out what's in here. Lucci said pulling up the door on the storage.

When Lucci opened that storage. We got the shock of our life. There were about twenty huge boxes that was marked police evidence. "What the fuck is this?" Lucci questioned. I looked at Lucci and asked, "Is Your cousin the police?"

"Hell, naw but, he might be a snitch. Come to think about it I don't even know. The nigga did do a bid up state for like three years. You never know what a nigga will say when they be in those interrogation rooms." Lucci said rubbing his hands over his beautiful jet-black waves.

"Snakes in the grass just can't get rid of them. Damn they everywhere." I said to Lucci. Me and Lucci started opening the boxes. There was coke, weed, pills and guns. What shocked me the most were the guns; there was a box that came from a company called Gun Shred a company that is supposed to destroy guns. "What the fuck are these guns doing in here? Chyna Doll look at this." Lucci said.

When I looked he was looking through a big yellow

envelope. What I seen in these folders blew my fucking mind. These were the real pictures of me when I was under investigation. The cops photo shop but, these was the originals. In these pictures there was no transactions or nothing illegal going on. I slammed the picture down. "We gotta find out who's name this storage is in. Lucci this shit is deeper than I thought." I said. "Yea it is but, what we going to do with all this shit?" Lucci asked me? Shit we gon sale this shit. You know I'm always on a money mission!" I said. "How?" Lucci asked. "Shit there's **A HUNNID DIFFERENT WAYS** WE CAN GET THIS MONEY I said pointing to all twenty boxes in the storage **TO BE CONTINUED...**

A Hunnid Different Ways: Tales OF A Queen Pen 2 COMING SOON!

If you are an established author or an inspiring author and you would like to be a part of the team please send your submissions to loyallegacypublishing@gmail.com. Send your first three chapters, your synopsis, and your biography. Please check out other LLP books below All reviews are appreciated. Thank you for your love and support. Happy reading ENJOY!!

BOOK LINKS FROM LOYAL LEGACY PUBLISHING

Intimacy: Ronnie & Kendra Part 1:
https://amzn.com/B074Z5DMK1

Fake Engagement FREE: https://amzn.com/B01MQ4Y0SF

Fake Engagement 2: https://amzn.com/B07329FPHY

No Love Just Sex FREE: https://amzn.com/B01KJ6I312

Blu Blaze https://amzn.com/B01LXAJWMO

Scar'D https://amzn.com/B01JXYH4QG

The One Holds My Heart FREE:
https://amzn.com/B01M6W71VF

The One Who Holds My Heart II
https://amzn.com/B01M3Q2545

The One Who Holds My Heart III:
https://amzn.com/B06XG1C1JH

A Toxic Kinda Love: https://amzn.com/B076TGG782

Broken Bonds: https://amzn.com/B0799CSK31

ABOUT THE AUTHOR

Tammera Townes, Pen name First Lady (Lead by Force), is a 34 year old native of Pittsburgh PA, #STEELERNATION. A mother of three, and a Certified Nursing Assistant at a Veteran Hospital. Tammera loves her Veterans and has the utmost respect for the men and women who served this country. She treats her Veterans like they are her family, with Compassion, Respect, Dignity and Pride!

Tammera started writing when she was ten years old. An English teacher gave a topic on the chalkboard. Just one word and the class would have to write a short story out of one word. She excelled at writing short stories and in reading/writing all through school. Reading and Writing is very therapeutic to her.

That talent still endures with her in adulthood. In 2014, while working night shift, she started writing this story about a girl named Chyna, in the notes section on her phone. About mid December 2017, Tammera transferred everything to her laptop. It was seven chapters, she was amazed! She did not realize how much she had written.

She thought to herself, *'I might as well keep writing.'* With that, she wrote her first novel and submitted it to several publishing companies. Where she was chosen by Loyal Legacy Publishing, and she is excited to be there.

Tammera is currently attending community college. Where she majors in English Literature. She is also taking some creative writing classes to strengthen her writing skills. (EMPOWERING WOMAN) you are in control of your own destiny, doors will open that no man/woman can close!

~Author First Lady hopes each of you enjoys her novel!

Made in the USA
Middletown, DE
22 December 2018